D.C. NOIR

c1

D.C. NOIR

EDITED BY GEORGE PELECANOS

AKASHIC BOOKS
NEW YORK

ALSO IN THE AKASHIC NOIR SERIES:

Dublin Noir, edited by Ken Bruen

Brooklyn Noir, edited by Tim McLoughlin

Brooklyn Noir 2: The Classics, edited by Tim McLoughlin

Chicago Noir, edited by Neal Pollack

San Francisco Noir, edited by Peter Maravelis

FORTHCOMING:

Manhattan Noir, edited by Lawrence Block

Baltimore Noir, edited by Laura Lippman

Twin Cities Noir, edited by Julie Schaper & Steven Horwitz

Los Angeles Noir, edited by Denise Hamilton

London Noir, edited by Cathi Unsworth

Miami Noir, edited by Les Standiford

Havana Noir, edited by Achy Obejas

Lone Star Noir, edited by Edward Nawotka

Wall Street Noir, edited by Peter Spiegelman

This collection is comprised of works of fiction. All names, characters, places, and incidents are the product of the authors' imaginations. Any resemblance to real events or persons, living or dead, is entirely coincidental.

Series concept by Tim McLoughlin and Johnny Temple
D.C. map by Sohrab Habibion

Published by Akashic Books
©2006 George Pelecanos

ISBN-13: 978-1-888451-90-0
ISBN-10: 1-888451-90-4
Library of Congress Control Number: 2005925467
All rights reserved

First printing
Printed in Canada

Akashic Books
PO Box 1456
New York, NY 10009
Akashic7@aol.com
www.akashicbooks.com

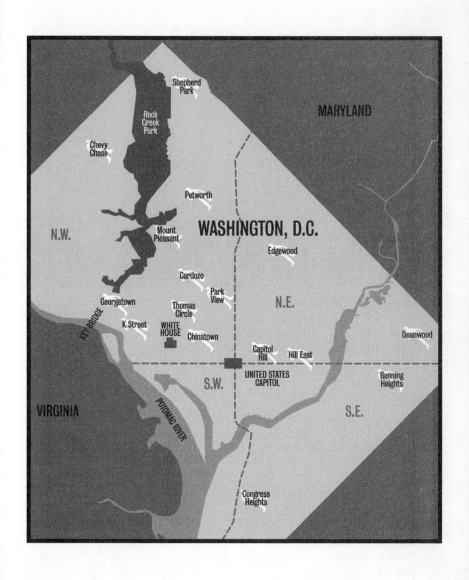

TABLE OF CONTENTS

PART IV: THE HILL & THE EDGE

INTRODUCTION
Notes on *D.C. Noir*

Recently, on the way to a witness interview on the 1600 block of W Street, S.E. with detectives from Washington, D.C.'s MPD Violent Crimes Branch, I passed through the low-rise, government-assisted dwellings off Langston Place in Ward 7. There, in a dirt and concrete courtyard patched with the last of winter's snow, was a makeshift memorial of sorts to a teenaged murder victim who had allegedly been in the life himself. Grouped around a steel pole were various forms of stuffed animals, teddy bears and the like, along with plastic flowers and some balloons, long depleted of their helium, lying on the ground. The site contained no *R.I.P.* tags or name identifications of any kind. It's what's known as a "tribute" in this part of town.

That night, in the comfort of my home, I sat down to read the *Washington Post*. The above-the-fold story on the front page of the Style section, which jumped inside and took up many column inches, concerned an author from wealthy, mostly-white Ward 3, who had written a book about the anxiety of today's Washington woman, who has to deal with "soul-draining perfectionism," shuttling kids to soccer matches, nighttime Girl Scout cookie meetings, and finding the right art camp and piano teacher for her kids. Buried in the Metro section of that same newspaper were the latest crime fatalities, all occurring far away from those houses on the high ground of Cleveland Park and Chevy Chase. The victims, many unnamed, all young, got two paragraphs of space inside the section.

By now you may think you know where this is going. But the truth is, it's just an anecdote that describes "that thing" D.C.-area residents live with every day. The reason so much space was devoted to the article about "today's Washington woman" was because it would be read by a large number of Washingtonians, who could relate. Yet just as many read the Crime and Justice capsule inside Metro, because they might have heard the gunshots outside their doors, or they might have known the victims or the shooters, or both, when they were children. Yes, this city is polarized, but that's a too-easy observation, and it denies the District's complexity as a whole. In fact, it would be inaccurate to repeat the notion that there are two D.C.'s.

Here's another myth debunked: This is not a transient city, as it is often ludicrously described. A very small percentage of the population comes and goes every four-to-eight years, blowing in and out of town with whatever presidential administration sets up temporary camp. The vast majority of the citizens, many who came up from the South, have lived here for generations. Others came and still come from overseas, or emigrated from other states, chasing opportunity and riding the great prosperity boom/hiring rush of the post–World War II years. Many arrived with a desire to be a part of early-'60s Camelot.

I imagine they stayed because they liked it. There are easier places to live, but few as interesting. Nowhere in this country is the race, class, and culture divide more obvious than it is in Washington, D.C. And the conflict does not bubble below the surface—this American experiment is dissected and discussed, in-your-face style, every day.

Other things: The citizens of Washington have no vote or meaningful representation in the House or the Senate of the U.S. Congress. *No taxation without representation*, except for the citizens of the nation's capital. The federal government controls the purse strings here, and the policymakers dole out the money according to their own motives. Since there is no vote to massage, politicians and presidents have historically ignored the neediest people of this city, as there's little upside to reaching out. Walk into any public high school in the District, take a look around, and see a stark illustration of an absolute failure of governance.

That the kids always suffer is nothing less than a national disgrace. But the communities, realizing that the financial gatekeepers have turned a blind eye toward their children, have dug deep and looked in their own backyards for solutions. Coaches, teachers, big brothers and sisters, mentors, church groups, and other volunteers are the real heroes of this city, and have stepped up in a big way to impact the lives of our young men and women. Still, there is a great deal of bitterness on the part of Washingtonians toward the federal government.

So don't expect all the locals to get misty-eyed over monuments, inauguration balls, or care about the society sightings inside Style. What might get them emotional is the sight of someone who shares their memories. The ones who remember Riggo breaking that tackle in '83, Len Bias's jersey number, Phil Chenier's baseline jumper, Frank Howard's swing, or Doug Williams throwing downfield like God was talking in his ear. The ones who saw Aretha as a child performing with her father onstage at the Howard, or Sinatra at the Watergate barge, or Trouble Funk at the old 9:30, or Hendrix at the Ambassador, or Bruce at the Childe Harold.

The ones who play Frankie Beverly or EWF at Sunday picnics in Rock Creek Park. The ones who have Backyard Band, Minor Threat, Chuck Brown, William DeVaughn, Shirley Horn, and Bad Brains in their record collections. The ones who know that Elgin Baylor came out of Spingarn, or that Adrian Dantley and Brian Westbrook were DeMatha Stags. The ones who hear the voice of Bobby "The Mighty Burner" Bennett on the radio and can't help but grin. The ones who bleed Burgundy and Gold. The ones who will claim that they know your distant cousin, or tell you they like the looks of your car, or, if it needs to be replaced, mention that it's a hooptie. Or the woman at the Safeway who hands you your receipt and tells you to "have a blessed day." Or the matriarch on your street with the prunish, beautiful face who raised six sons and now lords over a house holding many of their children.

It's about the collective memories of the locals, and also about the voices. If you close your eyes and listen to the people of this city, you will hear the many different voices, and if you've lived here long enough, the cadences and rhythms, the familiarity of it, the feeling that you are home, will make you smile.

This is a collection of short stories that, in the context of crime/noir fiction, attempts to capture those voices. Why crime fiction? It involves a high degree of conflict, which drives most good fiction. It also allows us to explore social issues and the strengths and frailties of humanity that are a part of our everyday lives here.

In the interest of inclusion, we have tried to explore every quadrant of the city and many of the neighborhoods within them, and have not forgotten the federal city and downtown. We have enlisted the well-known and the someday-will-be.

The writers include lifelong Washingtonians, imports and exports, a gentleman who is currently incarcerated, a police officer, an actor, bloggers, journalists, blacks, whites, Hispanics, males and females, and yeah, even a Greek American.

With pride, and always with hope and anticipation, here's a look at our D.C.

George Pelecanos
Washington, D.C.
November 2005

PART I

D.C. Uncovered

THE CONFIDENTIAL INFORMANT

BY GEORGE PELECANOS

Park View, N.W.

I was in the waiting area of the Veteran's Hospital emergency room off North Capitol Street, seeing to my father, when Detective Tony Barnes hit me back on my cell. My father had laid his head down on the crossbar of his walker, and it was going to be awhile before someone came and called his name. I walked the phone outside and lit myself a smoke.

"What's goin' on, Verdon?" said Barnes.

"Need to talk to you about Rico Jennings."

"Go ahead."

"Not on the phone." I wasn't about to give Barnes no information without feeling some of his cash money in my hand.

"When can I see you?"

"My pops took ill. I'm still dealin' with that, so . . . make it 9:00. You know where."

Barnes cut the line. I smoked my cigarette down to the filter and went back inside.

My father was moaning when I took a seat beside him. Goddamn this and goddamn that, saying it under his breath. We'd been out here for a few hours. A girl with a high ass moving inside purple drawstring pants took our information when we came in, and later a Korean nurse got my father's vitals in what she called the triage room, asking questions about his history and was there blood in his stool and stuff like that. But we had not seen a doctor yet.

Most of the men in the waiting room were in their fifties and above. A couple had walkers and many had canes; one dude had an oxygen tank beside him with a clear hose running up under his nose. Every single one of them was wearing some kinda lid. It was cold out, but it was a style thing, too.

Everyone looked uncomfortable and no one working in the hospital seemed to be in a hurry to do something about it. The security guards gave you a good eye-fuck when you came through the doors, which kinda told you straight off what the experience was going to be like inside. I tried to go down to the cafeteria to get something to eat, but nothing they had was appealing, and some of it looked damn near dirty. I been in white people's hospitals, like Sibley, on the high side of town, and I know they don't treat those people the way they was treating these veterans. I'm saying, this shit here was a damn disgrace.

But they did take my father eventually.

In the emergency room, a white nurse named Matthew, redheaded dude with Popeye forearms, hooked him up to one of those heart machines, then found a vein in my father's arm and took three vials of blood. Pops had complained about being "woozy" that morning. He gets fearful since his stroke, which paralyzed him on one side. His mind is okay, but he can't go nowhere without his walker, not even to the bathroom.

I looked at him lying there in the bed, his wide shoulders and the hardness of his hands. Even at sixty, even after his stroke, he is stronger than me. I know I will never feel like his equal. What with him being a Vietnam veteran, and a dude who had a reputation for taking no man's shit in the street. And me . . . well, me being me.

"The doctor's going to have a look at your blood, Leon," said Matthew. I guess he didn't know that in our neighborhood my father would be called "Mr. Leon" or "Mr. Coates" by someone younger than him. As Matthew walked away, he began to sing a church hymn.

My father rolled his eyes.

"Bet you'd rather have that Korean girl taking care of you, Pops," I said, with a conspiring smile.

"That gal's from the Philippines," said my father, sourly. Always correcting me and shit.

"Whateva."

My father complained about everything for the next hour. I listened to him, and the junkie veteran in the next stall over who was begging for something to take away his pain, and the gags of another dude who was getting a stomach tube forced down his throat. Then an Indian doctor, name of Singh, pulled the curtain back and walked into our stall. He told my father that there was nothing in his blood or on the EKG to indicate that there was cause for alarm.

"So all this *bull*shit was for nothin'?" said my father, like he was disappointed he wasn't sick.

"Go home and get some rest," said Dr. Singh, in a cheerful way. He smelled like one them restaurants they got, but he was all right.

Matthew returned, got my father dressed back into his streetclothes, and filled out the discharge forms.

"The Lord loves you, Leon," said Matthew, before he went off to attend to someone else.

"Get me out this motherfucker," said my father. I fetched a wheelchair from where they had them by the front desk.

I drove my father's Buick to his house, on the 700 block of

Quebec Street, not too far from the hospital, in Park View. It took awhile to get him up the steps of his row house. By the time he stepped onto the brick-and-concrete porch, he was gasping for breath. He didn't go out much anymore, and this was why.

Inside, my mother, Martina Coates, got him situated in his own wheelchair, positioned in front of his television set, where he sits most of his waking hours. She waits on him all day and sleeps lightly at night in case he falls out of his bed. She gives him showers and even washes his ass. My mother is a church woman who believes that her reward will come in heaven. It's 'cause of her that I'm still allowed to live in my father's house.

The television was real loud, the way he likes to play it since his stroke. He watches them old games on that replay show on ESPN.

"Franco Harris!" I shouted, pointing at the screen. "Boy was *beast*."

My father didn't even turn his head. I would have watched some of that old Steelers game with him if he had asked me to, but he didn't, so I went upstairs to my room.

It is my older brother's room as well. James's bed is on the opposite wall and his basketball and football trophies, from when he was a kid all the way through high school, are still on his dresser. He made good after Howard Law, real good, matter of fact. He lives over there in Crestwood, west of 16th, with his pretty redbone wife and their two light-skinned kids. He doesn't come around this neighborhood all that much, though it ain't but fifteen minutes away. He wouldn't have drove my father over to the VA Hospital, either, or waited around in that place all day. He would have said he was too busy, that he couldn't get out "the firm" that day. Still, my father brags on James to all his friends. He got no cause to brag on me.

I changed into some warm shit, and put my smokes and matches into my coat. I left my cell in my bedroom, as it needed to be charged. When I got downstairs, my mother asked me where I was going.

"I got a little side thing I'm workin' on," I said, loud enough for my father to hear.

My father kinda snorted and chuckled under his breath. He might as well had gone ahead and said, *Bullshit*, but he didn't need to. I wanted to tell him more, but that would be wrong. If my thing was to be uncovered, I wouldn't want nobody coming back on my parents.

I zipped my coat and left out the house.

It had begun to snow some. Flurries swirled in the cones of light coming down from the streetlamps. I walked down to Giant Liquors on Georgia and bought a pint of Popov, and hit the vodka as I walked back up Quebec. I crossed Warder Street, and kept on toward Park Lane. The houses got a little nicer here as the view improved. Across Park were the grounds of the Soldier's Home, bordered by a black iron, spear-topped fence. It was dark out, and the clouds were blocking any kinda moonlight, but I knew what was over there by heart. I had cane-pole fished that lake many times as a kid, and chased them geese they had in there, too. Now they had three rows of barbed wire strung out over them spear-tops, to keep out the kids and the young men who liked to lay their girlfriends out straight on that soft grass.

Me and Sondra used to hop that fence some evenings, the summer before I dropped out of Roosevelt High. I'd bring some weed, a bottle of screw-top wine, and my Walkman and we'd go down to the other side of that lake and chill. I'd let her listen to the headphones while I hit my smoke. I had made mix-tapes off my records, stuff she was into, like Bobby Brown and Tone-Loc. I'd tell her about the cars I was gonna be driving, and the custom suits I'd be wearing, soon as I got a good job. How I didn't need no high school diploma to get those things or to prove how smart I was. She looked at me like she believed it. Sondra had some pretty brown eyes.

She married a personal injury lawyer with a storefront office up in Shepherd Park. They live in a house in P.G. County, in one of those communities got gates. I seen her once, when she came back to the neighborhood to visit her moms, who still stays down on Luray. She was bum-rushing her kids into the house, like they might get sick if they breathed this Park View air. She saw me walking down the street and turned her head away, trying to act like she didn't recognize me. It didn't cut me. She can rewrite history in her mind if she wants to, but her fancy husband ain't never gonna have what I did, 'cause I had that pussy when it was new.

I stepped into the alley that runs north-south between Princeton and Quebec. My watch, a looks-like-a-Rolex I bought on the street for ten dollars, read 9:05. Detective Barnes was late. I unscrewed the top of the Popov and had a pull. It burned nice. I tapped it again and lit myself a smoke.

"Psst. Hey, yo."

I looked up over my shoulder, where the sound was. A boy leaned on the lip of one of those second-floor, wood back porches that ran out to the alley. Behind him was a door with curtains on its window. A bicycle tire was showing beside the boy. Kids be putting their bikes up on porches around here so they don't get stole.

"What you want?" I said.

"Nothin' you got," said the boy. He looked to be about twelve, tall and skinny, with braided hair under a black skully.

"Then get your narrow ass back inside your house."

"You the one loiterin'."

"I'm mindin' my own, is what I'm doin'. Ain't you got no homework or nothin'?"

"I did it at study hall."

"Where you go, MacFarland Middle?"

"Yeah."

"I went there, too."

"So?"

I almost smiled. He had a smart mouth on him, but he had heart.

"What you doin' out here?" said the kid.

"Waitin' on someone," I said.

Just then Detective Barnes's unmarked drove by slow. He saw me but kept on rolling. I knew he'd stop, up aways on the street.

"Awright, little man," I said, pitching my cigarette aside and slipping my pint into my jacket pocket. I could feel the kid's eyes on me as I walked out the alley.

I slid into the backseat of Barnes's unmarked, a midnight-blue Crown Vic. I kinda laid down on the bench, my head against the door, below the window line so no one on the outside could see me. It's how I do when I'm rolling with Barnes.

He turned right on Park Place and headed south. I didn't need to look out the window to know where he was going. He drives down to Michigan Avenue, heads east past the Children's Hospital, then continues on past North Capitol and then Catholic U, into Brookland and beyond. Eventually he turns around and comes back the same way.

"Stayin' warm, Verdon?"

"Tryin' to."

Barnes, a broad-shouldered dude with a handsome face, had a deep voice. He favored Hugo Boss suits and cashmere overcoats. Like many police, he wore a thick mustache.

"So," I said. "Rico Jennings."

"Nothin' on my end," said Barnes, with a shrug. "You?"

I didn't answer him. It was a dance we did. His eyes went to the rearview and met mine. He held out a twenty over the seat, and I took it.

"I think y'all are headed down the wrong road," I said.

"How so?"

"Heard you been roustin' corner boys on Morton and canvasing down there in the Eights."

"I'd say that's a pretty good start, given Rico's history."

"Wasn't no drug thing, though."

"Kid was in it. He had juvenile priors for possession and distribution."

"Why they call 'em priors. That was before the boy got on the straight. Look, I went to grade school with his mother. I been knowin' Rico since he was a kid."

"*What* do you know?"

"Rico was playin' hard for a while, but he grew out of it. He got into some big brother thing at my mother's church, and he turned his back on his past. I mean, that boy was in the AP program up at Roosevelt. Advanced Placement, you know, where they got adults, teachers and shit, walkin' with you every step of the way. He was on the way to college."

"So why'd someone put three in his chest?"

"What I heard was, it was over a girl."

I was giving him a little bit of the truth. When the whole truth came out, later on, he wouldn't suspect that I had known more.

Barnes swung a U-turn, which rocked me some. We were on the way back to Park View.

"Keep going," said Barnes.

"Tryin' to tell you, Rico had a weakness for the ladies."

"Who doesn't."

"It was worse than that. Girl's privates made Rico stumble. Word is, he'd been steady-tossin' this young thing, turned out to be the property of some other boy. Rico knew it, but he couldn't stay away. That's why he got dropped."

"By who?"

"Huh?"

"You got a name on the hitter?"

"Nah." Blood came to my ears and made them hot. It happened when I got stressed.

"How about the name of the girlfriend?"

I shook my head. "I'd talk to Rico's mother, I was you. You'd think she'd know somethin' 'bout the girls her son was runnin' with, right?"

"You'd think," said Barnes.

"All I'm sayin' is, I'd start with her."

"Thanks for the tip."

"I'm just sayin'."

Barnes sighed. "Look, I've already talked to the mother. I've talked to Rico's neighbors and friends. We've been through his bedroom as well. We didn't find any love notes or even so much as a picture of a girl."

I had the photo of his girlfriend. Me and Rico's aunt, Leticia, had gone up into the boy's bedroom at that wake they had, while his mother was downstairs crying and stuff with her church friends in the living room. I found a picture of the girl, name of Flora Lewis, in the dresser drawer, under his socks and underwear. It was one of them mall photos the girls like to get done, then give to their boyfriends. Flora was sitting on a cube, with columns around her and shit, against a background, looked like laser beams shooting across a blue sky. Flora had tight jeans on and a shirt with thin straps, and she had let one of the straps kinda fall down off her shoulder to let the tops of her little titties show. The girls all trying to look like sluts now, you ask me. On the back of the photo was a note in her handwriting, said, *How U like me like this? xxoo, Flora.* Leticia recognized Flora from around the way, even without the name printed on the back.

"Casings at the scene were from a nine," said Barnes, bringing me out of my thoughts. "We ran the markings through IBIS and there's no match."

"What about a witness?"

"You kiddin'? There wasn't one, even if there was one."

"Always someone knows somethin'," I said, as I felt the car slow and come to a stop.

"Yeah, well." Barnes pushed the trans arm up into park. "I caught a double in Columbia Heights this morning. So I sure would like to clean this Jennings thing up."

"You *know* I be out there askin' around," I said. "But it gets expensive, tryin' to make conversation in bars, buyin' beers and stuff to loosen them lips . . ."

Barnes passed another twenty over the seat without a word. I took it. The bill was damp for some reason, and limp like a dead thing. I put it in the pocket of my coat.

"I'm gonna be askin' around," I said, like he hadn't heard me the first time.

"I know you will, Verdon. You're a good CI. The best I ever had."

I didn't know if he meant it or not, but it made me feel kinda guilty, backdooring him the way I was planning to do.

But I had to look out for my own self for a change. The killer would be got, that was the important thing. And I would be flush.

"How your sons, detective?"

"They're good. Looking forward to playing Pop Warner again."

"Hmph," I said.

He was divorced, like most homicide police. Still, I knew he loved his kids.

That was all. It felt like it was time to go.

"I'll get up with you later, hear?"

Barnes said, "Right."

I rose up off the bench, kinda looked around some, and got out the Crown Vic. I took a pull out the Popov bottle as I headed for my father's house. I walked down the block, my head hung low.

Up in my room, I found my film canister under the T-shirts in my dresser. I shook some weed out into a wide paper, rolled a joint tight as a cigarette, and slipped it into my pack of Newports. The vodka had lifted me some, and I was ready to get up further.

I glanced in the mirror over my dresser. One of my front teeth was missing from when some dude down by the Black Hole, said he didn't like the way I looked, had knocked it out. There was gray in my patch and in my hair. My eyes looked bleached. Even under my bulky coat, it was plain I had lost weight. I looked like one of them defectives you pity or ridicule on the street. But shit, there wasn't a thing I could do about it tonight.

I went by my mother's room, careful to step soft. She was in there, in bed by now, watching but not watching television on her thirteen-inch color, letting it keep her company, with the sound down low so she could hear my father if he called out to her from the first floor.

Down in the living room, the television still played loud, a black-and-white film of the Liston-Clay fight, which my father had spoke of often. He was missing the fight now. His chin was resting on his chest and his useless hand was kinda curled up like a claw in his lap. The light from the television grayed his face. His eyelids weren't shut all the way, and the whites showed. Aside from his chest, which was moving some, he looked like he was dead.

Time will just fuck you up.

I can remember this one evening with my father, back around '74. He had been home from the war for a while, and was working for the Government Printing Office at the time. We were over there on the baseball field, on Princeton, next to Park View Elementary. I musta been around six or seven. My father's shadow was long and straight, and the sun was throwing a warm gold color on the green of the field. He was still in his work clothes, with his sleeves rolled up to his elbows. His natural was full and his chest filled the fabric of his shirt. He was tossing me this small football, one of them K-2s he had bought me, and telling me to run toward him after I caught it, to see if I could break his tackle. He wasn't gonna tackle me for real, he just wanted me to get a feel for the game. But I wouldn't run to him. I guess I didn't want to get hurt, was what it was. He got aggravated with me eventually, lost his patience and said it was time to get on home. I believe he quit on me that day. At least, that's the way it seems to me now.

I wanted to go over to his wheelchair, not hug him or nothing that dramatic, but maybe give him a pat on his shoulder. But if he woke up he would ask me what was wrong, why was I touching him, all that. So I didn't go near him. I had to meet with Leticia about this thing we was doing, anyway. I stepped light on the clear plastic runner my mother had on the carpet, and closed the door quiet on my way out the house.

On the way to Leticia's I cupped a match against the snow and fired up the joint. I drew on it deep and held it in my lungs. I hit it regular as I walked south.

My head was beginning to smile as I neared the house Leticia stayed in, over on Otis Place. I wet my fingers in the snow and squeezed the ember of the joint to put it out. I wanted to save some for Le-tee. We were gonna celebrate.

The girl, Flora, had witnessed the murder of Rico Jennings. I knew this because we, Leticia and me that is, had found her and made her tell what she knew. Well, Leticia had. She can be a scary woman when she wants to be. She broke hard on Flora, got up in her face and bumped her in an alley. Flora cried and talked. She had been out walking with Rico that night, back up on Otis, around the elementary, when this boy, Marquise Roberts, rolled up on them in a black Caprice. Marquise and his squad got out the car and surrounded Rico, shoved him some and shit like that. Flora said it seemed like that was all they was gonna do. Then Marquis drew an automatic and put three in Rico, one while Rico was on his feet and two more while Marquise was standing over him. Flora said Marquise was smiling as he pulled the trigger.

"Ain't no doubt now, is it?" said Marquise, turning to Flora. "You mine."

Marquise and them got back in their car and rode off,

and Flora ran to her home. Rico was dead, she explained. Wouldn't do him no good if she stayed at the scene.

Flora said that she would never talk to the police. Leticia told her she'd never have to, that as Rico's aunt she just needed to know.

Now we had a killer and a wit. I could have gone right to Detective Barnes, but I knew about that anonymous tip line in the District, the Crime Solvers thing. We decided that Leticia would call and get that number assigned to her, the way they do, and she would eventually collect the $1,000 reward, which we'd split. Flora would go into witness security, where they'd move her to far Northeast or something like that. So she wouldn't get hurt, or be too far from her family, and Leticia and me would get five hundred each. It wasn't much, but it was more than I'd ever had in my pocket at one time. More important to me, someday, when Marquise was put away and his boys fell, like they always do, I could go to my mother and father and tell them that I, Verdon Coates, had solved a homicide. And it would be worth the wait, just to see the look of pride on my father's face.

I got to the row house on Otis where Leticia stayed at. It was on the 600 block, those low-slung old places they got painted gray. She lived on the first floor.

Inside the common hallway, I came to her door. I knocked and took off my knit cap and shook the snow off it, waiting for her to come. The door opened, but only a crack. It stopped as the chain of the slide bolt went taut. Leticia looked at me over the chain. I could see dirt tracks on the part of her face that showed, from where she'd been crying. She was a hard-looking woman, had always been, even when she was young. I'd never seen her so shook.

"Ain't you gonna let me in?"

"No."

"What's wrong with you, girl?"

"I don't want to see you and you ain't comin' in."

"I got some nice smoke, Leticia."

"Leave outta here, Verdon."

I listened to the bass of a rap thing, coming from another apartment. Behind it, a woman and a man were having an argument.

"What happened?" I said. "Why you been cryin'?"

"Marquise came," said Leticia. "Marquise made me cry."

My stomach dropped some. I tried not to let it show on my face.

"That's right," said Leticia. "Flora musta told him about our conversation. Wasn't hard for him to find Rico's aunt."

"He threaten you?"

"He never did, direct. Matter of fact, that boy was smilin' the whole time he spoke to me." Leticia's lip trembled. "We came to an understandin', Verdon."

"What he say?"

"He said that Flora was mistaken. That she wasn't there the night Rico was killed, and she would swear to it in court. And that if I thought different, I was mistaken, too."

"You sayin' that you're mistaken, Leticia?"

"That's right. I been mistaken about this whole thing."

"Leticia—"

"I ain't tryin' to get myself killed for five hundred dollars, Verdon."

"Neither am I."

"Then you better go somewhere for a while."

"Why would I do that?"

Leticia said nothing.

"You give me up, Leticia?"

Leticia cut her eyes away from mine. "Flora," she said, almost a whisper. "She told him 'bout some skinny, older-lookin' dude who was standin' in the alley the day I took her for bad."

"You gave me *up?*"

Leticia shook her head slowly and pushed the door shut. It closed with a soft click.

I didn't pound on the door or nothing like that. I stood there stupidly for sometime, listening to the rumble of the bass and the argument still going between the woman and man. Then I walked out the building.

The snow was coming down heavy. I couldn't go home, so I walked toward the avenue instead.

I had finished the rest of my vodka, and dropped the bottle to the curb, by the time I got down to Georgia. A Third District cruiser was parked on the corner, with two officers inside it, drinking coffee from paper cups. It was late, and with the snow and the cold there wasn't too many people out. The Spring Laundromat, used to be a Roy Rogers or some shit like it, was packed with men and women, just standing around, getting out of the weather. I could see their outlines behind that nicotine-stained glass, most of them barely moving under those dim lights.

This time of night, many of the shops had closed. I was hungry, but Morgan's Seafood had been boarded up for a year now, and The Hunger Stopper, had those good fish sand-wiches, was dark inside. What I needed was a beer, but Giant had locked its doors. I could have gone to the titty bar between Newton and Otis, but I had been roughed in there too many times.

I crossed over to the west side of Georgia and walked

south. I passed a midget in a green suede coat who stood where he always did, under the awning of the Dollar General. I had worked there for a couple of days, stocking shit on shelves.

The businesses along here were like a roll call of my personal failures. The Murray's meat and produce, the car wash, the Checks Cashed joint, they had given me a chance. In all these places, I had lasted just a short while.

I neared the G.A. market, down by Irving. A couple of young men came toward me, buried inside the hoods of their North Face coats, hard of face, then smiling as they got a look at me.

"Hey, slim," said one of the young men. "Where you get that vicious coat at? *Baby* GAP?" Him and his friend laughed.

I didn't say nothing back. I got this South Pole coat I bought off a dude, didn't want it no more. I wasn't about to rock a North Face. Boys put a gun in your grill for those coats down here.

I walked on.

The market was crowded inside and thick with the smoke of cigarettes. I stepped around some dudes and saw a man I know, Robert Taylor, back by where they keep the wine. He was lifting a bottle of it off the shelf. He was in the middle of his thirties, but he looked fifty-five.

"Robo," I said.

"Verdon."

We did a shoulder-to-shoulder thing and patted backs. I had been knowing him since grade school. Like me, he had seen better days. He looked kinda under it now. He held up a bottle of fortified, turned it so I could see the label, like them waiters do in high-class restaurants.

"I sure could use a taste," said Robert. "Only, I'm a little light this evenin'."

"I got you, Robo."

"Look, I'll hit you back on payday."

"We're good."

I picked up a bottle of Night Train for myself and moved toward the front of the market. Robert grabbed the sleeve of my coat and held it tight. His eyes, most time full of play, were serious.

"Verdon."

"What?"

"I been here a couple of hours, stayin' dry and shit. Lotta activity in here tonight. You just standin' around, you be hearin' things."

"Say what you heard."

"Some boys was in here earlier, lookin' for you."

I felt that thing in my stomach.

"Three young men," said Robert. "One of 'em had them silver things on his teeth. They was describin' you, your build and shit, and that hat you always be wearin'."

He meant my knit cap, with the Bullets logo, had the two hands for the double l's, going up for the rebound. I had been wearing it all winter long. I had been wearing it the day we talked to Flora in the alley.

"Anyone tell them who I was?"

Robert nodded sadly. "I can't lie. Some bama did say your name."

"Shit."

"I ain't say *nothin'* to those boys, Verdon."

"C'mon, man. Let's get outta here."

We went up to the counter. I used the damp twenty Barnes had handed me to pay for the two bottles of wine and a fresh pack of cigarettes. While the squarehead behind the plexiglass was bagging my shit and making my change, I picked up a scratched-out lottery ticket and pencil off the scarred counter, turned the ticket over, and wrote around the blank edges. What I wrote was: *Marquise Roberts killed Rico Jennings.* And: *Flora Lewis was there.*

I slipped the ticket into the pocket of my jeans and got my change. Me and Robert Taylor walked out the shop.

On the snow-covered sidewalk I handed Robert his bottle of fortified. I knew he'd be heading west into Columbia Heights, where he stays with an ugly-looking woman and her kids.

"Thank you, Verdon."

"Ain't no thing."

"What you think? Skins gonna do it next year?"

"They got Coach Gibbs. They get a couple receivers with hands, they gonna be all right."

"No doubt." Robert lifted his chin. "You be safe, hear?"

He went on his way. I crossed Georgia Avenue, quick-stepping out the way of a Ford that was fishtailing in the street. I thought about getting rid of my Bullets cap, in case Marquise and them came up on me, but I was fond of it, and I could not let it go.

I unscrewed the top off the Night Train as I went along, taking a deep pull and feeling it warm my chest. Heading up Otis, I saw ragged silver dollars drifting down through the light of the streetlamps. The snow capped the roofs of parked cars and it had gathered on the branches of the trees. No one was out. I stopped to light the rest of my joint. I got it going, and hit it as I walked up the hill.

I planned to head home in a while, through the alley door, when I thought it was safe. But for now, I needed to work on my head. Let my high come like a friend and tell me what to do.

I stood on the east side of Park Lane, my hand on the fence bordering the Soldier's Home, staring into the dark. I had smoked all my reefer and drunk my wine. It was quiet, nothing but the hiss of snow. And "Get Up," that old Salt-N-Pepa joint, playing in my head. Sondra liked that one. She'd dance to it, with my headphones on, over by that lake they got. With the geese running around it, in the summertime.

"Sondra," I whispered. And then I chuckled some, and said, "I am high."

I turned and walked back to the road, tripping a little as I stepped off the curb. As I got onto Quebec, I saw a car coming down Park Lane, sliding a little, rolling too fast. It was a dark color, and it had them Chevy headlights with the rectangle fog lamps on the sides. I patted my pockets, knowing all the while that I didn't have my cell.

I ducked into the alley off Quebec. I looked up at that rear porch with the bicycle tire leaning up on it, where that boy stayed. I saw a light behind the porch door's window. I scooped up snow, packed a ball of it tight, and threw it up at that window. I waited. The boy parted the curtains and put his face up on the glass, his hands cupped around his eyes so he could see.

"Little man!" I yelled, standing by the porch. "Help me out!"

He cold-eyed me and stepped back. I knew he recognized me. But I guess he had seen me go toward the police unmarked, and he had made me for a snitch. In his young mind, it was probably the worst thing a man could be. Behind the window, all went dark. As it did, headlights swept the alley and a car came in with the light. The car was black, and it was a Caprice.

I turned and bucked.

I ran my ass off down that alley, my old Timbs struggling for grip in the snow. As I ran, I pulled on trashcans, knocking them over so they would block the path of the Caprice. I didn't look back. I heard the boys in the car, yelling at me and shit, and I heard them curse as they had to slow down. Soon I was out of the alley, on Princeton Place, running free.

I went down Princeton, cut left on Warder, jogged by the front of the elementary, and hung a right on Otis. There was an alley down there, back behind the ball field, shaped like a T. It would be hard for them to navigate back in there. They couldn't surprise me or nothing like that.

I walked into the alley. Straight off, a couple of dogs began to bark. Folks kept 'em, shepherd mixes and rottweilers with heads big as cattle, for security. Most of them was inside, on account of the weather, but not all. There were some who stayed out all the time, and they were loud. Once they got going, they would bark themselves crazy. They were letting Marquise know where I was.

I saw the Caprice drive real slow down Otis, its headlights off, and I felt my ears grow hot. I got down in a crouch, pressed myself against a chain-link fence behind someone's row house. My stomach flipped all the way and I had one of them throw-up burps. Stuff came up, and I swallowed it down.

I didn't care if it was safe or not; I needed to get my ass home. Couldn't nobody hurt me there. In my bed, the same bed where I always slept, near my brother James. With my mother and father down the hall.

I listened to a boy calling out my name. Then another

boy, from somewhere else, did the same. I could hear the laughter in their voices. I shivered some and bit down on my lip.

Use the alphabet, you get lost. That's what my father told me when I was a kid. Otis, Princeton, Quebec . . . I was three streets away.

I turned at the T of the alley and walked down the slope. The dogs were out of their minds, growling and barking, and I went past them and kept my eyes straight ahead. At the bottom of the alley, I saw a boy in a thick coat, hoodie up. He was waiting on me.

I turned around and ran back from where I came. Even with the sounds of the dogs, I could hear myself panting, trying to get my breath. I rounded the T and made it back to Otis, where I cut and headed for the baseball field. I could cross that and be on Princeton. When I got there, I'd be one block closer to my home.

I stepped up onto the field. I walked regular, trying to calm myself down. I didn't hear a car or anything else. Just the snow crunching beneath my feet.

And then a young man stepped up onto the edge of the field. He wore a bulky coat without a cap or a hood. His hand was inside the coat, and his smile was not the smile of a friend. There were silver caps on his front teeth.

I turned my back on him. Pee ran hot down my thigh. My knees were trembling, but I made my legs move.

The night flashed. I felt a sting, like a bee sting, high on my back.

I stumbled but kept my feet. I looked down at my blood, dotted in the snow. I walked a couple of steps and closed my eyes.

When I opened them, the field was green. It was covered

in gold, like it gets here in summer, 'round early evening. A Gamble and Huff thing was coming from the open windows of a car. My father stood before me, his natural full, his chest filling the fabric of his shirt. His sleeves were rolled up to his elbows. His arms were outstretched.

I wasn't afraid or sorry. I'd done right. I had the lottery ticket in my pocket. Detective Barnes, or someone like him, would find it in the morning. When they found *me*.

But first I had to speak to my father. I walked to where he stood, waiting. And I knew exactly what I was going to say: I ain't the low-ass bum you think I am. I been workin' with the police for a long, long time. Matter of fact, I just solved a homicide.

I'm a confidential informant, Pop. Look at me.

FIRST

BY KENJI JASPER

Benning Heights, S.E.

This shit has gone way too far. That's what the little voice in your head tells you. The black hoodie concealing your face is too warm for mid-April, and is thus putting your Right Guard to the test. However, it will keep you above description. And in this case, it's all that matters.

The radio's on but turned all the way down. More commercial breaks than there ever is music. Makes you curse your tape deck for being broken. Maybe it's a blessing though, one less thing to distract you.

After all there are three other men to worry about. The first, Sean, the one you've known since Ms. Abby's class at nursery school, is in the passenger seat sucking on a half-dead Newport as he loads a final shell into the sawed-off he stole from your first catch of the day. The four of you introduced his flesh to four pair of steel-toed Timberlands. You can still hear his ribs splintering, and that shrill scream he let out at the end, when Babatunde's fist split his nose in two.

Dante and Baba are in the '85 Escort behind the house, both in the same hot-ass hoodies you're rocking. Sean was the only one smart enough to go with short sleeves. But there are beads even on his brow, mostly near the sideburns. You've been telling him to cut that nappy 'fro of his for the last six months. It makes him look like a cheap-ass Redman. But he likes Redman.

"This jawnt is like that for '92!" he proclaims, continuing to take the critique as a compliment. You can't wait for '93.

"You ready?" Baba asks, his voice crackling with static through the pair of ten-dollar walkie-talkies you've purchased for this hit. The car sits different on your new rear tires. Rochelle slashed the old ones two weeks ago when you told her it was over. Maybe it wasn't too prudent for you to mention that Catalina had bigger titties.

You love titties, or breasts, as a more elegant politically correct nigga might say. But you ain't elegant and you definitely ain't PC. You're from Southeast. And there's four lives inside the rules say you gotta take.

It was definitely not supposed to turn out like this. You would have rather spent the last three hours in Catalina's basement, bumping and grinding in nothing but a latex shield. You should be squeezing her nipples with your fingers, and putting a thumb on that pearl down below.

You were supposed to be five grand richer by dawn. But that hammer hit the base of the shell and next thing you knew, Fat Rodney's skull was missing a chunk the size of your fist, his blood sprayed across your cheek as you took cover to the left of that door frame. It was your first time out and somebody had the fix in. Go fuckin' figure.

"So y'all ready?" Dante asks again. Burns Street is nothing but quiet, a block the cops hardly every patrol. Nothing over there but grandmas and kids and the P.G. line just a few up the hill. All of this for Boyz II Men at the Cap Centre. All of this because once again you didn't know when to pull out.

1.

You got up that morning Ferris Bueller style. Peered through the shades and there wasn't a cloud in the sky. Your new girl was still on your fingers, the smell of Claiborne all over everything else. You remembered the way her tongue felt against your chest and the way she said good night before she went out through the basement, knowing your moms always slept like a corpse.

You woke up with all of that on your mind and two dollars in your pocket. The weekend was on the way and Boyz II Men was coming to the Cap Centre with a bunch of other acts. Catalina loved those gump-ass niggas, and thus expected you to foot the bill for two tickets, preceded by dinner and hopefully followed by you getting some long-awaited ass. You'd been chipping away at that pussy for weeks, first base all the way to the edge of third. Now home was definitely in sight.

Things would've been simple if that coming Friday was a payday. But it wasn't. Add in the fact that you already owed Dante twenty dollars from the last time you took Catalina out and thirty to Sean for those tapes you were supposed to go in half on, then taxes, your pager bill, and cake for gas, and that forthcoming check was already spent. You needed some more dough and you needed it yesterday.

So you tried to come up with a plan in the shower, 'cuz that's where you do your best thinking. Under water your thoughts flow evenly. In the stream you cut through all the bullshit. So it was there, under the "massage" setting spray, that you thought about running game at the rec.

It was a Tuesday after all. Who the hell went to school on Tuesday, especially when you could buy off the rec manager with an apple stick and two packs of Now and Laters? What a pathetic price for a nigga as old as your father, whoever he is.

"You tryin' to play for time?" you asked your first mark, some light-skinned dude with a low-taper his barber shoulda got stabbed for.

You knew the kid had cake. He had that look in his eye, plus a Guess watch, the new Jordans, and a sweet pair of Girbauds cuffed at the ankle. You'd seen him around before, so you knew he wasn't some out-of-bounds hustler trying to move in on your racket. Yeah, that's right, it was already yours, even before the first shot.

"I'm tryin' to play for money," he said boldly, tapping a nervous finger against his thigh, the biggest tell in the world that he didn't have what it took. You had him on the rack six times in under an hour. The idea crossed your mind of majoring in pool when you got to college.

"My game's off today," he confessed earnestly after handing you three twenties without a flinch. "I guess my loss is your gain."

There was something about that phrase that didn't sit well with you. It wasn't the kinda shit niggas say on Ridge Road. Or if it was, you'd never heard it before. And that made you curious. You and your damn curiosity.

"And a nice little gain it is," you replied gloating, thinking of the words as a perfect move to finish him off.

"It ain't shit to me," he replied. "But I can see you need the money."

You told him he needed to watch himself, that he didn't know you like that. You turned open palms into fists, preparing yourself for battle. Yet all he did was grin. And that little grin made you think he might have heat, which meant you might be dead in the next few seconds. There you went again, acting before you could think on it.

He told you to chill. He didn't mean any disrespect. He

just thought that maybe the two of you could help each other out. After all, he'd seen you around the way and knew you were no joke. Truth be told, he even made it so he lost the first game or two of the previous series just to make you feel comfortable, just so you could feel like he was an easy mark. You took in all the words, but you didn't really understand them, except for when he said that he had a problem he wanted you to help him with.

"What you mean you want me to help you? I don't know you, nigga," was your response.

"It's ten G's in it for you," he replied. "Ten G's for some shit that won't even take ten minutes."

This was when you should have turned away. You weren't a fuckin' criminal. Sure you'd sold a few rocks back when everybody was doin' it, and sure you and Sean had run some chains off people outside of the go-go. But anything worth ten G's was way too hot for you to touch. Yet even though you were thinking these things, your mouth said: "Ten G's!? Shit, what the fuck I gotta do?"

Now according to the story, this dude who soon after introduced himself as "Butchie" had a little crack thing going down on Texas Avenue with a partner of his. The two of them had either bought (or run) some old lady out of her crib and were dealing there, but strictly to respectable clients (i.e., people who had all their teeth and wouldn't draw suspicion from the cop details). And it had actually worked out. They'd cleared just over 100 grand in six months.

This partner, introduced only as "D", handled muscle and management. Butchie dealt with the supplier and scouting out clientele. The only problem came in when D got hit with a rape charge on the other side of town. Not only was it a parole violation but the dude's second felony. Needless to say, D wouldn't be seeing daylight anytime soon. But there was money and some product still at his crib on Adrian Street, right over the hill from the rec where you met Butchie.

At this point, all the young man in front of you wanted to do was cash out, because there were no guarantees that D wouldn't give him up. However, he still wanted what was his, half the thirty-five grand in D's crib and whatever product was left over, so he could sell it wholesale and dump the money into a McDonald's he wanted to reopen out on Bladensburg Road. It was a plan you could respect. Shit, if you'd had the cake you would've done the same thing yourself.

Butchie went on to inform you that D lived alone and had even given him a key to the house. But he didn't want to pick up the loot himself just in case the cops were there waiting for him. Plus, he wasn't the kind of "go-hard nigga" that you were. As a matter of fact, he'd brought D into the equation because he wasn't from the street, because he needed somebody to have his back in an always competitive and treacherous marketplace. Thus, he was willing to give you almost a third of the cash sum if you'd just go in and get it for him.

Once again you were listening less to the plan and more to your own imagination. What would ten G's feel like in your hand? What couldn't you buy with that kind of dough? The possibilities were endless, and you, even with sixty-two bucks in-pocket, enough for the tickets and a little dinner, were now game on snatching this new ball of wax. Citing a prior commitment, he gave you his pager number before he headed toward the '93 Pathfinder on the asphalt. The deal would expire at the end of the day.

2.

"I don't know about this shit," Sean had grumbled as he passed you the remains of the blunt. Babatunde and Dante were on the other couch and Fat Rodney was upstairs cooking Steak-ums in the kitchen. If you were going to do this, you weren't doing it alone. So you got the crew together and sat them down in your mother's basement. These were the only dudes you trusted in the whole world.

"Me neither," Dante added. "This shit sounds way too easy for what he's payin' us."

"But then again, this nigga sounds weak," Baba fired back. "You know, like the kinda dude ain't never thrown a punch in his life. If the money's in there, we'd have it before him. Shit, if we wanted we could take it all and say 'fuck him.'"

"That's what I was thinkin'," Fat Rodney said with half a sandwich in his mouth. He was that kind of fat where his whole torso bounced with every other step. Five-foot-nine and 300 pounds at sixteen. Somebody needed to put his ass on a treadmill.

"We got five niggas," Rodney continued. "We go in there, get the money, and we're out. If he come around askin' questions, we let that nigga know who he's dealin' with."

Sean argued back that it was easier said than done, that as far as you all knew the house might not even belong to the alleged "D". Butchie coulda been a snitch for the cops or somebody's cousin you jumped a few weeks back at some party you can't even remember.

You rebutted that the cops didn't have a reason to be after y'all. Shit, you'd never been caught, never even been arrested, never even had to talk to a cop outside of the Officer Friendlys that blew through your elementary schools all those years ago. You'd dealt with a whole lot worse for a whole lot less. So why not give it a shot?

Dante looked nervous. Baba looked like he was already through D's door. Sean looked like you were all about to make the biggest mistake of your young lives. And Rodney, having finished his sandwich, actually looked full. Nobody wanted to put an answer on the table. So you did it for them. You were gonna tell Butchie that you were in, but stake the place out for a few hours before you made a move.

You paged Butchie that afternoon and he gave you a green light. It was around 3:00 when you the made the call so you all decided to waiting until after 10:00 when the block would be night and settled in. While you were waiting, Sean took the wheel of your Accord hatchback and headed over to the local arsenal, where he happened to have a running tab. He came out five minutes after he went in with a Glock 9, two snub .38s, and a .380, enough for all of you except Rodney, who "didn't do heat."

As it turned out, D's crib was the last house on the right at the bottom of Adrian, a little bungalow with a front and back yard. No basement and no alarm system, which appeared to mean that there were no problems. Texas Avenue was at the corner and Dupont Park was a block east.

Still, you decided to go with caution. Everybody took turns for three hours. The neighbors filed in car by car. By midnight all the lights in their cribs had gone dark.

Nobody went in or out of D's place either. It seemed deserted, just like Butchie said it'd be. All you had to do was go in and get rich.

Dante decided to stay in the car. Sean told him to honk the horn twice if somebody was comin'. Baba went around the back to make sure nobody was gonna sneak in from the rear. Sean was gonna stay at the front gate. You and Rodney were gonna go up the steps, turn the key, and stuff the Jansport you used for your books with more cash than you'd held in your seventeen years on the planet.

Each step brought you closer to the prize. You were thinking of Catalina and Claiborne, of having her lips wrapped around you in the privacy of your own bedroom. You slipped Butchie's key into the lock and it turned, putting a bigger smile on your face than Isaac from *The Love Boat*. You turned to Rodney for some sign of approval. You looked just in time to see the buckshot take half his head off.

It was only God that kept you from going out with him. The blast was deafening. You tripped over the porch railing and did a double-back into the bushes underneath. From what you could tell, Sean returned fire, trading blasts with your fat homeboy's killer. Babatunde picked you up and dragged you toward the car. Next thing you knew, Dante had parked at the river. The night sky didn't have a star in it, but you had a full clip and one in the chamber, one you wanted to use on yourself.

Sean didn't have a problem reminding you that he'd told you so. Dante's hands were trembling. Baba wanted blood. You wanted a time-traveling DeLorean so you could go back and stop your boy from a closed-casket funeral. But once the shock wore off, you wanted answers.

Who the fuck were the niggas in there and why'd they open up on you so quick? If you'd been set up, what was the reason? If it was your bad luck, then why'd Rodney have to go out? The magnitude of it made your head hurt. But you couldn't go home. You didn't even want to make a phone call until the source of the problem was six feet deep.

Baba and Dante seconded the motion. Dante knew he should have covered the front with you. He was sitting in the car with a gun that could've saved his boy's life. Sean felt the same way too. He just wanted you all to be careful. This was a bigger game than any of you had ever played. So you had to be smart, or you'd be as dead as Rodney.

After debating until dawn, you all decided the only move was to reach out to Butchie, to act like shit had gone as planned and then see what move he might make. Sure there were better ways to play it, but not with a bunch of young niggas working on fear, regret, and not a minute's worth of sleep. You paged your betrayer just after 9:00 from a pay phone on Benning Road.

He called right back and you told him you had everything. You even mocked Scarface by saying you had "the money and the yayo." He laughed and told you to meet him at his crib, the white house at the corner of Chaplin and Ridge. He even gave you the street number. You *never* gave people street numbers.

Still, you pulled up to the given spot at the designated time, your lips greasy from the bag of sausage biscuits and hash browns you'd recently devoured. Why did you have to be so fucking greedy? Now you were leading a crew of five down to four, running on nothing but revenge.

You literally saw red when he opened the door in a Mickey Mouse T-shirt and some boxer shorts. He said that you were early. You said that he was a dead motherfucker. Baba and Sean came in through an open window at the rear and you all let him have it.

Babo and Sean took the crib. They broke the glass-framed pictures and knocked over the credenza with all of his mom's good dishes. Then they went to work on him, while you asked the questions.

It turned out that Butchie had been doing a little double-dealing. Just to make sure he got paid, he pitched the same offer to some dude named Rico who lived over by the fish place on Burns Street. Apparently they'd gotten there long before you did. Maybe they'd come through the back or on the side you couldn't see so good. So they were on their way out with the goods as y'all were headed in.

However, Butchie hadn't heard from them, which told you maybe they'd gotten caught by the cops, probably with the money and the weight in hand after the shoot-out. Did Rodney's mom even know yet? Was there enough of his face left for a positive ID?

The bloody boy was talking so fast that he could've been speaking in tongues. He gave you Rico's first and last name and told you where the place was. Sean and Baba found about $1,000, a half a brick, and a pump-action sawed-off with a bunch of shells. Had you actually been thinking, you would've pressed him for all the money he had, cake you knew had to be stashed somewhere. But now all you wanted was Rico. Rico would close the circle so y'all could get the shirts and suits ready.

3.

This was no longer about what you wanted. It was about what had to be done. That's what you told yourself in the mirror as you changed into that hot-ass hoodie, that this was the way things worked in the streets, that it was an eye for an eye and all that other shit.

But then, for a moment, you thought about your mama, about the two jobs she worked to keep a roof over your head, about all the efforts she made to get you out of that fucked-up neighborhood school and into that pre-engineering program. You thought about all those dreams you had of getting out of

Southeast someday, of being a better dad than the one you never knew. You thought about all of those things and then shook them off when you closed the door behind you.

Dante brought his car so you could work in teams. Baba bought the walkie-talkies from the corner store on his block. You were in business. All you had to do was go to the designated crib and designate Rico's ass—that is, if he happened to be home. Still, you hesitated when you turned your key in the ignition. It was as if you knew you'd made the wrong choice.

Ten minute's later Dante crackles across the radio line, asking if you're ready. Sean's right next to you, down to see this thing through even if he was against it from day one. You can see people moving inside of the house from the street. There will never be a moment more perfect.

"Yeah," you say into the plastic device. "Let's do it."

You and Sean storm out of the car and rush the front, assuming your boys are doing the same at the rear. Your weapons are locked and loaded and the enemy will be caught unaware. Then you hear the fucking sirens, followed by the flood of gold and blue cruisers on both sides of the street. They're in the alley at the back too. The whole world is one big roar of karma's siren.

This was going to be your first kill, your first foray into the kind of streetlife that made gangsta rap sell millions. One pull of the trigger and you and your boys would've moved into a whole new area code. Instead you're in the back of a cruiser knowing that bloody Butchie crawled to the phone and made the call. Maybe he felt guilty. Or even worse, maybe he was smarter than you.

They won't get you for murder. Truth be told, if you rat

Butchie out you might only get a year at Oak Hill. You're only seventeen with no priors. Make it through twelve months in that place and you can still have a future, so will the others. But Rodney won't. He's the first casualty of a war that never got started.

You'll think about him for the rest of your life, never understanding how that blast didn't take you with him. If you live long enough, you'll try to understand how this era even existed, how so many lives were snatched away over shit as equally silly. You'll pour out a little brew every time you have a drink and never eat a Steak-Um again. You're lucky to be alive, player. This is the first day of the rest of your life.

CAPITAL OF THE WORLD

BY JIM PATTON
Chinatown, N.W.

Two in the morning, a steamy Saturday night in July, Sherman Brown was standing by the jukebox in the notorious Sunbeam Lounge, wondering what the hell he was doing here. With a wife, a little girl, twins coming, and no way to live anywhere near the District on a cop's pay, the idea was to earn some nice money, short-term, for a down payment on a house in peaceful Howard County, Maryland. But still, a D.C. cop—a good cop, who liked to think of himself as a good *man*—moonlighting as a bouncer in a dive like this? He wasn't the first, wouldn't be the last, but—

A gunshot. Marvin Gaye was wailing from the jukebox, a dozen or so brothers were whooping as the girl onstage humped the pole, but Sherman knew he'd heard a shot. A Metro cop heard plenty of them. Anyone who grew up in a project like Barry Farms had heard plenty. This one came from in back, the other side of the plain brown door Sherman had never passed through.

Tyrone, behind the bar, heard it. So did Antwain, the whale, who'd been up near the stage ogling the girl and stood there now with his mouth hanging open. Some of the brothers had heard it—they were getting up from their tables and streaming out. The girl stopped humping the pole.

LaPhonso, the boss, wasn't around. He'd been in and out as always—keeping an eye on things, going in back with one of the girls for a while, stepping outside to get high or do some kind of business.

Sherman crossed to Tyrone at the bar—Antwain right beside him, all 300 pounds. "Where's LaPhonso?"

"Ain't seen him in a while," Tyrone said.

"You got a key so I can check it out? Or you want to check it?"

Antwain butted in—"Naw, man. You the law. You gettin paid. Go on."

Sherman eyeballed him. He never liked mouth from a punk, 300 pounds or not.

"Go on. The Man ain't here," Antwain said, "and when he ain't here, *I'm* The Man." He told Tyrone, "Give him the key, dawg."

Tyrone handed it over.

"Go, boy," Antwain said.

Sherman wanted to hurt him—this whale, this punk, calling Sherman Brown *boy*. But not now. He turned and headed toward the anonymous door. He heard Antwain right behind him, the labored breathing.

The door opened to a dim hallway. Approaching the first door on the left, Sherman reached for the Glock 17 holstered under his shirt at the small of his back. In the room he found crackhead Donita, one of the strippers, blowing a cornrowed brother called Junebug. They hadn't heard anything, or didn't care.

In the next room a short, stocky guy called Cannonball was humping the new girl called Golden. No sign of any shooting here. Sherman pulled the door shut and went back the other way, Antwain close behind him, wheezing.

In the first room at the other end, a girl he'd never seen was on the bed clutching the sheet up under her chin, scared, as if she'd seen or at least heard something—a white girl, dark hair, foreign-looking. Sherman had heard about foreign girls back here who never appeared out front.

"You all right?"

"Ho-kay. Ho-kay," she said, nodding furiously. Foreign, definitely. Sherman wasn't sure she understood him.

Approaching the last door, he heard someone rattling the knob from inside, then working a key in the lock. Had to be LaPhonso.

"Yo, LaPhonz!"

Quiet, then. The key no longer working the lock.

"Boss!" (What LaPhonso liked to be called, though Sherman could rarely bring himself to say it.)

Nothing.

"Whoever you are! I got my piece and I'm coming in!"

He turned his key in the lock and opened the door a crack. There was someone there. A girl—a pale shoulder, an arm, part of a slip or negligee.

She backed up, whoever she was. "Sorry!" She too had some kind of accent, and sounded shaken.

The cordite smell told Sherman the shot had been fired in here. He raised his Glock and eased the door open with his left foot. "What's going on? You got a gun in here?"

The girl stared at him, wide-eyed. Behind her was a king bed and a pile of clothes on the floor—sandals, denim shorts, purple polka-dot boxers, and a wad that looked like the wifebeater T-shirt LaPhonso had been wearing tonight.

The girl pointed off to her right. Sherman, unable to see over there from the hallway, eased into the room.

There was a gun on the floor, probably a .38, near a closed door. Sherman picked it up, jammed it in his waistband and turned to the girl. "What happened?"

She stared with the wide eyes, didn't say anything.

"Who's in there?" Sherman said.

"Who *where*, man?"—Antwain, out in the hall.

Sherman went to the closed door and pushed it open. It was a little bathroom, nothing but an old toilet and sink— and *The Man*, LaPhonso Peete, sprawled on the floor, dead as a flat rat. Brain matter all over the wall behind the toilet, blood pooling under his head.

"What the *fuck?*"—Antwain right behind Sherman now. "Bitch!"

"Chill, man," Sherman said.

"Who you tellin *chill*, boy? Bitch *kilt* my nigga! You *dead*, bitch. Gimme that," he told Sherman, meaning the Glock.

Sherman wasn't about to.

Antwain glared. "*You* gonna take her out, then."

Out of his mind.

"You hear me, nigga? You been gettin fat here. You wanna keep that cabbage rollin in? You take this bitch out, I get ridda this here"—jerking a thumb toward LaPhonso's corpse, an inconvenience—"and we back to normal tomorra, nobody know nothin."

Sherman shook his head. It couldn't work. Besides, he was a police officer and this was a murder, even if LaPhonso had been nothing but a piece of garbage.

"*Yeah*, you gonna do her," Antwain said. "Then she ain't tell nothin bout our business. Do her or we gonna do *yo* ass."

Sherman looked over at the girl in her slip—pale and thin, but with a pretty face and something in her eyes.

"All right, then," he told Antwain, and told the girl, "Come on. Get some clothes on."

A few minutes later he had her out in his old Cutlass.

Now what? Antwain wouldn't believe he'd blown her away unless there was proof. He'd want to see the body.

He felt the girl looking at him as he pulled out of the lot. Did she believe he was one more sorry nigger, a killer?

He headed downtown on New York Avenue. Approaching Chinatown a few minutes later, he still didn't know what to do.

One of his favorite spots, the China Doll, was open till 4 a.m. on weekends. He turned left on 5th, right on H, and parked under a streetlight. He looked over and the girl was so pale, the eyes so big. Striking.

He wondered what the moment felt like to her. Wondered who she was, where she was from, what her story was.

As if she'd read his mind, she said, "I'm Mariana. From Moldova." Heavy accent, but understandable.

"Mol—?"

"Moldova. My country."

It sounded familiar, but only vaguely. Sherman felt stupid.

"Your first time in Washington?" he said. "Nation's capital?" And felt stupider yet.

"Capital of the world," she said. "Is what we learn in school. We study English language and much about United States."

"How'd you end up here?"

She shrugged. "Why you ask? Man say you kill me. So?"

"I'm not going to kill you," Sherman said. "I'm police, not a killer."

No reaction. Maybe she didn't believe him.

At a loss, he asked her again how she happened to get to the U.S. from . . . "Moldavia?"

"Moldova."

"I don't even know where it is," Sherman said.

"Is far. You know Romania? On other side. Far."

They sat there for most of an hour, under the streetlight, while she told her story. She said Moldova was one of the old Soviet states, one of the poorest countries in the world. In their capital, she said, men who worked in hospitals had been arrested for chopping up corpses and selling the flesh as meat at open-air markets. She grew up in a village called Droki, in a little house where the electricity rarely worked—her and two sisters and their mother, after her father drank himself to death. She quit school at fourteen and worked in a beetroot factory. Two years ago, when she was seventeen, an aunt in a neighboring village sold her out—told her about job opportunities abroad and dropped her off for an interview, supposedly, but the "interviewers" were Albanian gangsters who locked her up with some other girls and later drove them across Romania and Serbia to Macedonia, where they were locked in little rooms in back of a *kafane*, a club—like the Sunbeam, Sherman imagined—and forced to service twenty, thirty men every night. Slaves. After sixteen months she was saved by a man who bought her and took her to the authorities. The authorities arranged her passage back to Moldova. She got home only to find the Albanian Mafia had not only snatched her sister Nataly but murdered their little sister Lena, who had witnessed the snatching. Nataly had been gone for nearly a year. Their mother had received a single card from her, which said she'd been taken to Italy and forced into prostitution.

Sherman tried to take it all in. *You thought growing up in Barry Farms was tough?*

She—Mariana—said she'd gone to Albania then, last year, and *asked* to go to Italy as a prostitute, "my only hope to find my sister." She was sold at an auction and put on a speedboat across the Adriatic at midnight with other illegal immigrants. Gangsters in Italy took her first to a beautiful seaside town called Rimini and then many other places. Everywhere, she showed a picture of Nataly, but no one knew her.

The life was brutal, as in Macedonia. Threats, beatings, torture. When one girl was suspected of talking to the *polizia*, the men gathered all the others, tied the "bad" one in a chair, pulled her tongue out with pliers and sliced it off. Mariana saw girls killed for no reason than to put the fear in the others. Three girls killed themselves.

Sherman was sweating, hearing it. He started the Cutlass and ran the AC.

She said she was finally reunited with her sister. The gangsters had murdered a Nigerian girl and believed Mariana might go to a priest about it. One night they took her to a warehouse and produced Nataly—with a knife at her throat, and did Mariana still want to talk to the priest?

To get them out of Italy, away from the authorities, the gangsters flew them to Mexico. Then they were trafficked into the U.S. and sold again. Eventually they were brought to D.C.

"Together, at least," she said. "But they take me one place, Nataly another. I no see her. Sometime I hear something, but I no see her."

Sherman didn't know what to say. He sure as hell didn't know what to do. He couldn't take her to a police station—no telling who might be connected with LaPhonso or LaPhonso's people. If he took her to any authority at all, including the FBI's human-trafficking unit, he was asking for trouble—he'd have to say how he happened to know her, have to tell about the Sunbeam. He'd immediately be put on administrative leave and would probably wind up out on his ass. It was illegal for a cop to work anyplace that served alcohol—aside from the dealing, prostitution, and everything else at the Sunbeam. The MPD brass looked the other way if you wanted to take your chances, but if things blew up they'd hang you out to dry.

That was the *best-case* scenario. It would get a lot worse if they found out LaPhonso was dead and Sherman hadn't reported it.

And beyond the authorities, there was Antwain. Sherman would be as good as dead when Antwain found out he hadn't taken this girl somewhere, straight from the club, and murdered her.

This girl. *Mariana.* From Mol*dova.* Her life more harrowing than Sherman's, LaPhonso's, Antwain's.

"At this place they lock me in the room," she was saying, "and I know what I must do. Every day, every night. And this man—this man—"

"LaPhonso?"

"—he come sometime, too, and I must do for him. Anything. Sometime he want this and this and I say no and he hit me, hurt me. Sometime I want him to *kill* me. I'm dead inside, so no matter. Except for my sister. I live for my sister. I know she live for me."

She told it with no emotion at all. Spooky, as if she *was* dead inside. Except Sherman didn't believe she was. This girl could be saved, if he only knew how.

"Now," she said, "is okay I die. No matter. You kill me, is okay."

Sherman didn't understand. "I'm not going to kill you. And you just said you need to *live*, for your sister."

"No. Dead, my sister."

"Dead? You said . . ."

"Yes, dead. A girl come from the other place and say they kill a girl for nothing. I know is Nataly—hair, scars on the hand where men in Italy burn her with cigarette. Yes. And now, why I live? They kill me?—okay. You kill me?—okay."

Jesus.

"I'm not going to kill you," Sherman said. "Let's go in the restaurant and figure out what to do with you. Eat if you want."

"No eat. No."

Sherman couldn't eat either. They went into the China Doll and the graveyard waitress, Lejing, brought them tea. Mariana seemed not to even notice.

"So," Sherman said finally. He had to hear the rest.

"Yes." She looked off at the mirrored wall. "Is why I shoot this man. Many times—Macedonia, Italy, United States—I dream I have a pistol, but no. I can do nothing."

"But you got your hands on one tonight."

"Yes. He come and hurt me again. Drunk, or he use the drugs. He close his eyes later and I think he sleep. I go bathroom. Come back, I step on his clothes on floor. Something hard. When I lie down, he wake up and go bathroom, close door."

Sherman pictured LaPhonso on the crapper, in all his glory.

Mariana stared at her trembling hand on the tabletop. "So fast. I go touch hard thing under clothes. A pistol, after so many times I dream. This man, maybe he no kill my sister, but maybe yes. What I know, he is like these men everywhere. I take pistol, open door, shoot. Then think to kill myself, but—no."

She stared at the mirrored wall again. Sherman wondered if she saw their reflections there or was only seeing what was in her head—LaPhonso toppling off the can, the back wall already bloody. The many other bad men. The sister who'd been murdered recently. The little sister murdered in Moldova. Lord only knew.

He still didn't know what to do. He sympathized, he understood why she killed LaPhonso, but the bottom line was she'd killed a man, and he, Sherman Brown, was a police officer.

She might get off. There were no witnesses—a decent lawyer might get her off on self-defense. Then the authorities might get her back to Moldova.

He'd be through, of course. Not only off the force but *dead*, as soon as Antwain realized he hadn't killed her.

Still . . . "I want to help you," he said.

"No. My sister dead, my mother no expect see me again—"

"But she *can* see you again."

She turned away, staring out at lit-up H Street. Sherman wondered how it looked to her, this foreign place. He wondered how the capital of Moldova, where men sold human flesh at open-air markets, would look to him.

"I remember first night here," she said. "Men take me in car and I see Washington Monument—something I see in book when I'm a girl. Now, I am here. Land of the free. I see people on street, I want to cry for help—'Save me! This no happen in United States, in Washington, capital of the world!' But I can no scream. No one hear me outside. Feel I'm under the water, you understand?"

Sherman understood. Underwater, trying to be heard, and it was impossible. He remembered how he felt as a kid, the times he saw the nice part of D.C. Those people didn't see a little black boy from Barry Farms, and if they did, they wouldn't *hear* him—if he dared to speak. And he wouldn't dare. Even as a teenager, a little bit of a player in Barry Farms, he wouldn't talk to anyone in the D.C. you saw on TV. Show up, even, and people looked at you like they couldn't wait to call the police.

Lejing appeared, exhausted. "Solly, Mista Sherman. We close."

Sherman held out a hand to Mariana. "Let's go."

Without any idea where. No idea what he was going to do. Expecting a call from Felice any minute, when she woke up to go to the bathroom and realized he wasn't there. *It's 4 in the morning. What're you doing?*

Thinking of Felice, little Cheri, the twins on the way. His career, his livelihood. Whatever he did, whatever he didn't do, he was taking a big chance.

They were on the sidewalk, H Street, heading toward the Cutlass, when his cell phone rang. Caller ID told him it was Antwain.

"Officer Brown here."

"*Officer.* Shit. Where you at, *officer?*"

"I'm here. You need me?"

"Wanna know whassup. Where that ho-bag at?"

"Where you think?" Sherman said. "*Out.* You know what I mean?"

"I *don't* know. How you think *I* know? Tell me."

"She's out, trust me."

"Trust you, boy? Uh-huh." Sherman heard him chortle. "Listen—"

That was when the girl bolted in front of him, across the sidewalk, off the curb, lunging in front of a speeding Lexus, somebody probably high as the sky at 4 in the morning. Driver never had time to slow—Sherman heard the impact a split second before the screeching noise.

She flew up on the hood and across the windshield and ended up sprawled across the center line, a lane over.

Even as he ran to her, Sherman was looking around wondering who'd seen them together, wondering what to do. Save himself? Say he never saw her before, she came out of nowhere?

Blood running out her mouth, her pale face scraped raw from the pavement. No way she survived.

She hadn't wanted to. So did it matter what he said?

He knelt beside her. Mariana from Moldova, in the capital of the world.

THE NAMES OF THE LOST

BY RICHARD CURREY

Shepherd Park, N.W.

Liebmann locked the front door and walked through his store to the back. He propped the rear door open and picked up what was left of the boxes. He never had more than three or four boxes at the end of a day, most of them gone to the people who did not come in to buy liquor but for these sturdy weight-bearing cartons perfect for moving or for storage. Tonight there was a Wild Turkey box jammed into the corrugated white carton that Mogan David shipped in, both of those slipped into the wider brown flat that held a case of Iron City beer.

He carried the nested stack across the alley and lofted it into the dumpster.

It was November in the city of Washington and the dark came early and deep now. Liebmann paused in the falling cold, the same metallic chill he grew up with in Germany. Washington's weather turned European in November, the same dank gray, skies lowered and closed and withholding. Just a few weeks until Thanksgiving and Christmas and New Year. If the weather was never his favorite, it was Liebmann's best season in business, the only liquor store for ten miles in any direction to stay open until midnight on New Year's Eve. The liquor kept selling until the ball fell in Times Square on the little portable black-and-white TV he kept in his office. And he had no other place to go. If the second thought might have carried an element of dejection, Liebmann felt only a distant surge of something akin to melancholy: He was a businessman, he told himself, and business was good.

Down at the end of the alley a car clocked past on Kalmia Road, its headlights sweeping the misted gloom. He looked back into the glow spreading from inside his store, thinking that it would soon be 1968. He had been in America for twenty-two years, the owner of this liquor store for sixteen of them. One day to another and he was still here, surviving. He stood a moment longer in the chill before he went inside to close out for the day.

Liebmann was married once. His wife died. Cancer, in 1962. There was nothing anyone could do. He met her at the Shepherd Park public library on the corner of Georgia Avenue and Geranium Street. She caught his eye and he knew immediately that she was a survivor like himself. They talked for a few minutes in English and then he went to German and she smiled broadly. After a moment of shy quiet there on the steps of the library, she spoke the single word, *Mauthausen.* A camp in Austria. He understood that it was where she had been taken during the war.

He was standing a step below her and looked up and said: *Auschwitz. Und danach Flossenburg.*

They were married less than four months later, and lived together in the walk-up apartment. She brought a woman's touch. She cooked German, and made Liebmann buy a radio. They figured out the game of baseball and were regulars at Senators home games, sitting in their favorite spot above the third base line. She got him started with the long neighborhood walks around Shepherd Park.

He was not swept away by her, not at first, did not fall in

love the way lovers do who meet and capsize together into the heat and surprise and mystery of discovering each other. But it was a mystery nonetheless, his love building for her like slowly painting a picture of something he had never seen and could never have imagined. All they needed to know was where they had been and that they had found their way to this place and to each other. They were companions. Affection anchored them. They worked the store together. They saved to buy a house. His wife wanted to live on Morningside Drive—she took him walking there and admired the big four-square homes with their precise lawns and the satisfying geometry of their flower beds and careful flagstone walks.

They imagined together what it would be like when they could afford to move.

When she was sick and it was clear her time was short, Liebmann sometimes could not sleep and got up at night to sit beside the bedroom window in the apartment, looking down on Georgia Avenue. He touched the tattoo on his left forearm.

There was nothing anyone could do.

He was transferred from Auschwitz to the camp at Flossenburg to work in the granite quarry there. The Nazis had killed off most of the older prisoners with overwork and starvation and random executions by that point in the war. Liebmann was young and still able to stand on his feet and swing a pick. When the Americans liberated Flossenburg, he was among the few left alive. In the holding settlement where he was clothed and fed and gained twenty pounds in as many days, Liebmann made it clear that he wanted to come to America, that he never wanted to see Germany again. Refugees were assigned to cities when they arrived in

America, and Liebmann was given Washington, D.C., a part of town called Shepherd Park. An apartment was held in his name, where he lived rent-free for a year, after which time he was expected to support himself and pay his own way.

Twenty-two years later and Liebmann was still there, a four-room walk-up at 7701 Georgia Avenue. It met his needs.

Shepherd Park cornered into the northern edge of the District of Columbia and up against the Maryland town of Silver Spring. A few blocks to the west of Liebmann's apartment building was a sylvan grid of tranquil streets with red-brick colonials and tudors and substantial brownstone duplexes, the part of the neighborhood where his wife wanted to move. Further west, along 16th Street, there were pillared mansions on half-acre lots arching down to Rock Creek Park. But where Liebmann lived, at the corner of Georgia and Juniper Street, the area was failing. He had watched his six or seven blocks ebb and drift in a long collapse, falling faster and harder in the last few years. Stores and cafés and the bakery and the pharmacy and the neighborhood dry cleaner had all closed or moved to the suburbs. There was an open-air shopping mall out in Wheaton, a new invention of commerce drawing shoppers like nothing before, and merchants were moving north to Maryland and the money.

Liebmann was robbed once as the neighborhood faltered, held up by a frenzied black man with one clouded eye. The thief yelled and waved a gun around. Liebmann emptied the contents of the register into a paper sack and the man took it and bolted. Four mortified customers left quickly without purchasing anything. Liebmann filed a police report; one of the young officers who answered the call suggested he buy a handgun, for protection. *In case this happens again. And the way things're going around here, it will.*

A few of Liebmann's friends urged him to sell and move. They would stop in for a couple bottles of Mogan David or Manischewitz and talk to him as they paid. Jacob, they'd say, it's time to go. Rent a place in Wheaton. Your business won't miss a beat. But Liebmann didn't see it. Liquor sold everywhere and on any day. His wife was gone. He had no children. There was nobody he cared about who needed a different kind of life. He saw no reason to make any change at all. He took the policeman's advice and bought a .22 caliber pistol, a little revolver with white plastic grips that cost fifty dollars used. He got a quick tutorial on the pistol's operation from the gun store owner. Took the gun back to the store, loaded it and spun the cylinder and set the safety, and locked it in the lower left drawer of his desk in the office cubicle.

The war had left him appalled by firearms. He abruptly realized he could not imagine using this one.

He was forty-one years old and felt twice that age most of the time.

He did not own a car, had never thought to buy one, although he could easily afford anything on the road. He walked where he needed to go, or took the streetcar and later the bus. He ate most of his meals next door at Jimmy's Café or sometimes at Crisfield's, just over the District line in Silver Spring. And after the nights when images of his sister and parents came back too plainly in his dreams, he would take the longer walk to the synagogue on 16th Street and sit in the back and try to locate comfort in the rituals of his people.

On Sundays, the only day he closed the store, Liebmann rode the bus without any particular destination, his excursions a way past the dismay that could still run under his thoughts at any given moment, memory rivering through and working, down beneath the ordinary rhythms of his shop-keeper life.

On this Sunday in the middle of November, he crossed the street to catch the downtown bus, stepped up and greeted the driver and dropped the fare, and found his seat midway back. He preferred sitting on the right side of the bus although he could not explain the preference. Washington's decline slid past the smeared window, the boarded storefronts of Petworth and the catastrophe of Shaw, the choked streets around Howard University gone to every manner of destitution and loss.

The bus wheezed into downtown and hit the turnaround at Federal Triangle and gave up the last two passengers. Liebmann kept his seat. The driver scouted back down the aisle, picking up trash and the crumpled transfers left on seats or tossed on the floor. He stopped and sat in the seat across from Liebmann.

"Mr. Liebmann," he said. He sighed heavily as he lowered himself against the red vinyl. He was a big man, overweight from the hours passed behind the wheel.

"How are you today, my friend?" Liebmann asked.

"Not too bad," the driver said. He was perhaps fifty years old and had the practiced mix of resentment and acceptance that Liebmann noticed in many of the black men who lived in the neighborhood. "You out for your weekly pleasure trip?"

Liebmann said yes.

"Well," the driver said, "that's good. 'Course, for me it's the same as ever. No pleasure about it. The job I do. I'm just happy the damn rain's let up."

The Nazis came when Liebmann was seventeen. His family lived in Berlin, in a yellowing apartment building filled with other Jewish families. Later, after his family was lost, he would wonder that his and so many other families continued to live together, in the same neighborhoods, the same buildings, huddling on the same streets, long after they understood what the Nazis were doing, after so many others had been taken.

He had not understood then what little his father or any of the fathers could have done—Germany's borders closed and the jobs gone and the food gone and the possibility of hiding or shelter or refuge little more than fragrant wishes and the net pulling tighter day by day. The SS finally came in 1943, at dawn, stomping up the stairwells of the building, pounding on doors and shouting, and the staccato barking of the leashed shepherds in the hallways.

Liebmann roused his sleeping sister, gesturing that she hurry, get up and dress. For some reason he was afraid to speak, as if talking would give them away to the soldiers already in their building and moving room to room. He struggled quickly into his clothes, his half-top boots left untied when he heard the front door of the apartment give way and his father objecting and a louder voice ordering them out, downstairs, into the street. He heard something break—a dish or glass—and the door of his bedroom swung wide. The SS trooper standing there seemed massive but he was not much older than Liebmann. He was holding some sort of machine gun across his chest. The gun was black and gleamed with oil. The soldier stood easily, calm, expressionless, looking first at Liebmann and then his sister, still in her nightgown, only eleven years old.

The soldier may as well have been evaluating the fate of two barnyard animals. After a moment he simply waved them forward with the barrel of his gun and stood aside in the doorway as they walked out.

* * *

Liebmann stayed aboard the bus past his stop on the return trip. He thought he might get off at the National Guard Armory in Silver Spring and go across the street for a cup of coffee at the diner before he walked back up Georgia, into the District and home to his apartment. Three teenaged boys got on at the Kalmia Road stop, shoving and jockeying past the driver and down the aisle.

Liebmann recognized one of them immediately. An episode at the store a month or so back. Today the kid had a couple of buddies along. Blue-collar kids, but with the open pink faces that marked them as suburban, maybe in from the white-flight neighborhoods out in Glenmont or Aspen Hill, in the city and drunk on the jolt of getaway freedom that came with crossing the District line and wandering loose where nobody cared who they were or where they were going.

The driver called them back for the fare and the tallest of the boys, the kid that Liebmann had thrown out of his store, swaggered to the front of the bus.

"Seventy-five cents," the driver said, pointing at the coin box. The kid stretched it out, gazing at the side of the driver's head. He leaned against the coin box, scratched his genitals, looked back to his friends for the designated response. They were piled into a seat across the aisle from Liebmann and snickered on cue.

"I thought it was a quarter to ride." The kid had a blond crewcut, wore a white round-neck T-shirt under a black leather motorcycle jacket.

The driver brought the bus to a stop at a red light. "There's three of you," he said. "Twenty-five times three. Or is that too hard for you to figure?"

The kid looked away from his appreciative audience,

back to the driver. "You got a smart mouth on you, don't you?" he said.

The driver said nothing. Reached across to the lever on his right and pulled it to open the door behind the kid.

"Off," he said.

"I'm not gettin off," the kid said. "This ain't my stop."

It had been a Saturday night when one of Liebmann's clerks spotted the same kid slipping a pint of vodka under the same leather jacket. The kid was eighteen—or had a driver's license that said he was—old enough to buy in the District. But he was trying to steal a bottle.

The traffic light went to green.

The driver looked at the kid, waiting, and the kid said, "I told you. I ain't getting off. I'll get off when it's my stop."

A car behind the bus honked.

When Liebmann had asked for the bottle under his jacket, the kid said something about how he had to steal because of the "Jew prices" in the place. But he had given up the bottle and left, ambling out, making an elaborate show of being in no particular hurry, meeting the gaze of the store's patrons with slack-jawed hostility.

The driver put the bus in neutral and set the brake and put on the safety flashers. The kid said, "You can't put me off the bus, man. It's against the goddamn law."

"My goddamn bus. My goddamn law." The driver's voice was low and controlled. "Get off now, so's I don't need to do it for you."

The kid backed toward the door, slipped on the top step and caught himself. "What you need to do, man, is kiss my white ass."

"You just keep your white ass moving right out that door."

The kid looked back into the bus. There were only a few riders. A man three seats in front of Liebmann held his gaze on the window, peering out, waiting for the episode to be over, to resolve itself in one way or another.

Liebmann stood and stepped into the aisle, watching the kid still standing at the front of the bus.

"Oh, now, look at this," the kid said. "We got us a kike in the mix. You gonna kick my ass too, hymie? Come on up here and kick my—"

The driver was up and reached across and had the collar of the kid's leather jacket. The kid sucked for air, rocked forward onto the balls of his feet. He struggled against the driver's grip a moment, then stopped and hung there, his cheeks flaming.

"Get off the bus," the driver said. "I won't be telling you another time."

"You best get your goddamn nigger hand off me." The kid's voice shook but he worked to hold the arrogance.

The driver let go and the kid stumbled backwards down the two steps to the curb. The driver squeezed the door closed, shifted into gear, and jerked the bus through the intersection.

The kid lifted his arms and shot the air with both middle fingers as the bus roared past him.

Liebmann sat down again. Glanced across at the buddies, sitting sober now, hangdog cowboys left in the lurch.

The driver called back, voice booming. "Fifty cents, fellas. Hike it up here."

The two filed up and dropped their coins and came back toward Liebmann, this time passing him to go all the way to the back of the bus, away from the other riders.

* * *

The driver brought the bus to a stop on the north side of the Armory in Silver Spring, and cut the motor. The two kids got off at the rear door and walked a few paces, then broke into a worried run and disappeared beyond the Armory building. The other riders left from the front.

Liebmann waited until everybody was off, then walked up and stood next to the driver. "I know that boy," he said. "He came in my store. He tried to steal from me."

"Little turd," the driver said.

"I threw him out."

"Looks like that's all he's good for," the driver said. "Gettin thrown out of places. Little peckerwood son of a bitch."

"I'm sorry."

The driver heaved a sigh and looked up toward Liebmann. "No, man, *I'm* sorry. Sorry you got spoken to that way on board my bus."

Liebmann shrugged slightly. There was a moment of silence between them.

"Are you off work now?" Liebmann asked.

"Yeah. Gotta park this thing, but I'm through for the day."

"Then I will see you next time," Liebmann said.

"Let's hope we get ourselves a nice quiet ride."

After he got home, Liebmann sat in his apartment, at a window overlooking the street. He lifted the window in spite of the cold and pulled a kitchen chair close and sat with his coat on. The trees along Georgia Avenue were skeletal, black silhouettes in the endless afternoon. A few days after he had kicked the kid out of his store for trying to steal a bottle of vodka, Liebmann came to work to find the words

JEWS SUCK SHIT spray-painted in red on the store's front window.

He stood looking at the words painted unevenly on the glass, the morning traffic moving behind him. Thinking of it now in his apartment, he touched a point on his coat sleeve above the tattoo on his forearm. He always believed he could feel it there no matter how many layers were above it, the tattoo carved between his skin and the blood underneath.

The man who gave Liebmann the tattoo at Auschwitz was said to have once been the finest tattoo artist in Berlin. There was talk of his freehanding elaborate sailing ships and floral hearts and the names of mothers and lovers in elegant cascading script. But he was a Jew. Now branding his own people, one after the other, letters and numbers, working through the line. He was thin with a long face and beagle eyes and wire-rimmed glasses, and he never looked up, never looked at the faces of the people he marked, trading their names for numbers. Everybody knew he had no choice.

It was weeks later when the guards came to the dormitory and ordered everybody out.

Near dawn. The dormitory shouted awake and everybody made to stand outside in the crusted snow, freezing in rags. When this happened a prisoner was often singled out and led away. This time an SS major pointed at the tattoo artist. Two corporals pulled the man out of the group and pushed him around the side of the building. Within a few seconds came the sound of a pistol shot. A flat, dry snap echoing away into the dark forest beyond the wire.

The two corporals and the major came back around the side of the building as if they had been to the latrine or were returning from a smoke break. They ordered everybody back inside. Liebmann filed into the dormitory and lay down on the pine slat that passed for his bed. He realized that he did not know the tattoo artist's name, and now the man and his name were lost with all the others, disappeared. Liebmann repeated his own name to himself, over and over, *Jacob Liebmann, Jacob Liebmann,* suddenly convinced that doing so might stand as some sort of protection, an incantation prayed to all the names of the lost gone silent in a thousand forsaken nights, in the trackless abandoned last winter of the war.

Liebmann walked the streets of Shepherd Park. It was after midnight, in the week between Christmas and New Year. A gentle snow had fallen earlier in the day, leaving a half-inch dusting on the rooftops and cars and in the trees.

When Liebmann could not sleep he often gave up on the effort, got up and dressed and went out to walk the silent world. The cover of snow left the night even quieter, and he turned south outside his building, crossed Georgia Avenue and followed several blocks down to Fern, turned right to track the fenceline of the grounds of Walter Reed, the sprawling army hospital. Turned into the residential area on 13th Street and saw the snowfall had spangled shrubbery and porch railings and fences. The houses were mostly dark, a lamp here or there in a living room or behind an upstairs bedroom curtain. As he rounded up toward the corner where Alaska Avenue met Georgia, he saw lights moving inside his store.

He approached the intersection of Georgia and Alaska Avenues and Kalmia Road, and then stopped directly across from the front windows of his store. Lights flicked and darted somewhere inside. Liebmann was at first confused, then he understood—flashlights. In the quiet out on the street, even at his distance, he heard glass shattering, as if somebody was breaking one bottle with another. And laughter.

Someone inside smashing bottles and laughing.

Later, Liebmann would not remember any thought or specific plan as he cut around the rear of his store to edge in close to the wall. The glass plate in the back door was punched out. He crouched and eased through the opening, taking care to avoid the shards around the edges of the frame. He stood and saw three figures in a furious pleasure, flinging pints and fifths of whisky and vodka and gin against the wall, wailing and hooting when a bottle hit and exploded. One of them swung something sideways into the shelves, scattering bottles that popped like firecrackers as they hit the floor and burst.

A fierce alcohol reek, overheated, sick and pungent, the fouled sweetness everywhere.

The three carried on, oblivious to Liebmann, who moved into his office and found a key on the ledge over the door and unlocked the lower left desk drawer. He took out the little pistol, pushed the safety off, and stepped back out into the store. He held the gun straight up over his head at arm's length and squeezed the trigger.

The sound inside his store was nothing like the flat snap a Luger made in the open, frosted air of Germany—this was contained thunder, the sudden combustion of something unbridled and wild.

The three figures startled and crouched and froze where they were, faces ratcheted toward him. Liebmann stepped forward, crunching broken glass, felt the floor wet and precarious.

Two of them bolted, slipping and flailing as if they were on ice, making their way for the door. One of them fell, sliding on the floor, riding the glass, yelping in pain.

Liebmann ignored them to come within ten feet of the kid with the crewcut. The kid was wearing the motorcycle jacket. A baseball bat dangled in his right hand.

"You just couldn't do it," Liebmann said. "Mind your own business. Leave me alone."

The kid stared a moment, the same slack-jawed insolence as when Liebmann kicked him out of the store, when the bus driver tossed him off the bus. Then he said, "I'm outta here, man." He started to move.

Liebmann lifted the pistol into view, holding it up beside his face, pointed at the ceiling. "Not so fast. I thought maybe we have a little talk."

The pistol gave the kid pause but he worked quickly back into his moody swagger. "So, what, you gonna shoot me? For this? We was just havin a little fun."

"It was you who painted the words, yes?"

"What words?"

Liebmann lifted the pistol and fired into a wall. The kid hunched backward, cried out, dropped the bat, and lifted his hands as if to shield himself.

"The words," Liebmann said, after the echo of the gun blast subsided. "Red paint. The front window."

The kid straightened, let his hands move back to his sides. "So what if I did?" He started to work his way across the glass.

Liebmann pointed the pistol directly at the kid, tracking him as he moved. The kid kept a few yards between himself and Liebmann and said, "You can't do nothin crazy here, man. We was just screwin around."

Liebmann shifted the pistol to the right of the kid and fired again, this time into the wall. He moved the barrel a degree and fired again. A case of Coca-Cola hissed, spitting and fizzing and boiling over. Moved the barrel and fired again. The kid was howling now, hands over his face, knees going soft.

Liebmann fired into a flank of Alsatian whites, Rieslings, and Gewurztraminers. The rack of bottles ignited and blew apart in glittering spray, silvered glass and golden wines showering into the aisle.

The echo and reverberation of the gun was everything now, throbbing against the walls and ceiling, otherworldly, pure and untrammeled and wanton. The sound had severed something in Liebmann.

The kid was sobbing and sagged to his knees on the floor. "Crazy motherfucker," he said, heaving, all his imagined power drained away. "You're gonna kill me, right?"

A car passed outside, headlights searchlighting the room, the extent of the damage visible for several seconds. The floor gleamed with spilled and flooding booze and the jeweled light of shattered glass.

Liebmann looked back to the kid, held his gaze a long moment. Finally he said, "You do not deserve to die. You are not worthy of such an honor." His voice shook when he spoke. He was breathless, tainted in some way that was just coming to him. He lowered the pistol to his side.

"You're stone crazy, ain't you?" the kid said. "Crazy Jew."

Liebmann gazed at the boy for another moment, and then said, "Go. Get out."

The kid lurched to his feet, slipping, working for purchase on the wet floor.

Liebmann turned and crunched across the glass back to the cubicle office at the front of the store. He opened the desk drawer and returned the gun to its place. The kid made his way toward the door, slipped once and went down on one knee and grimaced as he caught himself with the heel of his hand. There was a blood smear on the floor when he lifted his hand away, black in the half-light.

Liebmann was no longer watching. He sat at the desk, his back to the room. "Get out," he said, speaking toward the wall. "I never want to see you again. Nowhere. Ever. Never in this life."

The kid paused near the office. "You just did all that to make me piss myself. Well, I did. Hope you're satisfied."

Liebmann did not answer.

The kid said, "Crazy fuck."

Leibmann sat long after the kid was gone and the night's silence regained. An occasional car hissed along the wet street outside. He sat in the dark and looked at the wall and marveled that no police had come, no fire truck, not a curious neighbor, nobody seemed to have heard a thing. Shepherd Park is not the neighborhood it once was, he thought. The idea brought no feeling one way or another. In the morning he would call the police and the insurance company to file the reports and pretend that he happened on the devastation when he opened the store in the morning. Just another morning coming to work, only this time to a bad surprise. He would describe his distress at what he discovered. Because what could anybody do? Besides, he could never explain. Or say why it happened, even if it was possible to carry it that far. Or why he had not called the police when he saw the lights in the store and heard the sounds of the damage being done. Now, looking at the wall, exhausted, vaguely ill, Liebmann knew he could not explain his shame to strangers. There had been a problem, and it was his, and he had taken care of it—he would leave it at that, in his own mind. He was not about to relate the way he had gone down under the heel of time, how a simple animal rage had blossomed against the ways his life was taken from him.

He had no language for that kind of story.

Three cops came, two uniforms with a plainclothes officer who picked around in the ruins, trying to protect his shoes. The uniforms glanced at the scene from the door and went back to sit in their cruiser at the curb out front.

"Any idea of the damages?" the officer asked.

"Not yet," Liebmann said. "I need a few days. I have to inventory."

"Right," the officer said. "I understand." He slipped, but caught himself against a shelf. "Damn. This is some kind of mess. Who would've done this?"

Liebmann was sweeping glass with an industrial push-broom. He said nothing.

The officer looked around with the expression of a man who needed to move on to some other part of his day. "No enemies, huh? No big fights with anybody? Upset customer?"

"No," Liebmann said.

The officer shrugged. "Vandalism. It's getting worse. We're seeing more of it all the time. Tough to connect anybody to these things, though. Not unless you walk in on them red-handed."

The insurance adjuster came a few hours later. Older than the cop, world weary, wearing black-frame eyeglasses and a tired off-blue suit. By the time he arrived Liebmann had swept paths through the glass. The floor was sugared with congealed liquor and the insurance man's wing tips stuck and sucked to the floor as he walked. He had a clipboard. He looked closer and harder at the damage than the police officer had, made notes as he moved through the wreckage, then left his business card with Liebmann, mumbling something about how sorry he was.

From time to time Liebmann's sister would appear and speak in his dreams. He had never seen her again after that morning in their bedroom in the family apartment in Berlin. Outside on the street the Nazis had separated the males and females—he watched his mother and his sister led away. An officer was saying over a bullhorn that everybody was being relocated for their own safety, away from Berlin and the Allied bombing runs, and he watched his sister in her little brown shoes, holding his mother's hand, walking off. Just before he lost sight of her, she turned back and smiled and waved.

Dreaming, Liebmann heard her voice lift in the open happiness of a child, speaking in a language he did not understand, that seemed more like bells heard at a great distance than any sort of words he might recognize. As she spoke, her tiny white face hung suspended in the opalescent air of his vision.

Neither the police officer nor the insurance adjuster noticed the bullet holes in the outside wall. Liebmann found them when he came to the store the next morning. They were there if somebody cared to look. But he knew nobody would.

Reports were filed. Liebmann hired a clean-up crew, and inventoried, and replaced the losses, and filed his receipts with the insurance company. He sold the pistol to a dealer at a gun show at the Armory for twenty-five dollars, and about six weeks later a check arrived from the insurance company for the damages. Business went on as usual. Thrived as usual. People still came in every day to get the boxes they wanted for storage, for shipping, for whatever they needed. A few of the regular customers offered consolation. Sorry about what happened, Jacob. Maybe it's time to get out of here. Move up the road to Wheaton.

Liebmann nodded. Maybe, he said. Maybe I need to think about that.

PART II

Streets & Alleys

EAST OF THE SUN

BY JENNIFER HOWARD

Hill East, S.E.

In that neighborhood, they said, you learned fast where trouble came from. All you had to do was keep your sense of direction and walk the other way. Hill East was still a little rough around the edges but most of the people wanted to be friendly. Stay away from the hot spots and say hello to everybody: That was the rule.

A month after we moved to Potomac Avenue we knew the places to avoid—mostly north and east, like the intersection of 17th and Independence, where the crackheads hung out, and the New Dragon, an all-night takeout joint over at 13th and C that sold liquor to go. You didn't want to mess with the kind of people who patronized that joint. They didn't go there for the food.

The Dragon was where the local pusher known as the Wheelchair Bandit did business. Having a disability didn't make a person any more law-abiding than anybody else, apparently. Instead of a motorized chair, the Bandit had an old pit bull—I know it's a cliché but it's the truth—who used to pull him around when he wasn't staked out for customers just outside the restaurant. Some people on the neighborhood listserv said you could hear the jangle of his keys—he carried at least fifty of them on a belt chain—and the panting of his dog before you saw the man himself. If you heard those sounds, they said, you'd better get yourself clear.

Nobody knew whether the food was any good at the New Dragon or whether in actual fact they even served any. Nobody moved to Hill East for the food anyway. Good pizza, decent Mexican, KFC—that pretty much covered the range. Thai takeout, if you were an office type with a little more disposable cash than the longtime residents, the federal workers and postmen and steady jobbers who'd bought their places forty years ago and couldn't believe what those old houses—nothing fancy, just solid 1920s brick numbers with modest front porches and envelopes of land front and back—went for these days. Couldn't believe their property taxes, either. They cashed in or they stayed put until they couldn't afford to stay put any longer. I used to wonder, once in a while, where they went when they left.

Drugs and real estate: two good lines of work to be in on the Hill if you weren't a Republican or a lobbyist, or maybe even if you were. We didn't care for the Republicans or the dealers, but none of that made trouble, not for us. It was just life in a town lousy with people who had too much money—the folks looking to buy up anything they could get their hands on—and even lousier with people who didn't have enough to do anything at all. Not everybody could be a winner.

Overall I couldn't complain about how things were going. Baseball had come back to town after thirty-five years—the Nationals were even on a streak, the winning kind—and after years paying good dough to bad landlords, we had a house of our own.

We felt lucky, finding that house. Lucky to have a front porch and a little bit of land to call our own, lucky to have a bedroom for each kid—Dani, who was almost four, and her baby brother Jack—when a lot of people we knew had theirs double-bunking. Especially if they lived in the older row houses to the west, over in the lockdown zone around the Capitol and the Supreme Court where the Homeland Security folks concentrated their loving attention. For the most part they left Hill East alone. There was nobody fancy here to protect, no essential governmental personnel, unless you counted the famous residents of Congressional Cemetery two blocks over. John Philip Sousa and J. Edgar Hoover were good neighbors.

I couldn't say that of everybody. In the mornings, on my way to the Metro, I got in the habit of picking up the Styrofoam containers and soda cans thrown out of car windows by the people who blew down Potomac Avenue. You could find all kinds of things in the bushes along that strip— condoms (used), CDs (unplayable), every type of wrapping known to the fast-food industry.

The weirdest thing I found was a baby doll the color of an old copper penny. I say I found it but in fact it was Dani who did, on one of the aimless stroller expeditions she and the baby and I used to take down the alley behind the house when we had time to kill before dinner. The backyards of our block were as diverse as the residents. A couple had been shrubbed and landscaped until they looked like pages out of *House and Garden*. Others, like ours, were crammed full of kiddie gear, plastic slides, and sandboxes shaped like enormous frogs and ladybugs. A few, including William and Ida's next door, had evolved over decades from outdoor storage to junkyards where unwanted objects went to die: broken-down jalopies, odd pieces of wood from home-renovation projects abandoned halfway through, steel meat smokers that looked like mini-submarines.

Next to William and Ida's on the other side was a group house for the mentally disturbed, muttering sad cases who boarded a van each weekday morning and were taken off to some useful occupation and brought back each night to Potomac Avenue. At home, if the weather was nice and even if it wasn't, they drifted along the sidewalk like so much human litter. That's not a very nice way of putting it. But whenever I saw Louis and Juanita and the other residents, whose names we didn't know, they looked emptied out like the discards I picked up along the margins of the avenue. If they were sad, though, they didn't know it. They used to try to bum cigarettes off us. They never could remember that we didn't smoke.

The backyard of the group house was a wasteland where even grass was too depressed to grow. One scraggly tree managed to stay alive there and shelter, under its few remaining branches, a row of those cheap molded-plastic chairs you could pick up for a song at Kmart or Wal-mart. Early in the morning and late in the afternoon, the inmates of the group house would park themselves in those chairs like so many city birds—what my mother would call "trash birds," grackles and starlings and the like—and smoke themselves closer to an early grave. I could have done without the smoke that some-times carried across William and Ida's backyard and into our kitchen windows.

The alley doglegged across the block, connecting the streets—16th and Kentucky—that angled into Potomac on either end. Two lines of garage-style, brick-walled storage units faced each other across a narrow strip of concrete, sealed off from the alley by a chain-link fence that didn't look like it would keep the rats out, must less any would-be bur-glars. That eyesore filled the lot right across from us, although it was interesting to speculate what might be hid-den in those units. William said he'd seen a Rolls Royce in one of them, but that might just have been wishful thinking.

The day we found the doll, Dani was investigating a section of wall on the storage unit that bordered the alley. Three or four bricks had come out and created a gap. Right on the edge of it sat the doll, naked as the day it came off the Chinese assembly line. Other than that it looked right at home.

Over Dani's strenuous objections I took it inside, put it in a place where she wouldn't see it—who knew where that thing had been?—and forgot about it. I put a note in the alcove where we'd found it—*We have your doll, come ring the bell at . . .*—and then I forgot about that too. You forget a lot of things when you're looking after a couple of kids.

Dani asked me if it belonged to William and Ida. I told her I didn't think so. They had been there as long as I'd been alive, long enough for him to be called Mister William by most of the young people in the vicinity, while Ida stayed just plain Ida. They'd raised their kids and now they liked things quiet.

As for the young people, well, I didn't much care for the teenagers who liked to hang out and yell at each other in the little park across the street, one of those orphan triangles of public space you find in D.C. where three or four streets come together at crazy angles. The teenagers scared me the first few nights we were in the house, but they weren't real trouble. They just acted like they were. They liked to shout it up after hours when the rest of the neighborhood had locked itself behind doors for the night, but I never heard that they did anything but make noise. They weren't part of the New Dragon posse. If you really wanted to freak them out, all you had to do was drive by slowly, roll down a window, and say hello in a big cheerful voice.

Weirdly enough, it was Juanita, not the teenagers, who freaked *me* out. Like most of the group house inmates she looked older than she probably was—hair gone gray years before its time, half her teeth gone too, skin the color and texture of dried apricots. What really got to me was how she liked to wear latex gloves, the kind doctors put on for intimate exams. Lord knows where she got them, but they didn't conjure up good associations.

One morning I came out and found one inside out on the sidewalk in front of our house. The fingers were still half-folded in on themselves, as though it had been pulled off in a hurry. Juanita stood about ten feet away watching me.

It was April, barely. March had come in colder than usual and stormed out again without leaving much in the way of spring behind it, and the first days of April struggled to catch up. I felt sorry for the flowers who'd pushed their way up expecting sunshine and mellow air and instead gotten the dismal leftovers of a winter that wouldn't shake itself loose.

I was in a hurry that morning, trying to get my daughter in the car. Ida had stopped by to watch the baby for a few minutes; Dani was late for school already, and it wasn't a day to linger out of doors. Juanita was out there having the first smoke of the day, bundled up and shapeless in the ratty down parka that had found its way to her through some dubious act of hand-me-down charity. I gave her a good morning that was as cheerful as I could make it under the circumstances.

"Man keys. Godababeedahl?" She cleared a wad of phlegm out of her throat—did she have to hawk it onto the sidewalk?—and looked at her shoes, Chuck Taylor All Stars a size too small and almost worn through at the toes. Without a full set of teeth she might as well have been speaking Chinese. On a good day I caught every third or fourth word.

She was gesturing now; her arms windmilled furiously. "Fur man. Keys."

"No cigs, Juanita." I shrugged as I got Dani buckled into her car seat. I didn't like her getting too close to any of the group house residents. I had no reason to think they were dangerous, but with people like that you might not know until it was too late. "We don't smoke." I nodded in Dani's direction as if that explained everything Juanita needed to know.

Her hands dropped to her sides all of a sudden, as if her battery had run out. Then she groped in her pocket for something that turned out to be a piece of paper. It looked familiar. When she handed it to me I saw why. It was the note I'd left in the alley in case the lost doll's owner came looking for it.

Juanita handed me my own note and wrapped her arms around herself, the gesture of someone cold or in need of comfort, and shook her head back and forth so hard it looked very likely she was doing her damaged brain more harm. "Babee. Doll. Man keys. Man keys!"

"We didn't know it was your baby."

"I'm a big girl!" Dani shouted from the backseat of our car.

"Not you, honey." I hated myself a little every time I used the word "honey" with one of my children, especially when I was in the kind of mood I was in this morning. "She's talking about *her* baby."

"Baby DOLL." The Ls of the last word hung in the cold air. Juanita gave me a big gummy smile that looked more anxious than happy. I saw now why she kept her arms wrapped around herself—she was shaking. "You get it back." Her head bobbled forward and back, forward and back. "Keys. He need it."

"All right," I said. She was more nuts than I'd thought. I made a mental note to tell Dave to keep an extra-close eye on the kids when she was around. "Sure."

"You get it, okay? Okay?" The arms were flailing again.

Dani made a noise that might have been a giggle and might have been something closer to fear. Kids always know when someone isn't right.

"I'll try." I gave Dani's car seat straps one more tug, even though I knew they were tight enough. She let out a howl of protest. "Sorry, honey. Mommy's finished." Juanita watched us pull away from the curb, her mouth forming the same words over and over.

That weekend I dug out the doll Dani had found. It was in even worse shape than Juanita. It had been loved hard, if you could call that kind of treatment love. Some people did. The doll's head hung at an angle that would have killed a human baby, and if there were a Doll Social Services they'd want to know who'd tried to open up Baby's belly with a screwdriver and where her missing leg had gotten to. I flipped the switch on her back—she was supposed to cry, probably, or say *ma-ma*—but nothing happened. A piece of crap like that wasn't worth wasting a couple of good batteries on. I had enough baby noise in my life already.

If Juanita wanted a baby, I thought, she could at least have one in decent shape. When Dave took the kids to the park for the usual Sunday afternoon run—"I'm going to run 'em like dogs," he told me, "tire 'em out good"—I rummaged through the plastic bins of discarded toys in the basement. Sure enough, there was a baby doll in one of them, a chubby thing in a onesie with stains all down the front from Dani's attempts to feed it pureed peas. Dani had moved on to other things—horses, Barbies, getting her little brother into trouble. The doll's blue eyes looked a little crazy now, and it was a couple shades lighter than Juanita's, but at least it had all its appendages.

I took it over to the group house—I'd never had cause to venture up those steps—and knocked hard enough to be heard over the TV that was always on. The day caregiver, one of a rotating 24/7 crew whose names I never learned, answered the door. He was a beat-up-looking guy in his fifties who wore the same shapeless clothes as his charges. If you spent enough time around people like that you couldn't help picking up a few of their habits.

He looked ticked off when I told him what I wanted, but he shouted Juanita's name into the dim interior of the house anyway. From one of the upstairs rooms I heard a radio playing salsa and wondered if it was WHFS, the indie radio station I'd listened to growing up. It had gone Latin a few months ago. I didn't listen to the radio much anymore, but I missed that station. It was the soundtrack of my youth.

Juanita came down the stairs like a ghost. She grabbed the doll from my arms, held it out a little distance from her, and gazed into its crazy eyes as if she saw the very truth of heaven there.

"Nut job," the caretaker said under his breath.

I thanked him anyway and left Juanita alone with Baby.

I had a bad dream that night, the kind that makes you wake yourself up just to stop it. But when I was fully awake I couldn't remember what had scared me. I sat up in bed and listened—no noise at all from the children's rooms. I listened for the teenagers but they had all gone home. It was almost 5 o'clock. A mockingbird sang his morning warm-ups in the park across the street. Dave breathed next to me, the intake and outtake of his breath regular as waves along a quiet beach. The only noise from the street was a bus that groaned its way to a halt at the four-way stop on our corner, then heaved itself into motion again and was gone.

The noise reminded me—trash day. The trucks would be coming through before it got much lighter, and as usual Dave had forgotten to put the can out the night before. I shrugged on my bathrobe and felt my way down the stairs to the back door.

I'd just pulled the can out from its spot next to the garage when I saw her. She lay face down in the little walkway that cut between the rental storage units across the alley. Someone had dragged her behind the chain-link fence to die.

She had on that ratty parka, the green of it dark where it had absorbed some of the blood. I couldn't see where it all came from, just that there was a lot of it spread out around the body, dark and congealed into wrinkles like the skin on a cup of chocolate pudding.

"Mommy?" All of a sudden Dani was standing next to me, eyes full of sleep. I didn't have time to stop her from seeing what lay there—I hadn't heard her follow me out the door. She was pointing at an object half-covered by Juanita's body. "Mommy, is that my doll's leg?"

"Don't tell them you gave it to her." Dave sat at the kitchen table with a cup of black coffee between his large hands. He never drank his coffee black. That's how I knew it was serious—as if a body in the alley hadn't told me that already. "You're asking for trouble."

"Trouble is finding a woman shot dead in the alley behind my house."

"They don't have to know it came from you." Family life

had brought out the conservative, don't-make-waves side of Dave. It wasn't my favorite thing about him. "What possessed you, anyway? You hate those people."

"I don't hate them. I just worry about the kids."

The cops were still out back doing whatever cops do when they have a murder scene on their hands. It only *looked* like they were standing around shooting the shit with cups of coffee in their hands. They'd sat me down at my own kitchen table and taken a statement, then gone over it again to make sure I had my story straight. There wasn't much to tell, after all.

"Haven't had a bag lady in a while," one of them, a fat little guy whose belly kept trying to bust out of his uniform, said to his partner. I liked the partner—he'd kept himself trim and he had nice manners for a cop. "Little long in the tooth to be playing with dolls."

"She wasn't a bag lady," I said. "She lived down the block."

The fat one laughed in a way that really soured me on him. "Different kind of bag lady, lady." He pushed his hat back on his head. His hair could have stood a couple of good latherings with industrial shampoo. "Know what a mule is?"

The Thin Man saved me the trouble. "She ran drugs for a cripple who works the territory east of here."

"East of the sun," I said. I didn't mean anything by it. Just some old story I used to read as a kid, a story about a girl who has to find her one true love east of the sun and west of the moon. "Over at the New Dragon. The Wheelchair Bandit— that's what the neighborhood listserv calls him."

"Nice neighbors you have." Fatty picked a dark speck out of his teeth.

"Sometimes they try to cut a deal on the side and make a

little extra cash," Thin Man said. "They're not real smart, these people."

When they finished with me, they went out in the alley and walked up and down, making notes in those pads they carry around. I watched them for a while and that's when I realized I hadn't said anything about the doll. They'd found most of its parts spread through the alley. If I hadn't mentioned it to Dave first, I probably would have gone straight out and told Thin Man, who had parked himself against the patrol car that blocked the alley. He was making more notes. Notes about splatter patterns and exit wounds and time of death. Notes about the grisly end of a woman whose worst crime, as far as I'd ever known, had been to try and bum cigarettes off people who didn't have them. What was she doing with scum like the Bandit? She was probably too crazy to know what she'd gotten mixed up in. All she'd wanted was a baby of her own.

"Think of the kids," Dave said. We'd been sitting there awhile. His coffee must have gotten cold by then, but he didn't even complain like he usually would. "You want them to get dragged into this? You want Dani on the stand telling a courtroom full of people how her mother gave her toys away to the drug dealer down the block? The cops have all the information they need."

I couldn't see how any lawyer in his right mind would put a four-year-old on the stand to tell a story about a doll, but I let Dave talk me out of what I knew I ought to do. He had a way of making certain things seem unnecessary, like you'd be a damn fool to hassle yourself.

It wasn't a dream that woke me up that night. As I passed the doors to Dani and Jack's rooms I heard the baby give out a creaking little sigh and settle himself back to sleep. I went down to the basement and got out Juanita's first doll, the one she'd never see again. I held it in my hands and tried to get the head to stay straight, but it couldn't. When something gets that broken, you can't fix it.

I got a flathead screwdriver out of Dave's toolbox. I turned the doll over and looked at the screws that held the doll's battery compartment shut. They were almost stripped, but if I pressed hard enough into the metal groove I could catch just enough traction to get them turning. You had to want it bad, though, to get that job done. After I dug the last one out of its hole, I used the tip of the flathead to jimmy the cover off. It popped out more easily than I was expecting and the tip of the screwdriver slammed into what should have been a battery—but whatever it was gave under the point.

In the space where Baby's batteries should have been— and crammed inside her torso and up into her poor dangling head—were plastic bags about the size of the half-sandwich-sized Ziplocs I used to pack up snacks in to take to the playground. I didn't need to know the name of what was in these.

I sat on the floor in the laundry room in my nightgown and stared at that doll and it stared back at me and its eyes weren't crazy at all, not one bit. It knew the score. It knew that one of these nights I'd hear the noise of the Wheelchair Bandit's keys and hear the panting breath of that pit bull and my family would never get clear, ever.

Unless.

I put every screw back in as tight as I could get it. I worked the flathead until my knuckles ached. A little bit of residue had settled into the gap where the doll's head had separated from its neck; I blew every last speck of it out. Then I collected the doll and myself and found the back door key and let myself out onto the deck. I didn't bother to get my slippers. I had to get that thing out of the house.

The lonely streetlight by the storage units shed an orange glow that just reached the spot where I'd found her. I could see the dark circle on the ground where Juanita had bled her life out with only an empty doll for company. I could see the gap in the bricks where Dani had found the thing I held in my hands.

I set that hateful thing back in the darkness where my daughter had found it and told myself I didn't hear the jangle of keys, the dog panting right behind me. I told trouble I didn't want any part of it. Nobody does, when you think hard about it. Isn't that the truth?

SOLOMON'S ALLEY

BY ROBERT ANDREWS

Georgetown, N.W.

Solomon's alley parallels M Street, Georgetown's main drag. Running behind Johnny Rockets, Ben & Jerry's, Old Glory Barbecue, and the Riggs Bank, the alley connects Wisconsin Avenue on the west to 31st Street one block east.

Battered blue dumpsters line the alley. Solomon had puzzled over the dumpsters for several years. Finally, he'd decided that their BFI logo stood for *big fucking incinerators*. That job done, he'd taken on thinking out the likely origins of the five ancient magnolia trees that shaded the stretch of alley where he parked his two Safeway carts.

On this Tuesday morning in September, he sat in his folding canvas deck chair, part of him pondering the magnolias while another part got ready for his day job, watching the Nigerian. At 10:00, like clockwork, the white Dodge van pulled up across Wisconsin at the corner of Prospect, by Restoration Hardware.

"Hello, Nigerian," Solomon whispered. He settled back to watch the sidewalk come alive. Each morning's setup was a ballet, a precisely choreographed routine, and Solomon was a discriminating critic.

Most mornings the performance went well: every move efficient, rhythmic, smooth. Some mornings it didn't: some mornings everything fell apart in a cranky series of busted plays.

The driver eased the van forward so its front bumper toed the white marks on the pavement. He switched off the ignition and got out to go round to the back.

Waverly Ngame was a big man. Two-fifty, six feet and a couple of inches, Solomon figured. His skin blue-black . . . shiny . . . like the barrel of a .38.

First out, a long rectangular folding table, the kind you see in church basements. Ngame locked the legs open. With his toe and wood shims, he worked around the table until it rested solid on the uneven brick sidewalk.

He disappeared into the van and came out with racks of white plastic-coated wire-grid shelving under both arms and a grease-stained canvas bag in his left hand.

In swift, practiced motions, he picked the largest of the shelves and braced it upright on the side of the table facing the street. With one hand he held the shelf, with the other he reached into the canvas bag and came out with a large C-clamp. Twirling it with sharp snaps of his wrist, he opened the jaws just enough to slip over the shelf and the table edge. He tightened the clamp, and moved to repeat the process on the other side of the table.

More shelving and more C-clamps produced a display stand.

Now the van disgorged Ngame's merchandise in large nylon bags and sturdy blue plastic storage boxes. Soon, Gucci and Kate Spade handbags hung alluringly from the vertical shelving while Rolex watches and Serengeti sunglasses marched in neat ranks across the top of the church-basement folding table.

He slow today, said Voice.

"He did good," Solomon contradicted. He didn't want to give Voice shit. He did that, give Voice any slack, Voice start up. Voice need his pills? Solomon tried to remember the last time he trucked to the clinic, then gave it up. Long as it was only one Voice, he could handle it. It only got bad when he had to put up with the whole goddamn family yelling and screaming, scrambling things inside his head.

Ngame climbed into his van. That was Solomon's cue. He got out of his chair and walked to where the alley ran into Wisconsin. There, he could keep a closer eye on Ngame's stand.

Ngame eased the van across Wisconsin and into the alley, waving to Solomon as he passed by. He pulled the van into a slot by the florist shop on 31st Street where he had a deal with the manager. Locking the van, he walked back up the alley toward Solomon.

"Nobody bother the stand, Waverly."

Ngame palmed Solomon a folded five.

"A good day, Solomon."

As a boy in Lagos, Ngame had learned his English listening to BBC. He sounded like a Brit announcer except that he had a Nigerian's way of softly rounding his vowels and stressing the final syllables of his sentences.

Solomon shook his head. "Watch yourself today."

Ngame gripped Solomon's shoulder.

"Voice tell you that?" he asked. He searched Solomon's face with clinical curiosity.

Ngame's concern irritated Solomon. "Hunh! Voice don't know shit," he said crossly. "Solomon telling you."

Something passed behind Ngame's eyes. He looked serious. "You hear anything?"

"Just feel," Solomon whispered to keep Voice from hearing, "just feel."

Ngame smiled. "You are a belt-and-suspenders man,

Solomon."

Solomon pouted and tucked the five away. "You don't have belt and suspenders, Waverly, you lose your ass."

Ngame took that in with a laugh. He squeezed Solomon's shoulder, then turned and made his way across Wisconsin.

In the street by Ngame's stand, a crow worried at the flattened remains of a road-killed rat.

And down the block from the stand, Solomon saw two men get out of a maroon Crown Vic. One black, one white. Both big. Both cops.

With a little finger, Ngame made a microscopic adjustment, poking a pair of sunglasses to line them up just so with its neighbors. He didn't look up from putting fine touches to his display.

"Detectives Phelps and Kearney. Good morning, sirs."

"How's business, Waverly?" José Phelps asked.

Ngame gave the sunglasses a last critical look, then turned to face José and Frank. He smiled a mouthful of perfectly straight glistening teeth.

"This is America!" Ngame exploded with exuberance. *A-mare-uh-CUH!* "Business is *always* splendid!" A wave of his large hand took in the sidewalk. "One is free to sell and free to buy . . . buy and sell." He caressed a handbag. "This purse, for example—"

José pulled Ngame's string. "Mr. Gucci gets his cut?"

Ngame got the tired look of a long-suffering teacher with a slow student. "Detective Phelps! Do you suppose this is a real Gucci purse?" He swept a hand over the watches. "Or that these are real Rolexes?"

José's eyes widened. "They aren't?"

"And do you suppose that any of these good people who

come to my stand *believe* they are buying real Guccis or real Rolexes?"

José opened his eyes wider.

Ngame spun up more. "And do you suppose that my customers could buy a *real* Rolex?"

"Oh?" José said, egging him on.

"So who is hurt?" Ngame was deep into it now, eyes wide in enthusiasm, hands held out shoulder-high, palms up. "Not Mister Gucci! Nor Mister Rolex! As a matter of fact, Mister Gucci and Mister Rolex ought to be pleased with me! Yes, pleased! My customers have learnt good taste here at my stand." Ngame's chin tilted up. "When they get wealthy, they'll buy the real Gucci and the real Rolex."

"Like Skeeter Hodges," Frank Kearney said.

Ngame gave Frank a heavy-lidded somber look. "He didn't buy here. He kept the real Mister Rolex in business."

"What's the talk?" José asked.

Ngame scanned the sidewalk. He did it casually, but he did it.

"Conjecture?" *Con-jec-TURE?*

Another glance, this time across the street. "The Puerto Ricans say it was the Jamaicans. The Jamaicans tell me it was the Puerto Ricans. And the American blacks"—Ngame shrugged—"they all point their fingers at one another."

"No names?" Frank asked.

Ngame shook his head. "No pretender to the throne. But then again, Detective Kearney, it was only last night."

Ngame paused a beat, then came up with a watch in his hand, gold-gleaming in the morning sun.

"A Rolex President? I will give a discount."

Solomon watched the two cops get in their car and leave. In

the street the crow continued working on the dead rat.

"You watch yourself today, Waverly," he whispered, and swung his gaze along the alley, past Ngame's van, toward 31st Street.

Motherfucker's runnin' late. Voice came up inside Solomon's head, peevish, accusing.

"He be along," Solomon told Voice, "he be along."

When?

As though on cue, tires squealed. A white Navigator roared in off 31st. Sprays of gravel ricocheted off dumpsters. Partway down the alley the Navigator turned right and disappeared into the Hamilton Court garage.

"See?" Solomon whispered to Voice.

Moments later, Asad the Somali appeared, coming up the ramp carrying a large brief case. A tall, thin man, he had a snaky, boneless way of moving. His tight-fitting yellow suit had a long jacket with five buttons and his skin was a light cocoa and his black hair lay slicked in thinning waves against his skull.

As usual, Asad's two goons flanked him. Gehdi and Nadif. Solomon had decided they were brothers. Maybe twins, whose orangutan mother had fallen out of an ugly tree.

Two weeks ago, Asad had come to Georgetown and leased a dingy storefront, paying cash. Solomon knew that storefront. A single window displayed garish men's clothes. The display had never changed. For years, players came and went. But he'd never seen any of them wearing those clothes. That shit only fools or Somalis would wear. Place never had sold anything legal. The Somali wasn't going to start now.

Asad didn't waste time setting up his network. He and his goons started with the street vendors. The vendors signed on to buy watches, sunglasses, and handbags from Asad.

Asad gave his new partners discounts on the junk. C-phones came with the deal. In return, Asad got a cut on the profits and he would know what was going on the streets. All the vendors had bought in except the Nigerian.

That first day, one of Solomon's carts had been sticking partway out into the alley. Gehdi misjudged his clearance and scraped the Navigator's fender.

Asad had stood there and watched with his hard black marble eyes while Gehdi and Nadif punched Solomon to the ground then kicked the shit out of him. They threw his carts out into the middle of Wisconsin Avenue. Things he'd collected, his precious things. The Nigerian had saved some, but the rest, his clippings, his notebooks, they'd been swept away with the street trash.

He'd been beaten before. But never in his alley. That they had done those things to him there shamed him. The alley had provided for him, and when danger came, he had been unable to defend the alley in return.

He gonna make the call?

"Sure he is." Voice didn't know its ass from apple butter sometimes.

Looking past Solomon and toward Ngame's stand, Asad reached into the briefcase and pulled out a fat c-phone/walkie-talkie. Flipping it open, he held it in front of his face.

Solomon saw Asad's lips move. A second or two passed and Solomon heard one crackling reply, then another.

"One more," he said to Voice.

Asad waited, holding the c-phone out from his face. Gehdi and Nadif swiveled their heads back and forth, searching the alley.

They expectin' Santy Claus?

A third crackle. Asad replied and stowed the c-phone

away in the briefcase. He said something to the two goons and the three began walking toward Solomon.

They gonna hit you? Hurt you today?

Solomon got a tightness in his chest. How it had been came back to him like it had every day since.

Curled up on the alley bricks. Crying and slobbering and puking. Waiting for the goons to swing another steel-capped toe.

They had grunted with the effort and they had cursed Solomon because beating a man while he was down was hard work and it made them sweat and they blamed him for that.

He lowered his head and pretended to doze. Through slitted eyelids, he saw the shoes approach, then pass.

"Not today," he whispered to Voice. "Not today."

As soon as he thought it safe, he lifted his eyes and followed the three Somalis approaching Ngame's stand.

And along Wisconsin, the other vendors watched.

Ngame saw them cross Wisconsin. He turned and busied himself tightening a C-clamp. He started counting silently. At nine, he heard the sliding scuffle of shoe leather on the sidewalk behind him.

"I need a decision," he heard Asad say.

He didn't turn, but continued fiddling with the clamp.

"You got mine," he said, "I don't need a partner."

"Every businessman needs a partner. Suppose you get sick?"

"I am healthy."

A twisting, tearing at his shoulders, and his elbows were pinned behind him as he was spun around to face Asad.

Gehdi stood to Asad's right, and Nadif held him tight, the goon's sour breath on his neck.

"You may be healthy," Asad whispered, smiling, "but men have accidents."

Gehdi dropped his hand into his jacket pocket.

Ngame flexed his knees and sagged, loosening Nadif's grip. Then with a violent burst, he straightened up. He raised his heavy boot and brought it down with all his strength on the top of Nadif's foot. He felt bones grind as Nadif's arch collapsed.

Nadif was still screaming as Ngame swung his foot forward. His toe caught Gehdi in the crotch, lifting him off the pavement. Gehdi gasped. His hand flew out of his pocket. A switchblade clattered to the sidewalk.

Almost casually, Ngame clenched Asad's collar with one hand, twisting it tight around his neck. Stooping slightly, he scooped up Gehdi's switchblade. He held it up before Asad's bulging eyes. He pressed the release. Asad stared hypnotically as the silver blade flicked open. Ngame slammed Asad up against a lamppost and brought the blade against the Somali's throat just below the Adam's apple.

Gehdi lay curled on the sidewalk clutching his balls, and Nadif, sobbing, stood on his undamaged foot, hanging on to a parking meter.

In a swift motion, he pulled the blade away from Asad's throat, cocked his arm, and brought the knife forward in a stabbing motion.

Asad let out a high-pitched scream. The crotch of his trousers darkened.

A fraction of an inch from Asad's ear, Ngame drove the knife into the lamppost, snapping its blade.

"You're right," Ngame said to Asad in his best BBC voice, "men have accidents."

* * *

The rest of the morning, Solomon watched Ngame at his stand. The Nigerian went about his business as though nothing had happened. Asad and his goons had disappeared into the storefront. The other vendors in sight of Ngame's corner were careful not to be seen paying attention, but it seemed to Solomon they moved like men tiptoeing around a sleeping beast.

Around 3:00, Solomon, eyes half-closed, was drowsing in his canvas deck chair. For seconds, he paid no attention to the car that pulled up to the curb by Ngame's stand, until the driver-side door opened and the black cop got out.

Oh shit, Voice said.

Solomon ignored Voice and sat up to get a better view of the cop and Ngame.

"You already find out who killed Skeeter?" Ngame asked.

José Phelps picked up a pair of Ray Ban knockoffs and examined them. "Not yet."

"Those are ten dollars."

José put the shades back, taking care to line them up just so.

"Little while ago, we were over at Eastern Market," he said. "Buzz was, you had a run-in with Asad."

"News travels fast."

José didn't say anything but left the question on his face.

Ngame shrugged. "A discussion. A business proposition."

"You know," José threw in, "DEA's interested in him."

Ngame nudged the shades José had held. "That's good. I'm not."

"You ever thought to moving somewhere else?"

Ngame gave José a hard look. "I have been here almost ten years. I am somebody here."

José picked up the Ray Ban knockoffs again. This time he tried them on. He leaned forward to check himself out in a small mirror hooked to the stand. He angled his face one way, then the other.

"Absolutely Hollywood," Ngame said.

José did another 180 in the mirror and handed over a ten. "You need anything . . ."

Toward evening the alley was getting dark. Solomon didn't need a watch to know Ngame would be closing up in an hour unless business was good. And today business hadn't been good. Not bad, but not good either. He saw Gehdi come out of Asad the Somali's store, stand in the doorway, and look down the block toward Ngame. Gehdi had a duffle bag slung over his shoulder. He stood there for a moment as though listening to a reply, then turned and said something to someone in the store. He shut the door and made his way across Wisconsin toward the alley. Solomon slouched in his canvas chair, pulled the American flag he used for a blanket up under his chin, and pretended to sleep.

Gehdi passed within a few feet of Solomon, and Solomon watched him disappear in the darkening alley toward the parking garage. Across the street, Ngame started disassembling his stand. Solomon began his night critique, judging how Ngame stowed the bulky handbags into the nylon sacks, taking care to dust each one carefully before putting it away.

Where Gehdi?

Voice surprised him. Feeling a flush of irritation and guilt, Solomon realized he hadn't been paying attention to his alley.

If Gehdi was going to bring the Navigator around, why wasn't he out by now?

Minutes passed. Ngame was working on the last of the handbags. Solomon squinted down the alley, trying to pierce the deepening darkness.

What's that? Voice asked.

"What's what?

That!

"You seeing shit," Solomon scolded, but even as he said it something moved, the slightest shift of black against the deeper black in the shadow of Ngame's van. And then nothing.

For a moment, stillness returned to the alley, then a figure crossed the sliver of light coming from between Old Glory and Johnny Rockets.

Paying no attention to Solomon, Gehdi walked by and returned to the store.

Solomon waited a moment or two, then slipped down the alley toward Ngame's van and the parking garage.

When he got back, Ngame was breaking down his stand, stacking the wire grate shelving, and bagging the C-clamps. His merchandise was packed away in the nylon sacks and the blue plastic storage boxes.

Up the street, Asad came out, followed by Nadif. Nadif walked with a heavy limp. In one hand, an umbrella he used for a cane. His other cluched Gehdi's shoulder. Asad locked up, keyed the alarm, and the three made their way toward him.

Solomon smiled. One gimpy Somali. Man gonna remember this day, long as he live.

The three passed by him and soon headlights swept the alley as the Navigator came up the garage ramp. It stopped where the alley intersected 31st, then took a right toward M Street and disappeared from view.

"Goodbye, Somalis," Solomon whispered. He got up, folded his flag carefully, and hung it over one of his Safeway carts. He crossed Wisconsin to stand guard over Ngame's goods while the Nigerian fetched his van.

It was 9:30 when Ngame slammed the doors of his van. He palmed Solomon their customary closing-of-the-day bill.

"This a twenty," Solomon said, offering it up.

Ngame waved it away. "We had a good day today."

"Business wasn't that good."

Ngame got into his van and started the engine. He leaned out the window and patted Solomon on the shoulder. "Business isn't all that makes a good day."

Canal Road runs northwest out of Georgetown along the Potomac River. Round a bend, the bright lights fade and it becomes a country road. After a mile, Waverly Ngame noticed headlights coming up behind him, speeding at first, then taking a position fifty yards or so behind and hanging in there. He checked his rearview. The lights behind him belonged to Asad's white Navigator.

And somebody in the passenger seat had an arm out the window, pointing something at him.

"Don't get so close," Asad said. "Drop back some."

Gehdi eased off the gas. He gave Asad a leer. "Fried Nigerian."

Asad laughed and pressed the button of the garage door opener. He imagined the sequence: the electronic command sent to the door opener's receiver, the receiver that would shoot thirty-six volts into the blasting cap, the blasting cap embedded in the quarter pound of C-4 plastic explosive that the magnet held to the gas tank of the Nigerian's van.

An hour later, José Phelps ducked under the police line tape.

Floodlights washed out color and turned the carnage two-dimensional: an axle with one wheel attached, its tire still smoldering, grotesque twists of metal strewn across the roadway and into the trees, a man's shoe obscenely lined up on the asphalt's center-stripe, a portion of the owner's foot still in it.

Renfro Calkins huddled with two of his forensics techs at the far side of the road, looking into the drainage ditch.

José walked over. "ID?"

Calkins shook his head. "Gonna have to be DNA. All we gots is hamburger." He pointed into the ditch. "That's the largest."

José walked over and looked. It took him several seconds to make out the thing that had been an arm. "What's that in the hand?"

"Looks like a switch for a garage door. Best guess, these guys set off a bomb in their own vehicle."

"How'd they manage that?"

Calkins shrugged. "They not gonna tell you, José."

Gonna be a quiet day today.

Solomon looked down his alley, then across Wisconsin to where the Nigerian was setting up his stand.

"For once," he said to Voice, "you got your shit together."

THE LIGHT AND THE DARK

BY ROBERT WISDOM

Petworth, N.W.

They called him Bay Ronnie but I don't know why. People in the neighborhood said he used to live around here but him and his people moved a long time ago. They said he was mean. Crazy-mean, like he'd rather take a switchblade to you than talk. He wore shades, a black dobb, Dak slacks or Sansabelts, silk socks, and Romeo Ballys. Black as tar, with pure white around the eyes. He would always come down singing from up Sherman Circle way. On Saturday morning, the 22nd of August, you could hear that ugly, husky voice: ". . . *It's a thin liiiine between love and hate/It's a thin line between love and hate . . .*"

Sunday, the 23rd of August, was a muggy and humid morning. It also marked the last sermon Reverend Yancey would preach at the old Gethsemane Baptist Church. Gethsemane had been on that hilltop at Georgia Avenue and Upshur Street for twentysome years. The church was set to be "tore down," as all the adults were saying around me. "It gon' be tore down by Monday mornin'." Torn down to make room for a Safeway. The church was so small I couldn't see how a big old grocery store was gonna fit, but I didn't know nuthin' about buildings. I was eight years old at the time. The youth and senior choirs would sing in a big service that day. My sister was in the youth choir and my mother taught Sunday school.

We moved into this two-story house on Crittenden

Street between Georgia Avenue and 9th Street in the '50s. There were a couple of white families when we came in, and everybody was friendly, but they had all left the neighborhood maybe a year after we moved in. Just as we started to play together, the white kids had to move someplace else. There were other friends too—Jon, Brian, Mark, and Lisa Rammelford—who lived around the corner on 9th Street before we arrived, along with Darryl Watson, a cousin of my sister's friend Joyce, who was around most of the time.

At some point, like most of the other people on the block, my mother and father started renting out rooms in our house. Some were family, like cousins Ivy, June, and Neville, and all of us Jamaicans and Trinidadians ate together. There was always loud laughter and somebody telling you what to do. When we first moved in, my parents took in some black Americans and a Chinese man, who were all real different from the West Indians—Miss Ruby, Mr. Palmer, Miss Lucy, and Mr. Price. Mr. Kinney and his come-and-go wife were Americans. They stayed in the room that looked over the backyard and were pretty nice and quiet. There was Tommy and Doris (or Clay and Liston, as my father called them), who were also American. All the Americans and Mr. Lee, the Chinese man, kinda kept to themselves and ate different foods, like grits, which Mr. Kinney taught me to make with butter for breakfast.

Mr. Lee was a mystery. He always locked the door to his room, even when he was home or just going to the bathroom. He was real polite. When he came home, he'd stand in the living room and look at everybody and bow and say something under his breath with a big grin, like, ". . . *Harerow* . . ." Sometimes his strange speaking went on for many minutes. Then he'd go upstairs for the night. My father loved it, he'd stand up and bow and smile. Then he'd have a big laugh when

Mr. Lee left and tell us, "That man got good manners." It got to the point that when I heard Mr. Lee's key in the front door, I'd go to the kitchen so I wouldn't have to do the greeting.

All three bedrooms in the house were rented out, which left the living room and dining room. My parents slept on a bed in the dining room and my sisters and I shared a foldout sofa-bed in the living room. This felt normal to us. My mother was always saying this setup was just for a little while and it helped them make ends meet.

There were a lot of times that I didn't like the folks who stayed at our house. I didn't appreciate my mom cooking for everybody, and I thought they were stupid when they asked where Jamaica was or turned up their noses at ackee and salt-fish or boiled green bananas and mackerel. But everybody knew food was always cooking at our house or at the home of one of our aunts or numerous cousins who lived nearby, so there were always people around and we always felt safe.

Still, there was a lot I wanted to understand about black Americans. Sometimes I would sneak into their rooms when they weren't home. Not that I was looking for anything, but I was curious to know who they were—their smells, how they were different from us. Mr. Kinney's magic shave smelled like rotten eggs; he said he used it so he wouldn't get razor bumps, but it stank. Snooping in his room one day, I opened the can to see what it looked like and spilled it all over the floor. I swept it up and put it back in the can and cleaned the floor, but then it started smelling like rotten eggs, so I left and prayed that the scent would disappear. If he ever knew what happened, he never said. In the other rooms I would find clothes that didn't get hung up, leftover fried fish sandwiches brought home from takeout, suitcases that never got unpacked, framed pictures and snapshots of smiling kids with missing teeth and shorts and barrettes. In some of the pictures taken long before I was born, the young men and women wore tweed suits and hats, their kids in front of placid monotone backdrops of trestled bridges over duck-filled English ponds, with Queen Elizabeth always somewhere in the background. But never any smiles. No Jamaican joy—only stern faces. All kinds of people were coming and going; why my parents chose them over other people was another mystery to me.

Everything became clear to me when I woke up that Saturday morning, August 22. The smells of cakes and pies being baked, greens being cooked, and chickens being fried settled like a cloud over the whole neighborhood. The Petworth Parents' Club, headed by Mrs. Florence Billops, was holding one of its four-times-per-year dinners and bake sales. The money raised from these events paid for annual community trips for parents and kids to places like the New York World's Fair, Hershey Park in Pennsylvania, and stuff like that.

So every mother in the neighborhood had started early in the morning, making her specialty. This meant me and my friends would have to hang around all day in case our mothers needed something from one of the corner stores, which they always did. Then we'd get the money and take off running through the alleys, pop over fences, shout at the friends who got to play kickball, and run in sweating to Mr. G's or Chuck & Danny's midnight delicatessen. Mr. G was this old—I don't know, eighty years old maybe—heavyset bald-headed Jewish man, his fingers thick and curled up. He spoke with an accent I never figured out, maybe German, and all he ever did was grunt when we slid the money on the counter or if we told him, "My mother said she'll pay you on Monday . . ." Then we'd take off again, racing three blocks to see who'd make it back to the front porch first.

Mom made peas and rice, cornbread, potato salad, greens, curry chicken, and fried chicken. We'd start taking the food to Mrs. Billops's by 10 o'clock, and people would be coming into the neighborhood and double-parking all afternoon. In the evening, all my father's buddies would start arriving for their weekly dominos games. Every week it was at a different house—this week it was ours. My father and his friends also worked "serving parties" in rich white households or embassies; you could tell when they had one of those jobs cause when they came over, everyone's arms would be filled with trays of hors d'oeuvres and bottles of scotch, rum, ginger ale, beer, and all kinds of expensive-looking stuff.

Mr. Christian, Mr. O'Connor, Mr. Palmer, Daddy Shaw, and my father would go to the basement to play "cards," as they called dominos. Upstairs in the kitchen, my sisters, cousins Ivy and June, my mom, and whoever else dropped by would heat up hot combs and turn the radio to WOL while they pressed each others' hair. The air in the house filled with the smells of "My Knight" hair pomade and curry chicken, and with laughter from the kitchen, the booming voices from downstairs, and Martha Reeves singing "Jimmy Mack."

I was in the living room watching Saturday night movies on TV when the screen door to the house swung open. It was Doris, who lived in the front room upstairs with her common-law husband Tommy, and you could tell she was drunk. Everybody in the kitchen went quiet.

"Hello, Miz Wizzdom, I'ma, I'ma . . . You fixin' Valda's hair? You shoulda waited for me, I'll do it. Hey, suga . . ." She was getting ready to squeeze my little sister's cheeks.

"Doris, gwan upstairs and sleep," my mother coaxed.

"Ah, Miz Wizzdom, y'all think I'm drunk, but I ain't been drinkin'. Where Tommy? He come back in yet?" She was slurring and thoughts were running from her mind to her mouth, getting her in deeper shit with the women in the kitchen. I was peeking out from my chair in the living room.

"Come here, Bobby, take this upstairs for me, will ya, hon?"

"No." Mom didn't allow any of the tenants to tell us what to do. "No, you take your things upstairs yourself. Bobby, gwan back to your TV."

"Shit. Y'all bein' like that, thinkin' y'all something special. Y'all ain't nuthin' but some black nigger Jamaicans."

Mom's hand was on cousin Ivy's arm. She was ready to jump.

"That's enough, *Doris.*" The name was spoken in a way that said this was the last bit of politeness coming. "You don't cuss me in front of me children. If you want food, there's food—"

"I ain't hungry." She was trailing a shirt or something on the floor behind her.

Doris was a big-boned woman, maybe in her thirties, from South Carolina. Black-skinned and thick. She wore red lipstick and nail polish and loved to party. She already had false teeth and sometimes pushed the bridge out when she talked. She was always smoothing her beehive—"I got good hair," she would say.

But tonight you could feel everybody was tight-jawed. From downstairs came the rumble of men's voices; they couldn't hear what was going on since the door to the basement was closed. Mom had always felt sorry for Doris and tried to help pull her life together. Mom had to put her out once already, then Doris came back and promised that she was on a good track. But this was the second weekend she had come in drunk. By now, everybody knew that when she had been drinking, it meant she and Tommy were gonna fight.

"Tommy, you up there . . . ?!" she shouted to nobody.

I walked around to the dining room and saw my mother staring at Doris with that red-hot comb in her hands. "Don't you dare talk fresh in my house!"

That was it. Even drunk Doris knew better than to push this woman.

"You tek yourself upsteers and don't bother comin' back down 'ere"—each word slow and quiet, with no fear. Doris went upstairs and we heard her door slam.

"She gon' have to go, Miss Inie, cause she nuttin' but trouble. You can't keep feelin' sorry for sumtin' like dat . . ."

Doris stayed up in her room, but the mood in the kitchen changed. Everybody spoke in hushes. *"Lawd have mercy,"* was my mother. *"I know, I know,"* was cousin Ivy. *"You should tell Daddy . . ."* from my sisters. *"No . . ."* from both older women.

This went on for half an hour until Ivy took June home. The game was breaking up downstairs, and we were pulling out the bed to get ready for sleep, then *Slam!*

Booming footsteps rolled across the ceiling above us, furniture was pushed, a body shoved . . . voices muffled, a man and a woman . . . My sisters and I looked wide-eyed at the ceiling and the swinging chandelier. The glass pieces were tinkling, catching some light from the streetlamps outside and making strange dancing patterns across the ceiling and walls.

BOOM! Two bodies fell together, like Bruno San Martino and Bobo Brazil, and it was as if we were watching from underwater.

Then the door upstairs opened and sound came rushing out.

"I'MA KILL YOU, MUTHAFUCKA !!" Doris banshee-screamed.

My father was up from the basement and in the hallway shouting. Tommy pushed past him, muttering, "She crazy, Mr. Wisdom, crazy and drunk. I'm through—"

Doris was running down the steps. "I'ma get you! You ain't no good, I know you been seein' that bitch!"

Tommy was out the door.

"Doris—" my father started to say.

"I ain't talkin' to you, you on his side. Where he at?!" Doris screamed.

My mother huddled us into a corner. "Unna just stay pon the floor . . . Elly, come back in, let that fool 'oman go."

Blam!

"Omigodalmighty!" My mother was on top of us. I was on the bottom, holding my little sister but wanting to look out of the window that we were now under.

Blam! Blam!

I could hear Tommy far off, shouting, "Woman, you crazy, you done shot that man!"

For a tornado of minutes there was more shouting, crying. I was straining to look out the window. My mother was yelling at me to get down, then yanked me away.

"What'd I do?" I demanded. "I didn't do nuthin' . . . Doris shot him!!"

"Don't say nuthin'! Just shut you mouth . . ." She was crying.

I could see that Miss Lucy, the other American tenant, had made it to the middle of the stairs and was humming and mumbling to herself: ". . . You let me see, hmmhuhp, those people are trouble, you know . . ."

My father was out front. "Ya nah come back in my 'ouse."

My mother: "Elly, don't let har back in."

By now, all the neighbors were out and we could hear police sirens coming down Georgia Avenue and around 9th Street. Doris was out front crying, "I'm sorry, I'msosorry, I'msorry . . . Tell Tommy don't leave me . . ."

My mother and older sister moved out to the door.

"Miz Wizdom, don't let the po-lice take me. I'm sorry, I didn't mean it."

To get my little sister to stop crying, we started jumping up and down on the bed, trying to reach the chandelier. Trying to make it start swinging again.

A little while later, I was falling asleep while the police stood in the hall talking to my mother and father. Miss Lucy was sitting on the steps picking at her feet and minding everybody's business. My sisters and I were in a heap on the bed. I heard Tommy come in to get some things. "Say good-bye to the kids for me."

A fresh breeze blew across my face. I opened my eyes to find that the sun was up. My mother came in to wake us at 7:30 a.m. on Sunday, August 23.

"Mom, is Doris in jail?" was the first thing I thought to say. I wanted to know if that room would be empty. If I could finally move up there and have my own room. It was the dead-center of the mid-Atlantic summer. Already the air was wet and heavy. The cool night breeze was all but gone and we would slowly drown the rest of the day in the sweltering summer heat. My older sister went upstairs to the bathroom. My little sister rolled up in her pillow for the last few minutes she could steal. I sat in the window. The street was quiet. I saw Reverend Gilmore come onto his front porch with his Bible under his arm and head to his car with his wife.

"Is everything all right over there, Mr. Wisdom?"

"Everyting is juss fine."

My father said good morning to someone else on the street. He must have been sitting out there on the porch all through the night. I just sat looking out, hearing the quiet, thinking how I wanted to go on up to Rock Creek Park and get lost in the woods. I glanced over and my mom was standing there silently. She eased my little sister's head off the pillow and sat her up. Then went into the kitchen to fix breakfast. I could hear her crying.

By 9 o'clock we were in the morning service. My mother, who taught Sunday school, always brought us early. My father only came to church for weddings, baptisms, and funerals. We were sitting in the middle section and the wooden chairs threatened to tip over with the big bodies. The junior choir had everybody on their feet and a fan cooled the sweating bodies. I was in my iridescent blue suit, white shirt, and tie. I just looked around at everyone and the smooth wooden floors and the feet walking by, carrying this one big woman after she got the spirit. The choir master was leaning back, mouth open, and the people were singing and clapping, but I couldn't hear a sound. I ran the toe of my shoe through a smooth groove in the floorboard. *Blam! Blam!* the only sound in my head. Everything else around me was a blizzard of empty details. Details that would be packed away inside me without being looked at, without letting them touch me. *Blam!* My hands were sweating into my little sister's—the only touch I let myself feel.

Fast forward: My stories don't really come all crafted into a nice tale. There are a whole bunch of things that come up as I tell this, and these are part of the story now. These little memories like bees in my mind's eye, threatening, buzzing around my head. Dangling threads that invariably lead to something deeper and darker . . . the innocence of learning to slow-drag with a girl on the dance floor and how the next day she was attacked and raped by a much older man. But nobody ever really talked about it. My friend was way different after that and nobody ever danced with her again. These are now just memories from the comfort zone of my current life, away from police sirens, getting jumped after school, and having to fight regularly just to get home. Long bus rides across D.C. to Spring Valley, to a world where there were no gangs, knives, anger, violence, roaches, and threats—at least, not in the streets where you had to look at it all the time.

You see, the cats I grew up with didn't hold on to our stories, we kept pure emotion hidden, cause we were the kids of the city. You had to be a quick study to survive. If you showed any feelings, much less reflection, you got your ass kicked over and over. Those kids who moved up from North Carolina and came into our neighborhood with their accents and their openness were laughed at till they conformed. If your parents cared, they fought to create some conditions so that you could value your life, your experiences—but on the street your story didn't have any value. *Top dog/dirty dog.* Only material things were valued on the street . . . *One day I'ma get me a* [insert Cadillac, $50 shoes, etc].

When I started going to an exclusive private school, I became convinced my stories didn't have value. So it was better to appropriate *their* stories—be like them, at least on the outside—because what could *my* stories contribute to the lives of these princes.

In college, there was an unspoken message to let go of the past, of my story, to move forward. When I came home for holidays and caught up with Green Jeans, Brock, or Black Joe, they told me stories, all the stories of who got locked up, broke down, shot, or OD'd. These stories were snuffed out and then forgotten, never to be recounted. College brought me pan-Africanism, the Nation of Islam, and other progressive movements meant to shape the black identity, to give us "real" stories. As these movements required new names, clothes, identity, I started feeling a strong pull back toward my own stories, though I still didn't have the will to tell them. An anchor dropped in high school kept me connected with the life stories I owned. My track coach, Brooks Johnson, drilled into me the importance of *character* and *pride*. His mantra took root in my life and became magnified through the men and women around me: my father and mother, my father's best friend Mr. Christian, other coaches, and my Episcopalian headmaster Canon Martin. These were fiery and gentle people whose lives seemed guided by their stories. The light *and* the dark.

I had to find ways to avoid being consumed by the myriad of dark impulses that came into my life. I had to figure how to *live* before I could recount, before I could truly own my story. It is very long and it continues. The stories I began but couldn't finish can now be looked at and coaxed back . . . I can take the gloves off, stop fighting life and instead hold it.

I left my neighborhood in the 1970s. Even though the razor-sharp edge of living in Petworth has dulled, I now hoard the memories. I find myself looking back, repeatedly—at street corners, empty stretches of Kansas Avenue, Sherman Circle—and these quiet scenes are arranged in my mind into strange, chaotic stacks, as if waiting for the day they will reveal themselves as the hidden alphabet that somehow spells out my life's meaning.

The potency is in the stacking. Laying them down in a brushed-steel coffin was too cold, I needed to heat them up with my experiences since that time and bring the life back to them. They needed to be honored. The characters and events struggled for a place in my soul. This is the richness I'm now willing to talk about.

A.R.M. AND THE WOMAN

BY LAURA LIPPMAN

Chevy Chase, N.W.

S ally Holt was seldom the prettiest woman in the room, but for three decades now she had consistently been one of the most sought-after for one simple fact: She was a wonderful listener. Whether it was her eight-year-old son or her eighty-year-old neighbor or some male in-between, Sally rested her chin in her palm and leaned forward, expression rapt, soft laugh at the ready—but not *too* ready, which gave the speaker a feeling of power when the shy, sweet sound finally bubbled forth, almost in spite of itself. In the Northwest quadrant of Washington, where overtly decorative women were seen as suspect if not out-and-out tacky, a charm like Sally's was much prized. It had served her well, too, helping her glide into the perfect marriage to her college sweetheart, a dermatologist, then allowing her to become one of Northwest Washington's best hostesses, albeit in the amateur division. Sally and her husband, Peter, did not move in and did not aspire to the more rarefied social whirl, the one dominated by embassy parties and pink-faced journalists who competed to shout pithy things over one another on cable television shows. They lived in a quieter, in some ways more exclusive world, a charming, old-fashioned neighborhood comprising middle-class houses that now required upper-class incomes to own and maintain.

And if, on occasion, in a dark corner at one of the endless parties Sally and Peter hosted and attended, her unwavering attention was mistaken for affection, she managed to deflect the ensuing pass with a graceful shake of her auburn curls. "You wouldn't want me," she told the briefly smitten men. "I'm just another soccer mom." The husbands backed away, sheepish and relieved, confiding in each other what a lucky son of a bitch Peter Holt was. Sally Holt had kept her figure, hadn't allowed herself to thicken into that androgynous khaki-trousered—let's be honest, downright dykish—mom so common in the area, which did have a lot of former field hockey players gone to seed. Plus, she was so great to talk to, interested in the world, not forever prattling about her children and their school.

Sally's secret was that she didn't actually hear a word that her admirers said, just nodded and laughed at the right moments, cued by their inflections as to how to react. Meanwhile, deep inside her head, she was mapping out the logistics of her next day. *Just a soccer mom, indeed.* To be a stay-at-home mother in Northwest D.C. was to be nothing less than a general, the Patton of the car pool, the Eisenhower of the HOV lane. Sally spent most of her afternoons behind the wheel of a Porsche SUV, moving her children and other people's children from school to lessons, from lessons to games, from games to home. She was ruthlessly efficient with her time and motion, her radio always tuned to WTOP to catch the traffic on the eights, her brain filled with alternative routes and illegal shortcuts, her gaze at the ready to thaw the nastiest traffic cop. She could envision her section of the city in a three-dimensional grid in her head, her house on Morrison and the Dutton School off Nebraska the two fixed stars in her universe. Given all she had to do, you really couldn't blame her for not listening to the men who bent her ear, a figure of speech that struck her as particularly apt. If she allowed all those words into her head, her ears would be bent—as crimped, tattered, and chewed-up looking as the old tom cat she had owned as a child, a cat who could not avoid brawls even after he was neutered.

But when Peter came to her in the seventeenth year of their marriage and said he wanted out, she heard him loud and clear. And when his lawyer said their house, mortgaged for a mere $400,000, was now worth $1.8 million, which meant she needed $700,000 to buy Peter's equity stake, she heard that, too. For as much time as she spent behind the wheel of her car, Sally was her house, her house was Sally. The 1920s stucco two-story was tasteful and individual, with a kind of perfection that a decorator could never have achieved. She was determined to keep the house at all costs and when *her* lawyer proposed a way it could be done, without sacrificing anything in child support or her share of Peter's retirement funds, she had approved it instantly and then, as was her habit, glazed over as the details were explained.

"What do you mean, I owe a million dollars on the house?" she asked her accountant, Kenny, three years later.

"You refinanced your house with an interest-only balloon mortgage in order to have the cash to buy Peter out of his share. Now it's come due."

"But I don't have a million dollars," Sally said, as if Kenny didn't know this fact better than anyone. It was April, he had her tax return in front of him.

"No biggie. You get a new mortgage. Unfortunately, your timing sucks. Interest rates are up. Your monthly payment is going to be a lot bigger—just as the alimony is ending. Another bit of bad timing."

Kenny relayed all this information with zero emotion. After all, it didn't affect his bottom line. It occurred to Sally that an accountant should have a much more serious name. What was she doing, trusting someone named Kenny with her money?

"What about the equity I've built up in the past three years?"

"It was an interest-only loan, Sally. There is no additional equity." Kenny, a square-jawed man who bore a regrettable resemblance to Frankenstein, sighed. "Your lawyer did you no favors, steering you into this deal. Did you know the mortgage broker he referred you to was his brother-in-law? And that your lawyer is a partner in the title company? He even stuck you with P.M.I."

Sally was beginning to feel as if they were discussing sexually transmitted diseases instead of basic financial transactions.

"I thought I got an adjustable-rate mortgage. A.R.M.'s have conversion rates, don't they? And caps? What does any of this have to do with P.M.I.?"

"A.R.M.'s do. But you got a balloon, and balloons come due. All at once, in a big lump. Hence the name. You had a three-year grace period, in which you had an artificially low rate of less than three percent, with Peter's four thousand in rehabilitative alimony giving you a big cushion. Now it's over. In today's market, I recommend a thirty-year fixed, but even that's not the deal it was two years ago. According to today's rates, the best you can do is—"

Frankennystein used an old-fashioned adding machine, the kind with a paper roll, an affectation Sally had once found charming. He punched the keys and the paper churned out, delivering its noisy verdict.

"A million financed at a thirty-year fixed rate—you're

looking at almost $6,000 a month and that's just the loan. No taxes, no insurance."

It was an increase of almost $2,000 a month over what she had been paying for the last three years, not taking into account the alimony she was about to lose, which came to $4,000 a month. A net loss of $6,000.

"I can't cover that, not with just $5,000 a month in child support." Did Kenny raise a caterpillar eyebrow at the "just." Sally knew that Peter paid well, but then—he earned well. "I can't make a mortgage payment of that size and pay my share of the private school tuition, which we split fifty-fifty."

"You could sell. But after closing costs and paying the real estate agent's fee, you'd walk away with a lot less cash than you might think. Maybe eight hundred thousand."

Eight hundred thousand dollars. She couldn't buy a decent three-bedroom for that amount, not in this neighborhood, not even in the suburbs. There, the schools would be free, at least, but the Dutton School probably mattered more to Sally than it did to the children. It had become the center of her social life since Peter left, a place where she was made to feel essential. Essential and adored, one of the parents who helped out without becoming a fearsome buttinsky or know-it-all.

"How long do I have to figure this out?" she asked Frankenny.

"The balloon comes due in four months. But the way things are going, you'll be better off locking in sooner rather than later. Greenspan looked funny the last time the Fed met."

"Funny?"

"Constipated, like. As if his sphincter was the only thing keeping the rates down."

"Kenny," she said with mock reproach, her instinctive reaction to a man's crude joke, no matter how dull and silly. Already, her mind was miles away, flying through the streets of her neighborhood, trying to think who might help her. There was a father who came to Sam's baseball games, often straight from work, only to end up on his cell, rattling off percentages. He must be in real estate.

"I own a title company," Alan Mason said. "Which, I have to say, is like owning a mint these days. The money just keeps coming. Even with the housing supply tight as it is, people always want to refinance. Rates go down, they want in. Rates squeak up, they panic."

"If only I had thought to talk to you three years ago," Sally said, twisting the stalk of a gone-to-seed dandelion in her hand. They were standing along the first base line, the better to see both their sons—Sam, adorable if inept in right field, and Alan's Duncan, a wiry first baseman who pounded his glove with great authority, although he had yet to catch a single throw.

"The thing is—" Alan stopped as the batter made contact with the ball, driving it toward the second baseman, who tossed it to Duncan for the out. There was a moment of suspense as Duncan bobbled it a bit, but he held on.

"Good play, son!" Alan said and clapped, then looked around. "I didn't violate the vocalization rule, did I?"

"You were perfect," Sally assured him. The league in which their sons played did, in fact, have strict rules about parents' behavior, including guidelines on how to cheer properly—with enthusiasm, but without aggression. It was a fine line.

"Where was I? Oh, your dilemma. The thing is, I can

hook you up with someone who can help you find the best deal, but you might want to consider taking action against your lawyer. He could be disbarred for what he did, or at least reprimanded. Clearly a conflict of interest."

"True, but that won't help me in the long run." She sighed, then exhaled on the dandelion head, blowing away the fluff.

"Did you make a wish?" Alan asked. He wasn't handsome, not even close. He looked like Ichabod Crane, tall and thin, with a pointy nose and no chin.

"I did," Sally said with mock solemnity.

"For what?"

"Ah, if you tell, they don't come true." She met his eyes, just for a moment, let Alan Mason think that he was her heart's desire.

Later that night, her children asleep, a glass of white wine at her side, she plugged figures into various mortgage calculators on the Internet, as if a different site might come up with a different answer. She charted her budget on Quicken—*if* she traded the Porsche for a Prius, *if* she stopped buying organic produce at Whole Foods, *if* she persuaded Molly to drop ballet, *if* Sam didn't go to camp. But there were not enough sacrifices in the world to cover the looming shortfall in their monthly bills. They would have to give up everything to keep the house—eating, driving, heat and electricity.

And even if she did find the money, found a way to make it work, her world was still shrinking around her. When Peter first left, it had been almost a relief to be free of him, grouchy and cruel as he had become in midlife. She had been glad for an excuse to avoid parties as well. Now that she was divorced, the husbands steered clear of her; a suddenly single woman was the most unstable molecule of all in their social set. But Alan Mason's gaze, beady as it was, had reminded her how nice it was to be admired, how she had enjoyed being everyone's favorite confidante once upon a time, how she had liked the hands pressed to her bare spine, the friendly pinch on her ass.

She should marry again. It was simple as that. She left the Internet's mortgage calculators for its even more numerous matchmakers, but the world she glimpsed was terrifying, worse than the porn she had once found cached on Peter's laptop, the first telltale sign of the trouble that was to come. She was so *old* by the standards enumerated in these online wish lists. Worse, she had children, and ad after ad specified that would just not do. She looked at the balding, pudgy men, read their demands—no kids, no fatties, no over-forties—and realized they held the power to dictate the terms. No, she would not subject herself to such humiliation. Besides, Internet matches required writing, not listening. In a forum where she could not nod and laugh and gaze sympathetically, Sally was at a disadvantage. Typing *"LOL"* in a chat room simply didn't have the same impact.

Now, a man with his own children, that would be ideal. A widower or a divorcé who happened to have custody, rare as that was. She mentally ran through the Dutton School directory, then pulled it from the shelf and skimmed it. No, no, no—all the families she knew were disgustingly intact, the divorced and reblended ones even tighter than those who had stayed with their original mates. Didn't anyone die anymore? Couldn't the killers and drug dealers who kept the rest of Washington in the upper tier of homicide rates come up to Northwest every now and then, take out a housewife or two? Why not?

* * *

In a school renown for dowdy mothers, Lynette Mason was one of the dowdiest, gone to seed in the way only a truly preppy woman can. She had leathery skin and a Prince Valiant haircut, which she sheared back from her face with a grosgrain ribbon headband. Her laugh was a loud, annoying bray and if someone failed to join in her merriment, she clapped the person on the back as if trying to dislodge a lump of food. On this particular Thursday afternoon, Lynette stood on the sidewalk, speaking animatedly to one of the teachers, punching the poor woman at intervals. Sally, waiting her turn in the car pool lane, thought how easily a foot could slip, how an accelerator could jam. The SUV would surge forward, Lynette would be pinned against the column by the school's front door. So sad, but no one's fault, right?

No, Sally loved the school too much to do that. Besides, an accident would take out Ms. Grayson as well, and she was an irreplaceable resource when it came to getting Dutton's graduates into the best colleges. Sally would need her when Molly and Sam were older.

Four months, according to her accountant. She had four months. Maybe Peter would die; he carried enough life insurance to pay off the mortgage, with plenty left over for the children's education. No, she would never get that lucky. Stymied, she continued to make small talk with Alan Mason at baseball games, but began to befriend Lynette as well, lavishing even more attention on her in order to deflect any suspicions about Sally's kindness to Alan. Lynette was almost pathetically grateful for Sally's attention, adopting her with the fervor that adolescent girls bring to new friendships. Women appreciate good listeners, too, and Sally nodded and smiled—over lunch, over tea, and, once 5 o'clock came around, glasses of wine. Lynette had quite a bit to say, the usual litany of complaints. Alan worked all the time. There was zero romance in their marriage. She might as well be a single mom—"Not that a single mom is a bad thing to be," she squealed, clapping a palm over her large, unlipsticked mouth.

"You're a single mom without any of the advantages," Sally said, pouring her another glass of wine. *Drive home drunk. What do I care?*

"There are advantages, aren't there?" Lynette leaned forward and lowered her voice, although Molly was at a friend's and Sam was up in his room with Lynette's Duncan, playing the SIMS. "No one ever says that, but it's true."

"Sure. As long as you have the money to sustain the standard of living you had, being single is great."

"How do you do that?" Asked with specificity, as if Lynette believed that Sally had managed just that trick. Sally, who had long ago learned the value of the non-reply, raised her eyebrows and smiled serenely, secretly.

"I think Alan cheats on me," Lynette blurted out.

"I would leave a man who did that to me."

Lynette shook her head. "Not until the kids are grown and gone. Maybe then. But I'll be so old. Who would want me then?"

Who would want you now?

"Do what you have to do." Another meaningless response, perfected over the years. Yet no one ever seemed to notice how empty Sally's sentiments were, how vapid. She had thought it was just men who were fooled so easily, but it was turning out that women were equally foolish.

"Alan and I never have sex anymore."

"That's not uncommon," Sally said. "All marriages have their ups and downs."

"I love your house." Logical sequences of thought had never been Lynette's strength, but this conversation was abrupt and odd even by her standards. "I love *you*."

Lynette put a short stubby hand over Sally's, who fought the instinctive impulse to yank her own away. Instead, it was Lynette who pulled back in misery and confusion.

"I don't mean *that* way," she said, staring into her wine glass, already half empty.

Sally took a deep breath. If this were a man, at a party, she would have laughed lightly and accused him of being a terrible tease. To Lynette, she said: "Why not?"

Lynette put her hand back over Sally's. "You mean—?"

Sally thought quickly. No matter how far Sam and Duncan disappeared into their computer world, she could not risk taking Lynette to the master bedroom. She had a hunch that Lynette would be loud. But she also believed that this was her only opportunity. In fact, Lynette would shun her after today. She would cut Sally off completely, ruining any chance she had of luring Alan away from her. She would have to see this through, or start over with another couple.

"There's a room, over our garage. It used to be Peter's study. He took most of the things, but there's still a sofa there."

She grabbed the bottle of wine and her glass. She was going to need to be a little drunk, too, to get through this. Then again, who was less attractive in the large scheme of things, Alan or Lynette? Who would be more grateful, more giving? Who would be more easily controlled? She was about to find out.

Lynette may not have been in love when she blurted out that sentiment in Sally's kitchen, but she was within a week.

Lynette being Lynette, it was a loud, unsubtle love, both behind closed doors and out in public, and Sally had to chide her about the latter, school her in the basics of covert behavior, remind her not to stare with those cowlike eyes, or try to monopolize Sally at public events, especially when Alan was present. They dropped their children at school at 8:30 and Lynette showed up at Sally's house promptly at 8:45, bearing skim milk lattes and scones. Lynette's idea of the perfect day, as it turned out, was to share a quick latte upon arriving, then bury her head between Sally's legs until 11 a.m., when she surfaced for the Hot Topics segment on *The View*. Then it was back to devouring Sally, with time-outs for back rubs and baths. Lynette's large, eager mouth turned out to have its uses. Plus, she asked for only the most token attention in return, which Sally provided largely through a hand-held massage tool from The Sharper Image.

Best of all, Lynette insisted that, as much as she loved Sally, she could never, ever leave Alan, not until the children were grown and out of the home. She warned Sally of this repeatedly, and Sally would nod sadly, resignedly. "I'll settle for the little bit I can have," she said, stroking Lynette's Prince Valiant bob.

"If Alan ever finds out—" Lynette said glumly.

"He won't," Sally assured her. "Not if we're careful. There. No—*there*." Just as her attention drifted away in conversation, she found it drifting now, floating toward an idea, only to be distracted by Lynette's insistent touch. Later. She would figure everything out later.

"You're not going to believe this," Sally told Lynette at the beginning of their third week together, during one of the commercial breaks on *The View*. "Peter found out about us."

"Ohmigod!" Lynette said. "How?"

"I'm not sure. But he knows. He knows everything. He's threatening to take the children away from me."

"Ohmigod."

"And—" she turned her face to the side, not trusting herself to tell this part. "And he's threatening to go to Alan."

"Shit." In her panic, Lynette got up and began putting on her clothes, as if Peter and Alan were outside the door at this very moment.

"He hasn't yet," Sally said quickly. "But he will, if I fight the change in the custody order. He's given me a week to decide. I give up the children or he goes to Alan."

"You can't tell. You *can't*."

"I don't want to, but—how can I give up my children?"

Lynette understood, as only another mother could. The truth would destroy her; the secret would tear apart Sally's life. And even if Peter agreed not to tell for now, the danger was still there.

"Would he really do this?"

"He would. Peter—he's not the nice man everyone thinks he is. Why do you think we got divorced? And the thing is, if he gets the kids—well, it was one thing for him to do the things he did to me. But if he ever treated Molly or Sam that way . . ."

"What way?"

"I don't want to talk about it. But if it should happen— I'd have to kill him."

"The *pervert*." Lynette was at once repelled and fascinated. The dark side of Sally's life was proving as seductive as Sally's quiet companionship.

"I know. If he had done what he did to a stranger, he'd be in prison for life. But in a marriage, such things are legal. I'm stuck, Lynette. I won't ruin your life for anything. You told me from the first that this had to be a secret. I just hope Peter will be satisfied with destroying me."

"There has to be a way . . ."

"There isn't. Not as long as Peter is a free man."

"Not as long as he's *alive*."

"You can't mean—"

Lynette put a finger to Sally's lips. These had been the hardest moments to fake, the face-to-face encounters. Kissing was the worst. But it was essential not to flinch, not to let her distaste show. She was so close to getting what she wanted.

"Trust me," Lynette said.

Sally wanted to. But she had to be sure of one thing. "Don't try to hire someone. It seems like every time someone like us tries to find someone, it's always an undercover cop. Remember Ruth Ann Aron." A politician from the Maryland suburbs, Aron had, in fact, tried to hire a state trooper to off her husband. But he had forgiven her, even testified on her behalf during the trial.

"Trust me," Lynette repeated.

"I do, sweetheart. I absolutely do."

Dr. Peter Holt was hit by a Jeep Cherokee, an Eddie Bauer limited edition, as he crossed Connecticut Avenue on his way to the Thai restaurant where he ate lobster pad thai every Thursday evening. The remorseful driver told police that her children had been bickering in the backseat over what to watch on the DVD player and she had turned her head, just for a moment, to scold them. Still distracted by the children's fight when she turned around, she had seen Holt and tried to stop, but hit the accelerator instead. Then, as her children screamed for real, she had driven another 100 yards in panic and hysteria. If the dermatologist wasn't killed on impact, he was definitely dead when the SUV finally stopped. But the only substance in the driver's blood was caffeine, and while it was a tragic, regrettable accident, it was clearly an accident. Really, investigators told Holt's stunned survivors, his ex-wife and two children, it was surprising that such things didn't happen more often, given the congestion in D.C., the unwieldy SUVs, the mothers' frayed nerves, the nature of dusk with its tricky gray-green light. It was a macabre coincidence, their children being classmates and all, the parents being superficial friends. But this part of D.C. was like a village unto itself, and the accident had happened only a mile from the Dutton School. In fact, Peter Holt had just left the same soccer practice that the driver was coming from. He had been seen talking to his ex-wife, with whom he was still quite friendly, asking her if she and the children wanted to meet him for dinner at his favorite restaurant.

At Peter's memorial service, Lynette Mason sought a private moment with Sally Holt, and those who watched from a distance marveled at the bereaved woman's composure and poise, the way she comforted her ex-husband's killer. No one was close enough to hear what they said.

"I'm sorry," Lynette said. "It didn't occur to me that after—well, I guess we can't see each other anymore."

"It didn't occur to me, either," Sally lied. "You've sacrificed so much for me. For Molly and Sam, really. I'm in your debt, forever."

And she patted Lynette gently on the arm, which marked the last time the two ever touched. Sometimes, when Alan was working late, Lynette would call, a little high and a lot tearful, and Sally would remind her that they shouldn't tie up the phone too long, lest the records of these conversations come back to haunt them or the children overhear anything. They had done what mothers should do. They had put their children first.

Peter's estate went to Molly and Sam—but in trust to Sally, of course. She determined that it would be in the children's best interest to pay off the balloon mortgage in cash, and Peter's brother, the executor, agreed. Peter would have wanted the children to have the safety and sanctity of home, given the emotional trauma they had endured. He wouldn't want them forced out in the housing market, cruel and unforgiving as it was.

No longer needy, armored with a widow's prerogatives, Sally found herself invited to parties again, where solicitous friends attempted to fix her up with the rare single men in their circles. Now that she didn't care about men, they flocked around her and Sally did what she had always done. She listened and she laughed, she laughed and she listened, but she never really heard anything—unless the subject was money. Then she paid close attention, even writing down the advice she was given. The stock market was so turgid, everyone complained. The smart money was in real estate.

Sally nodded.

PART III

Cops & Robbers

COLD AS ICE

BY QUINTIN PETERSON

Congress Heights, S.E./S.W.

Seventy-two-year-old Ida Logan was sitting in her rocker on her front porch when the gunman opened fire. She never knew what hit her. Neither did her five-year-old great granddaughter Aaliyah Gamble, who was sitting nearby at her red, blue, and yellow plastic Playskool desk, playing with Legos.

In but a few seconds, more than a half dozen hollow-point 9mm rounds ripped through each of them, their bodies performing the death dance that only the gunfire of automatic weapons can orchestrate, jerking to the staccato of the *rat-tat-tat-tat* of the machine gun, as though keeping time to the pulsating rhythm of a boogie rap tune.

To eyewitness Rodney Grimes, the carnage seemed to transpire in slow motion; amid the crimson mist of their splattering blood, the bullets appeared to strike the frail old woman and the fragile little girl forever.

The dreadful scene was punctuated, and made that much more grotesque, by Aaliyah's head exploding, bursting like a ripe melon dropped from a high place. The pink halo of her vaporized brain was visible only for an instant, yet the obscene corona lingered around what little remained of the back of her neatly braided head; a ghastly image frozen in time . . . emblazoned upon his troubled mind.

* * *

Rodney Grimes didn't think twice about cooperating with the police. His late father had taught him that "evil flourishes when good men do nothing."

Rodney Grimes was a good man, wasn't he? He liked to think so. And even if he had not truly been good up to that point, couldn't he be? Could he not rise to the occasion? Evil had been done and he was compelled to do his part to ensure that the gunman did not go unpunished. It was his duty. Voluntarily, he told the police who arrived first at the scene of the crime that he had witnessed the murders and provided them with a detailed description of the suspect, making sure to emphasize that the gunman had long dreadlocks and was very dark-skinned with unsettling bluish-gray eyes; and described the getaway car, a black late-model Ford Crown Victoria, like a cop car. And later that day, he assisted Detective John Mayfield, the lead on the case, by accompanying him to the Violent Crimes Branch headquarters and picking out a photo of a suspect from an array of nine mugshots. He'd also agreed to participate in the viewing of a lineup. "Sure, no problem," he'd told the detective. "Just let me know."

However, the day after the double shooting, the courage of his conviction diminished considerably when he looked up from the *Spider-Man* comic he was leafing through at the newsstand inside of Iverson Mall and noticed the killer with a lion's mane of long dreadlocks standing next to him, towering above him.

The shooter held the latest issue of *Superman*, flipping its pages, but not looking at the comic book. Instead, his cold, disconcerting bluish-gray eyes were fixed on him.

Rodney hoped it was just his imagination at the crime scene; that the killer had simply looked in his general direction, not directly at him, directly into his face. But the killer's presence here before him dashed that hope. The killer had seen him . . . and evidently knew who he was.

They stood there silent for a moment, an outlandish odd couple, Rodney Grimes's clean-cut, black yuppie appearance in direct contrast to that of the killer, who looked like a hip-hop Rastafarian.

"Hey," said the killer, finally breaking the ice, "you look familiar." He paused, waited for a response. When Grimes did not reply, he continued. "Do I look familiar to you?"

Grimes remained silent.

"No?" the killer said. "I musta made a mistake." The killer laughed. "I know what it is! Ever see that Eddie Murphy movie . . . um . . . *Harlem Nights*, yeah. Redd Foxx had on big, thick Coke-bottle glasses like yours, made his eyes look all big and shit, like he was wearin' magnifyin' glasses. Yeah, that's it, you probably just reminded me of him."

Grimes remained silent.

"Say," the killer continued, "just *how* good can you see with eyes *that* bad? I'll bet you be makin' mistakes all the time, don't you? Wavin' at people across the street, then be like, 'Oh, shit, that ain't whoever.' Yeah, must be hard recognizin' people with eyes as bad as you got."

Grimes remained silent.

"You kinda old to be readin' comic books, ain't you?" the killer asked. "What, you twenty-one, twenty-two? Sheeit, I gave up readin' them joints when I was a little kid." He snickered.

Grimes remained silent. The killer turned his attention to the comic book.

"You know," the killer mused, "funny thing about heroes, 'specially comic book superheroes, none of 'em wear glasses. Take *Superman* here. His disguise, his *costume*, is Clark Kent, all mild-mannered and shit, wearin' eyeglasses, 'cause Superman, he know that people who wear eyeglasses all weak and geeky and shit, so nobody will mistake him for a hero. So he can have some peace, un'erstand? 'Cause otherwise, people would bug his ass to death! 'Superman, get my cat out the tree.' 'Superman, tow my car to the shop.' Yeah, it just be Superman do this and Superman do that, all the goddamn time!"

The killer stared directly into Grimes's magnified eyes and continued: "But the point I was tryin' to make is, heroes don't wear them shits. The eyes is the windows to the soul: weak eyes, weak soul. People who wear 'em is just plain weak. It's a *fact*. But when it's time to go to work, Superman snatch off them horn-rims and that Brooks Brothers and show off his Krypton clothes. 'This is a job for Superman!' Right? Voice get deep and everything." The killer paused for a moment to let his point sink in, and then made his message plain. "Thinking your weak ass can take down a *super* villain could get you and other people you care about in some serious trouble and cause you some real heartache. Don't make no mistake, Rodney, don't try to be no hero. Heroes don't wear glasses."

Certain his point had been made, the killer put the comic book back on the rack, glared at Rodney Grimes a few long moments for good measure, and then turned and leisurely walked away.

Finally, after having been paralyzed like a deer caught in the headlights of a semi, Grimes returned the *Spider-Man* to the rack and, on unsteady legs, exited the newsstand.

He fretted and racked his brain, trying to fathom, *How did the killer find out who I am? How did he find me?*

The thought occurred to him that the killer might still be

around, lying in wait to . . . to do what? Knife him and leave him bleeding on the floor? Gun him down in the parking lot? He looked around, trying to make sure he was not in immediate danger, but he was sure that his nervousness betrayed him.

Warily, his mind reeling, he walked to the escalator leading to the second level of the mall, wondering if being a good man was worth it.

When he got to his car in the front parking lot of Iverson Mall, he found a folded piece of paper under the left windshield wiper of *Sweet Georgia Brown*, his mint-condition 1970 metal-flake candy-apple-red, black-ragtop-with-black-leather interior Volkswagen Karman Ghia Coupe, which he had painstakingly refurbished personally over the last two years. Her personalized D.C. license tags read, GEORGIA.

What with him attending Howard U on a full scholarship as a civil engineering major and only working part-time at various jobs—busboy, waiter, photo technician at Moto-Foto—restoring her had by no means been an easy task, but it had been worth it. Often women mistook it for a Porsche. Incredible! Yeah, *Sweet Georgia Brown* drew women's attention that men like him could not otherwise draw, and that was priceless.

Rodney Grimes's anxiety heightened when he opened the note and read it. The message, which was handwritten in a childlike scrawl, said: *Heros don't wear glasses.*

Heros—the ignorant bastard couldn't even spell *heroes*. Under different circumstances, Rodney would have found this amusing, but nothing was funny about the situation. This was the killer's subtle way of telling him that he knew not only who he was, but what car he drove. It was a good bet that he knew where he lived, too.

Grimes refolded the note and put it in his shirt pocket. He walked around the car, giving it a once-over to determine if any damage had been done. Satisfied that his sweetheart was still in great condition, he disarmed the alarm system and unlocked her, climbed in, started her up, and headed off.

The drive home to his tenth-floor apartment at the Wingate House East apartment complex on Martin Luther King Jr. Avenue in far Southwest Washington was no joyride. Rodney couldn't shake the fear and a sense of impending doom he had not felt in years, not since he was in the seventh grade at Hart Junior High School.

When he'd attended Hart, he had been beaten and robbed on a daily basis, by people like the killer, until he fought back one day and maced a thug in the face when he'd attempted to rob him. That had been his last day, since to remain would have meant certain death. His mother had used her cunning by giving her sister's apartment in a housing project on M Street, S.W. as his home address so that he could attend a school in another part of town, Jefferson Junior High. It had been smooth sailing from there and he had stopped living in fear. Until now.

But what he had experienced at Hart was nothing compared to the terror the killer instilled in him now. The killer had threatened not only him, but also "other people" Rodney cared about, and his concern for the safety of his friends and family was what really terrified him. His actions could cause them harm . . . but could he live with the consequences of inaction, of not cooperating with the authorities and letting the killer go unpunished? In fact, what would stop the killer from doing him and those he cared about harm once the danger of arrest and prosecution had passed? If something bad happened to April Knight, he'd never forgive himself.

As he parked his sweetie in the front parking lot of Wingate House East, Rodney Grimes could not shake the belief that he was damned if he did and damned if he didn't.

Detective John Mayfield had seen better days, both careerwise and in his private life. His early years as a homicide detective had been good days. His closure rate was high, the envy of his peers, in fact. His late wife had always been in his corner, even though most homicide detectives' marriages end in divorce. Understandable. Police work, with its constant shift changes, makes cultivating any meaningful relationship difficult, but this type of assignment, which requires a round-the-clock commitment, makes it virtually impossible. Few people can accept being married to a ghost. But his dear Katherine had put up with it and hung in there. She had deserved better than dying by the hands of a lowlife during a street robbery gone bad. The fact that her murder remained unsolved was a festering wound. To him, every murderer he brought to justice was Katherine's killer, but the wound would never heal, he knew.

His closure rate seemed to diminish in direct proportion to his failing health, not because he lacked the stamina he once had as some might argue, though he was painfully aware that he did indeed lack the vigor of his youth, but because of obstacles he now had to hurdle to bring the guilty to justice. Nowadays, witnesses were hard to come by. A thug strapped with a MAC-11 can open fire on a crowded street or sporting event or concert hall, and no one sees a thing. If the perpetrators fail to intimidate witnesses, then murder definitely does the trick.

Cases that shocked and outraged the public humiliated the mayor and his "law and order" administration, and the pressure to quickly rectify each situation was passed on to the chief of police. Shit rolls down hill, and this time around Mayfield was at the bottom of the heap. With a caseload of thirty-seven murders for the year, more than half of them unsolved, John Mayfield was under a lot of pressure. As his boss Captain Lynch had put it, "Work better and faster if you want to keep your job!"

Yeah, the good old days of being a superstar homicide detective were definitely long gone as far as Detective Mayfield was concerned. But today would be like the good ol' days, he mused. Today, he had a rock solid case against the prolific and ever elusive "Teflon Thug," Isaiah "Ice" Hamilton, the suspect in the double homicide on Chesapeake Street, S.E., not only with strong physical evidence, but with three eyewitnesses: urban pioneer Terri Daulby; pillar of the community Ruthann Sommers; and Whiz Kid Rodney Grimes, some kind of nerdy genius who had risen above the social forces that seemed to conspire to keep black men down by turning them into Ice Hamiltons to become well-educated and gainfully employed. Each of them, separately, had picked Ice out a nine-mugshot black-and-white photo array—black-and-white instead of color so that Hamilton's cold-as-ice, steely bluish-gray eyes wouldn't set him apart from the mugshots of thugs of similar age, facial structure, and dark complexion.

The witnesses would stand by in separate waiting areas down the hall in an office just inside the secured, combination-lock doors leading to the lineup room where, one by one, they would see if they could pick out the suspect who had opened fire in broad daylight a couple of days ago on a cool, early September Saturday afternoon while the intended target, Francisco "Big Boy" Longus, was standing in front of 740 Chesapeake Street, S.E.

Mayfield was driven by a burning desire to see Ice, the cold-blooded perpetrator—*alleged* perpetrator—of this and other sins before God, put away as soon as possible. But it was also important to him that by closing this case he got off his back the government officials, police brass, and community leaders who were all whipped into fever pitch by an outraged public.

Yes, closing this case swiftly had gotten him out from under not only the victims' family—he had notified Aaliyah's mother by phone as soon as the arrest warrant was issued—but from the good captain as well.

Detective Mayfield had arrived at the soot-stained, weather-beaten, and dilapidated municipal center, the Henry J. Daly Building, located at 300 Indiana Avenue, N.W., at around 7:45 a.m. for check-in at the Court Liaison Unit on the first floor, a prerequisite before he could log in at D.C. Superior Court across the courtyard for the long and ongoing "Simple City Massacre" murder trial at which he would testify against codefendants LaVon "Pooty" Kirkwood and Donzelle "Killa" Hilliard . . . whenever the prosecution got around to him.

After he had checked in to court and was placed on standby, to be paged shortly before they needed him on the witness stand, he'd returned to MPD HQ for his 10:00 a.m. appointment in the lineup room. He was anxious. Finally bringing down Isaiah "Ice" Hamilton had him wired.

Handcuffed and shackled, and escorted by two officers assigned to the Central Cell Block (CCB), the very dark-complexioned Isaiah "Ice" Hamilton, six feet four inches tall and lean but muscular, clad in the standard thug uniform of laceless sneakers, baggy low-riding jeans, and oversized T-shirt, stepped from the private express elevator that ran between the CCB in the basement and the prisoner holding area adjacent to the CID lineup room. Detective Mayfield, Detective Crawford of the Lineup Unit, and five plainclothes officers of similar build, age, and skin color, selected to participate in the lineup, were already there when Ice and his escorts arrived.

Ice Hamilton had been picked up at about 4:00 a.m. that morning, operating the suspect vehicle described by the three witnesses, a black late-model Ford Crown Vic, and bearing the tag number Ruthann Sommers had jotted down just before the shooter sped from the scene. Remarkable also was that the car had not been reported stolen, which was typically the case for vehicles used in the commission of felony offenses. Ice was pulled over by two Seventh District officers when they spotted him driving the wanted vehicle on Barnaby Street, S.E., a couple of blocks away from the scene of the crime. Luckily, Ice Hamilton had not been able to produce his license, so he was placed under arrest and his vehicle was impounded. As instructed, the arresting officers made no mention of the car being the suspect vehicle in a murder case.

When he got the news, Detective Mayfield had been amazed that the cunning and elusive Teflon Thug had made such a magnificent blunder, and he was still astounded by this development, but rationalized that perhaps Ice wasn't as smart as he had given him credit for. Hell, it wouldn't be the first time. Incredibly, pursuant to a D.C. Superior Court warrant issued posthaste through Mayfield's connections and served within ninety minutes of Ice being taken into custody, the search of the trunk of the Crown Vic had yielded a MAC-11 and two fully loaded magazines, clothes matching the description of that worn by the assailant, and black cotton work gloves of the type the witnesses said the shooter had worn. Furthermore, ballistics tests conducted by the Firearms Examination Section—also conducted posthaste within two hours of the arrest via Detective Mayfield's connections— had identified the MAC-11 as the weapon in the Chesapeake Street double murder, as well as tentatively linked it to a half dozen other shootings and seven other murders committed in D.C. over the last nine months. The discovery of the weapon and the ammo led to additional holding charges of possession of a prohibited weapon and possession of unregistered ammunition.

By the time Detective Mayfield interviewed Ice briefly in the Seventh District Detectives Office, the latter was only aware that he was being charged with failure to display his operator's permit, and possession of a prohibited weapon and unregistered ammo. Mayfield nonchalantly inquired as to (1) Ice's whereabouts on the afternoon of the previous Saturday, and (2) how he had come to be in the possession of the Crown Vic.

Ice's answers were simple: "Hangin' wid my boyz" to the first question, "Borrowed it from my boy" to the second. Ice didn't even bother to ask the detective why he wanted to know.

When questioned if he knew that the man he'd borrowed the car from, Carter Washington, was wanted on an arrest warrant charging him with murder, and if he knew Washington's whereabouts, Ice replied, "Naw, I didn't know he was wanted. I don't know where that nigger at."

At any rate, John Mayfield was certain that he had built a rock solid case against Ice Hamilton for the Chesapeake Street murders. The physical evidence and the statements of the three witnesses who had separately picked him out of a photo array was more than enough for him to obtain an arrest warrant and a lineup order.

Stifling a laugh, Mayfield smiled at Ice, who responded with a smirk.

"Ice," said Mayfield.

Ice nodded. "Detective."

"Been behaving yourself?" the detective asked.

Ice snorted. "Don't matter if I misbehave or not. Rollers always tryin' to pin somethin' on me. *Tryin'*. Like you tryin' *this* time."

Mayfield chuckled. "If at first you don't succeed, try, try again."

Ice glared at him. "My lawyer'll get me off, like always."

"Oooh," quipped Mayfield, "I'm shaking. Fact is, your very expensive lawyer, who just happens to be next door waiting to sit in on the lineup, by the way, is very, very good . . . but Johnny Cochrane couldn't get you out of this one. You got sloppy this time, Ice. You should stick with knives; guns aren't your speed." He nodded at an officer. "Unshackle him."

One of the CCB officers unlocked and removed the shackles from Ice's ankles, then stepped back, keeping a sharp eye him.

Hands cuffed behind him, Ice Hamilton eyeballed the plainclothes officers donning cheesy dreadlock wigs meant to mirror his magnificent mane. He chortled and shook his head.

"You know," said Ice, "even with them cheap-ass wigs, these lineups ain't fair to me, 'cause of my eye color . . ."

Mayfield opened a paper bag and took out five contact lens cases (purchased out of his own pocket because they weren't in the Lineup Unit's budget). He handed them out to the police officers participating in the lineup. "Put these on, fellows. Nonprescription disposable cosmetic contact lenses. Bluish-gray in color." He turned to Hamilton. "You were saying?"

Ice smirked and shook his head.

Detective Mayfield was more than confused and more than a little disappointed—he was concerned. He'd taken them in separately, making sure that the witnesses had no contact with each other. First Ruthann Sommers had failed to identify Ice Hamilton in the lineup, then Terri Daulby. What troubled him was how nervous each of them had been, more nervous than witnesses usually are. They were nervous and . . . apprehensive, yeah, that was it, apprehensive. As though someone had somehow gotten to them, threatened them. But how? How could Ice or his minions know the identities of the eyewitnesses? Certainly not through his lawyer. Ice's attorney, C.F. Carlton, had just now become privy to this information.

If Rodney Grimes was as nervous and apprehensive as the others and failed to identify Ice, the chances were that Ice, somehow, had gotten to them. If not, Ice would be fingered by at least one of the witnesses, which was better than nothing. If so, then Mayfield would make it his business to find out how.

Mayfield tried to take away his frown and put on his best face. He opened the door to the waiting area where his last witness sat. He assessed the clean-cut and neatly dressed Rodney Grimes for a moment. Rather than apprehensive, Grimes appeared anxious. Grimes's eyeglasses were not quite as thick as true Coke-bottle glasses, but magnified his eyes just enough for them to be called Coke-bottles, nonetheless.

There was something else, though, a feeling he couldn't shake since he'd first laid eyes on him: Grimes was oddly familiar to him, as though he'd seen him somewhere before. He just couldn't place him.

"Mr. Grimes," Mayfield said, "We're ready for you."

Rodney Grimes replied, "Certainly," as he got to his feet. "How's it going, Detective Mayfield?"

"Fine," Mayfield said flatly.

"Really?" said Grimes. "You seem . . . disturbed."

Mayfield was taken aback, though he hid it. At least, he *tried* to. Grimes was very perceptive. "No, no. Just been working long hours. Right this way."

Grimes followed Mayfield down the hall.

"What's the suspect's name?" Grimes asked. "Or is it against the rules for you to tell me?"

"No," Mayfield said. "First pick him out of the lineup, then I'll tell you his name."

"Fair enough," said Grimes.

To Mayfield's relief, Grimes passed with flying colors. He picked Ice out of the lineup quickly and with absolute certainty.

C.F. Carlton had smiled when he saw Grimes's thick glasses, and Mayfield knew for sure that the attorney would bring into question the witness' vision at the trial, as well as the fact that the other two, who did not wear eyeglasses, had failed to identify Ice. Still, Mayfield had an eyewitness to the crime and a mountain of physical evidence. He had a good case that should do well in trial.

Detective Mayfield escorted Grimes down the hall toward the elevators, passing a number of people who were on the floor seeking copies of police offense reports or police clearance background checks for job applications.

Speaking low so as not to be overheard by passersby, Mayfield said, "The suspect's name is Isaiah 'Ice' Hamilton."

"Tell me about him," said Grimes.

"Why are you interested in his background, Mr. Grimes?"

"Just curious," Grimes answered. "Tell me, detective, did the other eyewitnesses identify Hamilton?"

Mayfield shook his head.

"Is that what was bothering you earlier?" Grimes asked.

Mayfield nodded.

"What," said Grimes, "you worried somebody threatened your witnesses and made them clam up?"

"Did someone threaten *you*, Mr. Grimes?"

Grimes nodded.

"Who?"

"Ice Hamilton," Grimes replied.

"Ice Hamilton personally threatened you? When?"

"Sunday," said Grimes. "He came up to me at the newsstand in Iverson Mall . . ."

"Sunday? The day after the murders?"

"That's right," Grimes said. "He even knew what I was driving because he left me a note on my windshield . . ."

"A note? Saying what?"

Grimes removed a plastic Ziplock sandwich bag from his pants pocket containing a piece of paper. "See for yourself."

Mayfield took the plastic bag and could clearly read the note inside. He shook his head.

"I touched it, but as little as possible," Grimes told the detective. "I put it in the bag just in case you can lift the writer's prints."

Detective Mayfield smiled.

"Now that the other 'witnesses' are in the clear," Grimes said, "how do you propose to protect me?"

Detective Mayfield rubbed his chin. "Tell me everything Ice said to you."

John Mayfield, dazed and confused, lit a Winston as he stepped from the side entrance of D.C. Superior Court into the courtyard leading to the municipal center. He was absolutely flabbergasted. What had just transpired at Ice Hamilton's arraignment had been a travesty of justice.

Just as the proceeding was about to begin, Detective Fanta Monroe had rushed in and whispered the disturbing news to him and Assistant U.S. Attorney Dean Hatcher: Carter Washington, the owner of the black Crown Vic Ice was picked up in, had made a videotaped confession to the Chesapeake Street murders. And according to her, Washington could pass as Ice's brother, right down to the bluish-gray eyes. They were contact lenses, sure, but he said he wore them to emulate Ice, because he admired him for being such a bad motherfucker. She'd produced a color, digital "live scan" mugshot to prove it. Mayfield had to admit the resemblance was striking.

Detective Monroe insisted that she'd been trying to reach Mayfield via pager and cell phone for a couple of hours, but had not been able to get through, which was bullshit. His cell phone and pager were in perfect working order.

Fanta Monroe also informed John Mayfield that Captain Lynch was pissed about his "fuck-up," having given a news conference at noon in front of the Violent Crimes Branch announcing the arrest of Isaiah Hamilton in connection with the Chesapeake Street murders. Mayfield had seen it broadcast "live" on Fox 5. The captain planned to recover by having another news conference at 3:30 that afternoon to announce the closure of the case with the arrest of Carter Washington, thanks to the teamwork of John Mayfield and Fanta Monroe. Incredible.

In light of the circumstances, Assistant U.S. Attorney Hatcher asked that Defense Attorney C.F. Carlton, Detective Mayfield, and himself meet with the judge in his chambers. In that meeting, the new development was discussed and C.F. Carlton artfully pointed out that his client had an alibi: The evidence had been found in the trunk of a vehicle that was loaned to him by a man who he resembled, a man who had confessed to the murders; only one of Mayfield's eyewitnesses, "a man with questionable eyesight," had picked his client out of a lineup.

Mayfield told Judge Haddix how Hamilton had threatened the witness Carlton spoke of, and showed him the note in the sandwich bag Grimes had given him. The detective asked for time to test the note to find out if Ice Hamilton's prints were on it. He also conveyed to the judge that he suspected Ice had threatened the other two witnesses who had failed to pick him out of the lineup.

Judge Miles Haddix countered that Mayfield's argument was purely supposition when it came to the other two witnesses, as they had made no such claims. Furthermore, what the witness claimed Hamilton had said to him didn't constitute a threat, nor was he satisfied that it was actually Hamilton who had confronted the witness at the newsstand. The man hadn't identified himself as Hamilton. The man could have been Carter Washington, who, he pointed out by waving the live scan mugshot, bore a remarkable resemblance to Hamilton. He believed that it was more than likely that the witness had simply mistook Carter Washington for Isaiah Hamilton, like he apparently had at the lineup.

"Under the circumstances," said Judge Haddix, "I have

no recourse but to drop the charges against Isaiah Hamilton and release him."

Ice smirked at Mayfield when the judge announced his decision.

Dean Hatcher tried to console Detective Mayfield by pointing out that the case against the man who had confessed was a slam dunk, that putting away Carter Washington would be a piece of cake and all concerned would be satisfied that justice had been served. But the detective wasn't having any of it. The Teflon Thug had slipped through his fingers again.

Just before Ice Hamilton left the courtroom, Mayfield observed a look pass between him and the vivacious Detective Fanta Monroe. Sure, it could have simply been a man admiring a beautiful woman—she was a hottie, no doubt—but it was something more than that, Mayfield was sure. He felt it in his gut. Yes, Fanta and Ice were joined at the hip. He didn't know how or why, but the two of them were connected, somehow. He'd make it his business to find out.

Mayfield tossed his cigarette butt and pulled out his cell phone. He called Rodney Grimes and gave him the bad news. Understandably, Grimes was outraged.

"They're making a big mistake," Rodney Grimes protested. "I'm telling you, it was him! He killed that woman and that little girl and he threatened me!"

"I believe you," the detective assured him. "Trust me, Mr. Grimes, I believe you."

"What happens now?" Grimes wanted to know.

"Nothing, I hope. But . . . Ice Hamilton's been known to hold a grudge."

"I'll keep that in mind," said Grimes. "Protection's out of the question, I suppose."

"That's right, unfortunately," the detective sighed. "No case, no protection."

"Looks like I'm on my own."

After an uncomfortable silence, Detective Mayfield said, "I know this doesn't mean much, but thank you for coming forward, Mr. Grimes. I wish . . . I wish . . ."

"Keep up the good work, Detective Mayfield. Take care of yourself."

"Listen," said Mayfield, "I owe you. Let's discuss your options over a beer. What do you say?" *As if you have any options, other than move,* Mayfield thought.

"Sure," Grimes said.

"What time's good for you?"

"Well, I've got to work out tonight . . ."

Work out? Mayfield thought. *Him?*

". . . How about 9:30, 10?"

"Sounds good," said Mayfield. "I'll take you to a police bar so you can feel safe. See you then." Mayfield closed his cell phone and sighed.

Two more years before he would be eligible for retirement at the age of fifty. Two more years of this shit seemed like an eternity. But what was he going to do when he retired? What else was he fit to do? Hell, what else did he have to live for?

All retirement would mean to him was biding his time, waiting to die in an empty house, trying to fill lonely evenings and sleepless nights by listening to Miles Davis, Charlie Parker, Motown showstoppers.

Retire from the force in two years? He doubted it.

He felt like the man with the shovel following circus elephants who, when asked if he couldn't find a better job, says, "What, give up show business?"

Ice Hamilton pimp-walked up to his 1st Street, S.W. condo complex, unlocked the electronic fence of this "gated community" with a card key, and crossed the courtyard. Using a standard key, he unlocked the front door of his building and entered. A short walk to the second floor and he was at his door. He unlocked it and went inside.

Hamilton had several cribs, but this one, which was in his sister Beth's name, was decked out entirely in Ikea shit that Danielle, one of his classy ho's, picked out. The place was slammin'!

He tossed his keys onto the telephone table near the entrance and walked to the kitchen.

Ice took a bottle of Hpnotiq Liqueur from the fridge and poured himself a tall glass of the blue beverage. He drank deeply. Damn, that was good. He walked over to his couch, flopped down, and put his feet on the coffee table. He laughed aloud, recalling the day's events.

That look on Detective Mayfield's face. Priceless!

Carter "The Real Deal" Washington owed him big time, and taking the fall for Ice on the Chesapeake Street murders made them even. Of course, promising to kill Washington's entire family if he didn't take the fall had helped The Real Deal make the right decision. And, as usual, his baby Fanta Monroe had come through for him with the names and addresses of potential eyewitnesses, an invaluable service for which she had been well compensated, monetarily and otherwise. He'd turned Fanta out long before she'd joined the police force and was glad that she was still a-dick-ted! He laughed at his own pun, one that he had run into the ground over the years and was funny only to him, though others still laughed because they feared him.

No doubt about it, there was no substitute for having whores in all walks of life strung out on his enormous Johnson. Every woman he'd taken had come under his spell because, like Captain Kirk, he had gone where no man had gone before.

Hamilton took another swig and then got serious as he considered the fate of the punk who had dared to speak out against him. He had been ineffectual, sure, but the nerve! His power must be *absolute*, his reign unopposed. What Grimes had done was bad for business, and he had to pay the ultimate price so that others would know the way of the world: DON'T SNITCH ON ICE HAMILTON. As always, he'd see to it personally. Ordering murders was too risky because underlings who committed the hits might cut a deal with 5-O and rat on him. Besides, he *enjoyed* killing people.

And, of course, that punk muthafucka Francisco "Big Boy" Longus would get what he deserved, not only for trespassing on his turf, but also for the Chesapeake Street fiasco. Shit, it was Big Boy's fault that he had missed him and killed that old hag and that kid. Punk-ass should have stood still.

Yeah, that fat bastard was going to get what was coming to him. Soon.

How Big Boy thought that he could get away with peddling smack on the big dog's turf, Ice would never know. Didn't matter. People had to know not to step on Ice Hamilton's toes. He had a lot of turf, but he wasn't giving up an inch. Crack, weed, crank, ecstasy, or heroin, the new drug of choice (oh, yeah, it had made a comeback with a vengeance!)—whatever, he didn't care, he had people out there selling it. And nobody was going to take one penny of his profits out of his pocket. Nobody. At the age of only twenty-six, he could buy *anything* he wanted.

It was also necessary that he send a clear message to the police in general, and to Detective Mayfield in particular, that he was untouchable. He smiled. Yeah, Ice would send his message to Mayfield loud and clear. Tonight.

Breaking in to that sap Rodney Grimes's tenth-floor apartment was simple. He knocked on the door like a policeman beforehand, to make sure no one was home, then went to work with his locksmith's tools. He was inside and sitting on the man's couch inside of two minutes.

To make certain that Grimes would not be alerted to his presence when he returned to the apartment building, Ice kept the lights off and simply used a penlight to maneuver around.

From what he could see of Rodney's place, it was nice. Shit, Danielle, the ho who had hooked up his place, could have hooked up this one. True, it wasn't Ikea shit, but it was put together well, sort of an Asian thing going on. Not too much furniture, but it was well placed, and there were lots of plants. Nice artwork on the walls. Nerd-boy had it goin' on in here.

Ice smiled. He hoped Rodney Grimes had enjoyed this place. He also hoped that he had lived life to the fullest, but he doubted it. Whatever. Today was the last day of that geek's life.

Isaiah "Ice" Hamilton turned off his penlight and waited in the dark for his next victim to return home.

Rodney Grimes exited the elevator and walked down the hall to his tenth-floor apartment. He unlocked the door and entered, closing it behind him.

He hit the light switch and froze. Sitting on his futon couch was Ice Hamilton.

"Welcome home," Ice beamed. He flicked open a switchblade. "You can run if you want to, but I bet I can catch you."

Rodney just stood there.

"Brave, huh?" Ice chuckled.

Rodney put his gym bag on the floor.

"Been workin' out?" Ice asked.

Rodney did not reply.

"Well," Ice said, "let's see if you can kick my ass." Brandishing his stainless steel stiletto, he laughed and rose from the futon.

John Mayfield pulled into the front parking lot of the Wingate House East apartment complex at 9:45 p.m. He parked his unmarked police cruiser, a black 2000 Ford Taurus, and just as he lifted himself out of the car, the sound of breaking plate glass drew his attention upward, where he saw a man dangling from the railing of a balcony.

"*Sweet Jesus*," Mayfield whispered. He bolted toward the apartment building.

Someone began pounding on the front door, yelling, "Police! Open up!"

Grimes realized it must be Detective Mayfield. *He owes me a beer*, he thought. Wiping his Coke-bottle glasses, he turned and headed for the door.

Detective Mayfield, gun drawn, was surprised to see him. "Who . . . ?"

"Ice," Grimes replied.

Detective Mayfield passed quickly through the rubble of broken furniture and stepped onto the balcony. He was awestruck. Isaiah "Ice" Hamilton, battered and bloody, his eyes filled with an odd combination of terror and rage, was struggling to keep hold of the railing with one hand. The other, once-powerful arm, now as limp as a strand of overcooked spaghetti, merely swung back and forth like a pendulum.

"Help me, man!" Ice yelled. "Help me! My fingers is slippin'!"

While the detective considered what to do, Ice lost his grip. He screamed like a white chick in a horror flick all the way down.

Mayfield holstered his service handgun and turned back to Grimes. He was speechless. But as he looked at Grimes without his glasses, it suddenly came to him where he had seen the man before. The trophies toppled over on the bookshelves and the certificates and awards on the walls confirmed it. Rodney Grimes was a Tae Kwon Do champion, a tenth-degree black-belt. Over the past several years while lending his support to fellow officers who were involved with martial arts, Mayfield had seen Grimes compete at tournaments held at the old D.C. Convention Center. Grimes was a dynamo; Hamilton never had a chance. A Herculean effort was required for John Mayfield to conceal his amusement and deep satisfaction.

The detective noted that Grimes was as cool as a cucumber. No. *Cold.*

"Ice needed someone to save the day," said Grimes. "It's too bad I couldn't help him. But, like he said . . ." He slipped on his glasses and his magnified eyes stared directly at Mayfield.

Recalling the note Ice Hamilton had left on Rodney Grimes's car, Detective John Mayfield nodded, a smirk playing at the corners of his mouth.

GOD DON'T LIKE UGLY

BY LESTER IRBY

Edgewood, N.E.

The Fantasy Nightclub used to sit on the corner of 14th and U Streets, N.W., in what was then D.C.'s red-light district. Pimps, whores, players, drug dealers, and every other sort of hustler swarming the deadly streets of the Chocolate City frequented this establishment. Even a sprinkle of lawyers and local politicians wandered through from time to time.

The year was 1970. On a warm and pleasant Friday night in September, the folks inside of this enclave of sinful joy were at their partying best. Drinks were being gulped down at a rapid pace. Coke and "doogie" snorted even quicker, and couples gyrated, cutting the rug as the fiery sounds of the Temptations' smash hit "Ball of Confusion" heated the mood to an even higher pitch.

At approximately 12:30 a.m. the club was filled to its maximum capacity. A boisterous crowd of latecomers stood outside the club's front entrance pleading with the muscular bouncers to let them in.

"Look, muthafuckas," said Granite, one of the several mean men hired by the owner to keep peace in the house. "There ain't no mo' muthafuckin' room in the place, so shut the fuck up and get ta steppin', fo' I put a hot-ball inside somebody's ass."

Granite had a take-no-shit-off-nobody attitude and reputation. He also had pay-me-for-protection partners feared by many, so certain big-time entrepreneur/hustlers readily hired his crew to keep their businesses moving smoothly.

While Granite and the other bouncers were trying to quiet and disperse the crowd, two gorgeous hookers, one black and the other white, left the dance floor and entered the ladies' room to cool down and freshen up.

Several minutes later, awful cries for help were heard clearly over the loud music—screams eerily vibrating from within the ladies' room.

Inside the rest room, the five-foot-eight curvaceous and strikingly beautiful Sarah Ward was discovered dead. She hovered over the toilet with her head completely submerged inside the piss-filled bowl. She had been strangled and drowned, and, according to the pathologist who later performed an autopsy, "beaten unmercifully moments before," as evidenced by multiple facial bone fractures.

Who tortured and killed this beautiful woman?

My name is Felicia "Fee-Fee" Taylor. I attended the Fantasy Club that night. I am the sister of Raymond "Smooth" Taylor Jr., and I was once the number-one girlfriend of the notorious Zack Amos, the flamboyant yet smart, crafty, and feared drug kingpin of our nation's capital.

My ex-man and brother play major roles in the story that I am about to tell you, and they are significantly linked to the murder of Sarah Ward. I too am linked significantly to that terrible tragedy, as is undercover police officer Ted Jenkins, who was also present that night. But before I go into the details of that event, I desire and very much need to share some things about myself.

I was raised in the Edgewood section of Northeast D.C. Born January 13, 1952, the youngest of two children, I was spoiled rotten by my parents, Raymond and Patricia Taylor, and even more so by my grandma, Nanny Johnson. Along with my older brother (by four years) Raymond Jr., we all resided at 3618 Bryant Street. Both parents worked. My mother was a teacher at Mott Elementary, which my brother and I both attended. My father worked two jobs, construction four to five days a week and an evening part-time job stacking shelves at the Safeway on the corner of 4th and Rhode Island Avenue. We had a three-bedroom home— actually four, because my parents converted a portion of our basement into another bedroom. That was Nanny's Queendom and she simply loved her space.

I wouldn't say that we were a middle-class family during that period, but we were close, and that's saying something. It was extremely hard for black people to move up the economic ladder in the '50s, yet we lived very comfortably in what at the time was an integrated neighborhood.

Growing up I idolized my older brother. I can still remember when he walked me to school every day in kindergarten. I felt so happy, safe, and confident. Each day when he dropped me off with my teacher, he'd tell me: "Baby sis, you hang in there girl. I'll be right down the hall if you need me. And you better not cry."

Even at home I would follow him all around the place. His little shadow I was. Years later, as I thought about our childhood, I concluded that, periodically at least, I was a pain in his ass. Even when he had his friends over or when they were out playing in the streets doing their boy things, I'd make it my business to be a part of the action.

"No, Fee-Fee, stop!" my brother would shout. "Go play with the girls . . . No, you can't play stickball—get yo' butt outta here before I call Mama!"

Then I'd start to pout and cry and cry, and when I couldn't cry no more, I'd fake the tears until I got my way. I didn't realize it then, but my brother really knew how to manipulate people. Where I had it in my little child's mind that I was going to do exactly what my brother and the boys did, my brother would always talk me into something like an "important cheerleader role." And with my little dumb-ass self, I'd end up on the sideline shouting out some silly "Rah-rah-hip-hip-hooray-for-the-gang" bullshit as they played. Yet still loving every moment of it.

I can't pinpoint exactly when the high affection for my brother began its decline, but I do remember when he dropped out of high school in the tenth grade and started hanging out on the street with his friends instead of being at home. Both matters led to major arguments between him and my father, which months later erupted into a horrendous fight—right smack in our living room, as me, Mama, and Nanny looked on and begged them to stop.

Daddy ended up knocking Junior to the floor—then started shouting at him: "Nigger, get yo' ass up and get the fuck outta my house. You don't wanna go to school, you don't wanna work. Get the fuck out and don't come back until you get some sense."

Junior slowly got up off the floor, walked straight out the door, and I didn't see him again for months. He was sixteen years old at the time and I'd recently turned twelve.

Junior would drift periodically back into the house. During the few weeks or months that he was home, we'd share some good times. But something was missing. Things just weren't the same. The streets had taken over Junior, and I could see in his eyes how extremely anxious he was to get back out there to do whatever he was doing.

As I entered my teen years, my life became humdrum. My hero Junior was no longer there to play with, learn from, and help me to stay on course. My father continued to work two jobs and was too tired to do anything other than eat and sleep when he got home, and Mama had become much too strict and demanding for me to try to talk over anything with her. Nanny was rapidly aging. I was still her "precious little pumpkin," even as early stages of Alzheimer's set in.

Gradually, boys became the excitement in my life. Boys, boys, and more boys. I had to have them. I had a crush on this particular seventh-grade classmate named Richard Armstrong. This was one cool, ultrafine manchild. His coffee-with-a-splash-of-cream complexion fit so well on his handsome face. And his slim, trim yet muscular physique simply turned me on. Plus, he had this roguish, street-smart attitude and confidence about himself—with a sexy-ass swagger that immediately started my juices flowing whenever I saw him. Every girl in my school, Langley Junior High, worshipped this boy, and rumor had it that an estimated ninety-five percent of the young ladies who were virgins upon entering the school all became virginless within ninety days, and that Richard was single-handedly responsible for a whopping percentage of the deflowering. A fact for sure, though, is that I am a statistic in whatever Richard's true percentage is, because I happily lost—no, *gave*—my cherry to him at the ripe age of fourteen.

Word travels quickly, I learned, when a female is promiscuous. My brother was the first in the family to find out about my sexual activities and sneak-off-partying lifestyle. Even though Junior himself had completely adopted sinful ways, he still looked down on me and started to lash out. We would run into each other at various places, and every encounter turned into a fierce battle of nasty exchanges. He even smacked me so hard once that I discovered how a person can literally get the taste slapped out of her mouth. My hero didn't exist anymore.

My mother and grandmother died the same year, 1966, two months and three days apart. My mother had undetected diabetes—she suddenly fell into a coma and just as suddenly passed away. Nanny died of a heart attack.

After their deaths, nothing inside of the Taylor home was the same. Daddy went into a shell. He quit one of his jobs and merely went through the motions of working the other. We seldom talked or did things together, and it wasn't long before I was out on the streets nearly all the time, completely falling in love with the games, drugs, and fun. But equally so with a very powerful, handsome, and sexy new man.

I met Zack Amos when I was sixteen years old through my girlfriend Kim, who was his cousin. I knew about him and had seen him on a number of occasions, but we hadn't actually spoken until the day Kim told me that Zack was interested in meeting me, and that he'd arranged a gathering of four at his favorite club, Evelyn's. The four would be me, Zack, Kim, and her man, Oje Simpson.

Kim was very street smart and knew just about everybody in D.C., particularly all the major players in the hustling world. She was gorgeous, of the Pam Grier nature. It became very easy for me to function smoothly on the streets after being taken under her wing and taught the tricks of the trade.

Zack Amos was twenty-five then and he had already taken over much of the drug trade in D.C., which he inherited from his uncle, Hazel "Cookie" Ferguson. Cookie had been busted under the Rico Conspiracy Act three years earlier and is now incarcerated at Leavenworth Federal Penitentiary serving a life sentence.

Zack stood six-foot-two and had the same glorious physical traits as my former teenage lover, Richard Armstrong. But where Richard was a sexy manchild, Zack was a superman in every way, and I instantly fell in love with him.

Located at the corner of 9th and U Streets, N.W., Evelyn's Nightclub was a modest facility, unlike its counterpart, the Fantasy, which was a monstrosity of width, height, glitter, and raucous activities. Evelyn's was a classy spot that catered to a sophisticated and older jazz-loving crowd who also enjoyed a dose of mellow R&B.

By age fourteen, I'd developed a voluptuous, womanly body, and I had little trouble getting into any of the "adult only" places. Where Kim was considered by many to be drop-dead gorgeous, I was the star of the show when it came to physical traits. And yes, I proudly flaunted my stuff. Yet I will also admit that the main reason I was always allowed inside of Evelyn's was because I was the invited guest of "The Man," as Zack was known in private circles.

Kim and I were driven to Evelyn's by Oje in his spanking-new, money-green Eldorado Caddy. Oje was a ranking member of Zack's crew. He was deathly in love with Kim, and wished the feeling was mutual, but that's another long story and no time for that. Briefly, though, he was not the pretty-boy type that Kim preferred, but she still kept him under lock and key, basically to provide protection. Anyway, Zack was waiting at Evelyn's when we arrived, sitting at his reserved table in front of the stage.

It was at Evelyn's that night that I got my first real lesson on jazz. A local group calling themselves Miles's Boys did several of Miles Davis's magnetic tunes. Another local songstress named Brenda Mcphey took my breath away with what Zack later told me was a splendid version of the great Nancy Wilson's "Guess Who I Saw Today." That was just the beginning of a lot of things that I would learn from Zack.

I had a wonderful time and told Zack without hesitation that I would be more than happy to join him for a nightcap and whatever else at the Washington Hilton, where he'd reserved a beautiful and cozy room. The confidence and surity of that man was amazing.

Zack's lovemaking sealed it for me that night. Unspeakably perfect pleasure.

I knew from the beginning that I wasn't the only female in Zack's life. His womanizing reputation in D.C. was as legendary as his suspected crime involvements. None of that particularly bothered me. I knew what I wanted, what I needed, and where I was going. We talked openly about his desires and his need for multiple partners in his life. Women played major roles in his criminal activities and he needed strong, faithful people to keep things working smoothly. He had a deep yearning to be financially successful, and I envisioned a lucrative future as Zack's leading lady. I'd fallen madly in love with this fantastic man and nothing would tear us apart.

Zack's main woman when we first met was the beautiful Sarah Ward. Besides being gorgeous, she was a selfish, greedy, sneaky, no-good bitch. When I came aboard, friction instantly erupted between us. She had her sights on staying number one in Zack's life and complained constantly to him about me. Always telling him that I couldn't be trusted and that being involved with the sister of a competitor would eventually hurt him. Once she stole some product from one of

Zack's drug houses and tried to blame the shit on me. Zack investigated the matter and found that one of his workers had seen Sarah take the package. Zack showed her mercy, but she'd fallen way down on his list of people he could trust.

I don't know exactly when Sarah and Junior started sneaking around. By then my relationship with my brother had deteriorated to the point that we hardly saw each other, and the few times that we did cross paths, we rarely spoke. We had virtually become enemies, and rightly so, because I was now the woman of his hated rival—my Zack Amos!

By the mid '60s, Junior started to make a big name for himself. He'd formed a crew of stick-up boys who robbed banks, jewelry stores, and out-of-town drug dealers. Junior and his crew were nearly as feared as Zack and his organization.

In the spring of 1969, one of Zack's drug houses got knocked off by several masked men. Over $100,000 in cash and drugs were taken, and a few workers were badly pistol-whipped. There was no evidence of who the robbers were, but Zack kept saying that he had a gut feeling Junior was responsible. Zack kept his calm, though, and simply took it as a loss.

When word got around that Junior and Sarah had been seen partying at the famous Cecilia's Restaurant & Club at 7th and T Streets, N.W., adjacent to the Howard Theater where all of the major singers and comedians performed, Zack erupted with harsh words: "That bitch and brother of yours is crazy! Think that they can keep chumpin' me and get away with it. Gonna fix their asses," he told me.

Zack and I had recently visited Cecilia's for a night of fun. In popped Junior and Sarah, accompanied by several of my brother's crew. Men like Zack and Junior hardly ever traveled outside of their safe zones without protection, and Zack had his guys positioned throughout the club.

Neither man acknowledged the other at first, but as Junior, Sarah, and their entourage passed our table, the bitch looked down at me and had the nerve to say, "Whatcha lookin' at, ho?" For some reason I had a flashback to that day Junior smacked me so hard I momentarily lost my taste. I jumped up before Zack could say or do anything to stop me, but instead of smacking this heifer with my palm, I balled up my fist and knocked the living shit out of her. I tell you, the bitch went straight out.

That nearly led to a major confrontation right there between Zack and Junior, but the club's security stepped in and defused the matter. Plus, Zack had high respect for Cecilia and didn't want further mess to spread.

Junior cut menacing eyes our way, but didn't say a thing, he just helped bring Sarah back to consciousness. Zack decided it was best for us to leave, and as we made our exit, he hollered back at Junior: "You get a pass this time, nigga. Best you keep yourself and tramp in line!"

Chemically, blood is thicker than water, but in the case of me and my brother, a series of painful experiences had transformed that chemistry. Our hearts became harder and the blood diluted behind our sufferings. In our respective pursuits of foolish material gain, we had lost the love and care.

The year is now 1975, five years since the murder of Sarah Ward. Perhaps this is a shocking revelation to the reader, but I am writing this story from prison. A reporter named Frances Parker from the *Washington Post* contacted me and asked me to tell my story—she said she would cowrite it and turn it into a short story for her magazine. She also offered me a handsome fee. As I told Frances when I first met her, money is no longer important to me. At this stage of my life, I only want to clear my conscience and be granted God's forgiveness for all of the evil that I've done. I've grown close to Frances Parker since our first meeting of a year ago when she came to this prison and asked me to do a story. Initially I said no, but she kept coming back. A story to generate income for herself had been her original reason for contacting me, but after a year of really getting to know each other, we have become good friends. She has encouraged me to lift my burden and let the folks in D.C. and the rest of the nation know exactly what happened that night inside the Fantasy Club.

The night that Sarah was murdered, she had accompanied my brother to the Fantasy. Zack had invited them to this gathering under the pretense that a truce and the possible joining of crews would make all of our lives better. I was a willing accomplice to this deception.

Unknown to anybody other than Zack and myself, an undercover D.C. police officer was planted in the club. He was a personal friend of Zack's and one who was very well paid to be there that night. His name was Ted Jenkins.

Zack and I were sitting at our reserved table at the Fantasy that night, sipping drinks and watching the dancers move creatively to the beat on the dance floor. The DJ was playing high-energy sounds to keep up with the lively and frantic mood.

Junior and Sarah entered around midnight, extending greetings to those they knew as they made their way across the dance floor to our table. Zack rose and shook hands with Junior, and both he and Sarah gave me slight nods of greeting. A round of drinks was ordered as the two men began to make small talk over the booming rise of the music. Moments later, Zack and Junior told me and Sarah to split while they talked over some business.

Immediately, I asked Sarah to join me inside the ladies' room. "We girls need to do some talking and mending ourselves."

Two women were coming out as we approached the rest room. Drunkenly laughing and poking fun at each other, they purposely paused in front of the entrance so that we could hear them. This sort of plump-bodied but cute, short-afro-wearing woman said to her frail ugly-duckling-type girlfriend: "Girl, I just pulled this nigga tonight who is spendin' money like crazy. He's packin' meat, if you know what I mean. Child, I'm gonna spend his money, then fuck his brains out."

As they passed, Sarah and me entered the bathroom and moved to the far end by the wash basins and toilets. Large mirrors were positioned on the walls above the sinks, which had stools under them. We sat next to each other and began to chat.

I told her that I was sorry for all that had happened between us, that since she was my brother's woman we were sisters in a way, that none of us should be at each others' throats. It would take time for everything to mend properly between all of us, but me and Zack were willing to forgive and make a new start.

Then I got up slowly, patted her on the shoulder, and told her that I'd be right back—I had to get my purse for a few items I needed to freshen up.

As I dodged around the frantic dancers on my way back to our table, I turned to gaze back at the ladies' room entrance. At that instant, undercover officer Ted Jenkins darted inside the rest room without anybody other than me noticing. I proceeded to our table.

"Back in the nick of time, baby. Where's Sarah?" Zack asked.

"She's still in the rest room waiting for me to come back," I responded. "Came back to get my purse. Need to freshen up to keep looking good for you, Daddy. How's it going with you and Junior?"

"We've reached an agreement," Zack said. "But Junior needs to tell you something, so hold tight for a second. Run it, Junior."

I could see the hatred for me in Junior's eyes. But he spoke with remarkable calm. "Let's get one thing straight, Fee-Fee. I'm only here to prevent a stupid war between Zack and me. Fighting will only cost the loss of lives on both ends, and the loss of a whole lot of money. None of us need this shit, so Zack and me have agreed to stop going at each other. Sarah won't be going at you anymore and I expect you to stay clear of her. Another thing: I got what I want, you got what you want. We ain't brother and sister no more, and it's best that we keep it this way. Do I make myself clear?"

As I listened to my brother, I saw Ted Jenkins exit the ladies' room and lose himself in the crowd.

Before I could get a word out in response to Junior, all hell suddenly broke out. Screams of terror could be heard coming from within the rest room. The music and dancing abruptly stopped and the crowd rushed to see what had happened. Junior sprang from the table and ran toward the rest room.

Moments later, a squad of D.C. police were on the scene, directing the crowd away from the crime area. Three other officers led by Ted Jenkins hurried over to where Junior was trying to muscle himself through the crowd to the club's entrance. With their guns drawn, two officers grabbed Junior, slung him to the floor, and quickly handcuffed him.

The crowd went silent as Junior yelled out at his captors, "What the fuck is going on? Get the fuck off me, you pieces of shit. I ain't did nothing!"

"You are under arrest for the murder that just took place," Jenkins announced. "You have the right to an attorney . . ." and so forth, his words drowning beneath the chatter of the confused crowd, watching as the cops swiftly moved Junior outside to the waiting police car.

A year later, after a series of court hearings, Junior was tried and convicted of murdering his fiancée, Sarah Ward. Undercover officer Ted Jenkins told the court that he had been there at the club doing surveillance work and had witnessed a heated argument between the two in front of the rest room entrance before they both entered. That was right at the time of the murder. He hadn't thought that the argument would carry over to something violent.

"Couples are always arguing, then quickly making up," Jenkins concluded. "I just feel so bad that I probably could have prevented that fool from killing her."

Zack and I were summoned to the grand jury to state what we knew or saw. We both emphatically claimed that we didn't see, hear, or know anything.

Junior was convicted and given a sentence of twenty years to life. Throughout the entire process he insisted that he was being framed. He'd figured out that Zack and I set him up, but he didn't call names. Lacking evidence, it wouldn't have helped him anyway.

With Junior and Sarah out of the way, Zack was very much on cloud nine. He completely ran the city again, and we were loving the good life.

Junior had my father visit him in prison. He told him that

Zack and I had killed Sarah and set him up. Immediately, my father tried to get in contact with me. For months I avoided him, then finally agreed to sit down and talk. He told me what Junior had said. I denied everything and said that Junior had lost him mind.

"Remember one thing, girl," my father warned me, "God don't like ugly. If you had anything to do with the murder of that woman and the jailing of your brother, you will pay a terrible price for your sins. And God be my judge, I'll be the first to rejoice over your suffering if you did what your brother said you did."

My father's words have stayed with me, surfacing frequently and torturing me badly. They were spoken nearly four years ago, shortly after Junior's conviction. My father never found out what really happened, nor did he know that his words had weakened me and that he was one hundred percent right—that I would pay a terrible price for my sins. A month after talking with me, my father died in his sleep of heart failure. But I know that he really died of a *broken* heart.

Zack noticed my change instantly when I returned from the visit with my father, as well as my deepening depression after my father died. He did what he could to try and cheer me up, but I was locked into despair. The tough, selfish girl that I had been was gone.

Two weeks after my father's death, Ted Jenkins was gunned down by two masked men as he left his house on Longfellow Street, N.W. He was about to get in his car when the men pulled up and unloaded twelve .38 Special bullets into his body at point-blank range, four head shots killing him instantly. The newspapers reported that the motive could be revenge from loyal members of Junior's crew, but street rumor had it that Zack might be responsible.

Even in my lethargic condition, I found strength to question Zack about the officer's murder. He told me that he didn't have anything to do with it—that Junior probably had it done and that we had to be careful because his crew might be plotting in on us as well.

"You need to snap out of this shit you're going through, woman! We need each other, and I need you at your best," he'd tell me daily.

Approximately a month after the Jenkins murder, Junior was found stabbed to death in the mop room of his jailhouse unit. No witnesses to the crime, no one picked up for the murder.

I knew then that I was next.

Two days after I received word about Junior's death, I put six bullets inside of Zack Amos's head. I used his own gun, which I'd taken from his shoulder holster in the closet. Just for that night I found the strength to be my old self again—cunning and manipulative.

Zack had been in bed, waiting for me to come out of the bathroom and join him. He was so happy to have his baby back. I could tell that he was ready for a great night. I left the bathroom and entered the bedroom wearing the purple negligee that he liked best. He flung off the covers so that I could get a good look at his rock-hard, throbbing dick.

"Come get it, baby—come to Daddy," he said.

With the gun behind my back, I moved seductively toward the bed. I shot him immediately.

Then I called the police. Told them that I'd just killed my lover. Pleaded guilty in court and was sentenced to fifteen years to life.

I've told my story. To some degree it's been a cleansing process. I now feel straight with the street. Yet I may never be straight in the eyes of God.

COYOTE HUNT

BY RUBEN CASTANEDA

Mount Pleasant, N.W.

Cort DeLojero sauntered past the torched police cruisers, past wary cops in full riot gear gathered in groups of four and five.

He picked his way through hundreds of broken beer bottles strewn about the street.

A riot cop caught the forlorn look on Cort's face and cracked, "You missed the party."

Cort grimaced. He walked past a burned-out cruiser that had been driven by a deputy chief and muttered, "Goddamnit."

Cort was the night cops reporter for the *Washington Tribune*. He'd spent most of the night sitting in a company sedan in a parking lot at Bethesda Naval Hospital, working a deathwatch on President George H.W. Bush.

President Poppy was laid up with an irregular heartbeat. Night editor Chuck Ross caught the disappointment on Cort's face when he dispatched him. Chuck had said, "Think what a big story it'll be if the president croaks."

Cort had given Chuck a thin smile. They both knew that if Poppy croaked, the big guns from National would elbow them out.

Cort had been working on his fourth magazine when Chuck paged him at 1:30 a.m. They could slam stories into the paper as late as 2:00. Cort pulled the brick-sized company cell phone from his tan canvas satchel and punched in Chuck's number.

Chuck ordered Cort to ditch the deathwatch and get to Mount Pleasant. "There's been a riot. A black cop shot a Latino man, and there's rumors the man was handcuffed. They've torched about a half dozen cop cars on 16th Street, near Lamont. Didn't you hear it on the scanner?"

Cort's eyes flickered down to the silent black police scanner mounted under the car radio. He groaned. The riot was a guaranteed front-page story.

Chuck sighed. "I don't blame you. I would've sent you, but we needed to keep someone at the hospital."

Now, with his tan canvas satchel slung over his right shoulder, Cort walked slowly, absorbing the scene. The rain had quit, and the night was warm and humid.

To Cort's left, two dozen spectators, mostly Latino adults, stood in front of the faux-marble pillars at the top of the concrete steps of Sacred Heart Catholic Church.

The damage was concentrated in a three-block strip of 16th Street, dominated on both sides by medium- and low-rise apartment buildings.

On one corner, a lean, thirtyish, sandy-haired Franciscan priest in a thick brown robe talked with a group of officers. Father Dave Lowell, a Sacred Heart priest.

A few months before, Cort had written a feature story on the church, focusing on Father Dave, who'd worked at a parish in Guatemala. Cort shadowed Father Dave as poor immigrants streamed into his office.

A teenage girl who'd been raped by a family friend was distraught that she'd sinned. Father Dave gently assured her she'd done nothing wrong, and convinced her to call the police. Another woman brought in her toddler son for a special blessing; the kid had an infected eye. Father Dave blessed the kid, then had a church worker drive the woman and her son to a health clinic.

Father Dave was the real deal. Cort had grown up in a church where the parish priest dished out hellfire and brimstone, when he wasn't boozing it up. Cort had lost touch with his faith a long time ago. But he believed in Father Dave.

A month after the piece ran, an old girlfriend was visiting from California when she got word that her father had died in a car wreck. She cried all night. At daybreak, Cort took her to see Father Dave. He spent an hour with her while Cort waited outside the office. She emerged feeling better. Cort was grateful.

Cort waved to Father Dave. The priest trotted over.

"Cortez, I thought I might see you tonight. How are you?"

"Fine, Father." He looked around. "How'd this happen?"

"It's been brewing for a while. There's so much tension between Latinos and the police. The shooting was like a flame to a tinderbox."

Cort nodded. "What about the shooting?"

Father Dave shrugged. "I've probably heard what you've heard. The police say the man pulled a knife. There's rumors that he was handcuffed. There's probably a lot of misinformation going around."

Cort suppressed a chuckle. Driving over, he'd tuned in to an all-news station. A radio reporter had breathlessly noted that the violence erupted on the Mexican holiday Cinco de Mayo, and speculated on a connection. Mount Pleasant was Salvadoran territory, with Hondurans, Guatemalans, and Nicaraguans mixed in.

Cort said, "Yeah, bad information. Thanks, Father. I've got to roam now."

"Good to see you, Cortez. Drop by anytime. You're always welcome at Mass."

Cort stepped away, surveying the aftermath of the bedlam. His stomach churned as the dimensions of the missed opportunity sunk in.

"Goddamnit."

Even with the city clocking nearly 500 murders a year, Cort had to hustle for a byline. For every ten murders, one would yield a story, usually a fifteen-inch quickie buried inside Metro.

A yuppie victim was guaranteed decent ink. But a black or Hispanic homey gunned down in the hood? Well, that's what the Briefs column was for.

Cort reached the end of the riot zone, hooked a right, and ambled north on Mount Pleasant Street.

The street featured dollar stores, bars, greasy carryouts, liquor stores, old apartment buildings, and Heller's Bakery, which arguably produced the finest cakes in the city.

The MacArthur Park section of Los Angeles was Little El Salvador, and Mount Pleasant was its East Coast counterpart. Inside Haydee's, a Salvadoran restaurant, former Marxist guerillas drank beer with ex–Salvadoran Army soldiers as they argued over soccer games playing on a TV behind the bar. Nearby, Salvadoran day laborers stood outside 7-Eleven, or "*El Seven*," as they called it, waiting for work. Salvadoran vendors with metal carts dotted the street, hawking fresh mangos.

To the west, a series of quiet, tree-lined residential streets with row houses sloped down toward Rock Creek Park and the National Zoo.

The street was unscathed, except for El Seven. A window had been shattered and a store worker swept glass off the sidewalk.

Cort pulled out the cell phone and punched in Chuck's number. "Everything's quiet now. I'm heading back." He clicked off, muttering, "Goddamnit."

He was three blocks from the office when a high-pitched screech rang out from the police scanner.

A woman dispatcher said, "*Attention units paged. Third District officers at a stabbing at an apartment building, the corner of Park Road and Mount Pleasant Street. Homicide requested.*"

Cort pulled over to the curb. Mount Pleasant Street dead-ended at Park Road, three blocks north of 7-Eleven, one block over from 16th Street.

A murder on the edge of the riot zone? Huh.

Cort pulled out the cell phone and called Chuck.

"Yeah, I heard it," Cort said. "I'm heading back. Maybe it's connected to the riot. I'll call as soon as I know."

The brick apartment building was four stories high, with a fading, chipped white paint job and a well-manicured lawn decorated with shrubs and small shade trees.

A concrete walkway stretched thirty yards from the sidewalk to the glass double-doors at the front entrance. From the entrance, the building jutted out on both sides out to the sidewalk, in a half H configuration. A short, black iron fence surrounded it. Yellow crime scene tape was draped across the width of the fence.

The victim was halfway down the walkway, lying on his back, his head turned away from the street.

He was a stocky Hispanic man, in his early twenties, wearing faded blue jeans, a yellow polo shirt, and black canvas sneakers. The chest area of his shirt was stained a dark crimson. His right arm was crooked at an angle above his head, and his left arm was parallel to his body. Wooden crutches lay on either side of him.

Two crime scene technicians in navy-blue uniforms worked around the body. One leaned down and shot photos. The other, wearing disposable latex gloves and holding a flashlight in her left hand, was on her hands and knees, looking for evidence.

A uniformed sergeant Cort knew from previous shooting scenes stood just inside the front gate. An unmarked sedan and a squad car were parked in front of the building. The detective was probably inside the building, interviewing witnesses.

To the right, a handful of spectators had gathered on the sidewalk. A local TV newsman, Brad Bellinger, chatted them up while a cameraman rolled tape on the body.

Across the street, to the left, three young Latino men in jeans and battered sneakers stood underneath a streetlight in front of the Argyle convenience store. Two of the men looked anxious, they kept looking from the body to the third man and back again. The third man, slightly older, in his late twenties, leaned against the lamppost, his gaze steady on the body. He looked like he was doing a slow burn.

Cort soaked it all in as he walked deliberately toward the crime scene, his satchel slung over his right shoulder.

He stopped at the gate and asked the sergeant, "This related to the riot?"

"Unlikely." The sergeant nodded over his shoulder, toward the body. "Victim has an MS-13 tat on his forearm, my money's on a gang beef. The guy from Homicide's inside, he'll be out soon." MS-13 was a Salvadoran gang.

"Thanks."

Cort turned and sauntered toward the three Latinos. Maybe they'd seen something.

One man was wearing a white and red Budweiser T-shirt and a chain with a silver cross around his neck. The guy next to him wore a soccer shirt emblazoned with the light-blue and white Salvadoran flag. The older man wore a red Chicago Bulls T-shirt.

They clammed up when Cort got within earshot.

"*Buenas noches,*" Cort said.

Tentatively, the two younger men responded in kind. The older man gave Cort the once-over. In Spanish, he said, "Who are you?"

"*Periodista,*" Cort replied. In Spanish, Cort identified himself: "My name is Cortez DeLojero, I'm a reporter for the *Washington Tribune.*" He gestured toward the murder scene. Continuing in Spanish, he said, "Can you help me with what happened? Is this about the riot?" He kept his notebook and pen holstered; bringing them out too soon spooked some civilians.

The two younger men looked at their shoes.

The older man peered at Cort a long moment, then said, "This isn't about the riot."

Budweiser said, "His name was Roberto Arias. He deserved better."

No riot angle. Probably a gang beef. He could hear Chuck say, dismissively, "Brief it."

Cort put his palms out. "So, what happened?"

Chicago moved off the lamppost and squared up to Cort. "He was murdered by a *coyote.* He was behind in his payments, because he was hurt, and the son of a bitch killed him."

Cort felt an adrenaline surge. *This* was interesting.

"How do you know?"

Chicago pointed to an apartment building adjacent to

the murder scene. "The three of us live there, we share an apartment. Roberto lives, *lived*, next door, with his sister. We were walking home, Roberto was going to his place. He screamed. We ran over—Gato was standing over him. He pointed his knife at us and said, 'This is what happens to people who don't pay.' Then he wrapped the knife in a bandana and ran that way." Chicago pointed west, toward the neighborhood of row houses.

Halfway into the account, Cort had pulled out his notebook and pen, and was writing furiously. He jotted "Bud," "Sal," and "Chi," respectively, next to each man's statement.

"Did Roberto say anything?" Cort asked.

"He couldn't. He gasped, and he was gone," Chicago said.

A death scene—outstanding. Cort walked them through the evening.

Chicago said they'd been playing soccer at a nearby schoolyard. Roberto watched. When the game ended, the riot was raging. They went to a friend's apartment and waited it out. They had a few beers and walked home after calm was restored.

Cort nodded as he took down the account. "And why did Gato kill him?"

Budweiser explained: Four months before, Gato and two other men had driven the four of them and eight others in a van from their village near San Salvador across the Mexican border into California, then to D.C. Each man owed $1,800. Each man had to start paying off his debt two weeks after arriving in D.C.

Roberto had been working steadily in construction, and paying, until he fell off a second-floor scaffolding and broke his hip. A week after Roberto missed his first payment, his mom in El Salvador was kidnapped by the *coyote* crew. Gato told Roberto he needed to come up with a thousand dollars. Chicago gestured to his friends. "We all pitched in, others too. Roberto paid, and his mother was freed. But two days later, Gato told Roberto that was just a tax, he needed to keep up his payments."

Budweiser made a circular motion with his index finger near his head—the universal *loco* gesture. "Gato smokes PCP."

Jackpot.

Most victims were drug slingers, bandits, or enforcers. Editors didn't break a sweat over them. But this was what the Homicides called a *real* murder. This had front-page potential.

Cort said, "Describe Gato."

Chicago said, "He's about your size, but bigger, like he lifts weights. He's about twenty-five. His hair is short, slicked back."

"Anything else? A scar, anything like that?"

Chicago shrugged. Budweiser rubbed his chin.

Salvadoran flag said, "Yeah, the tattoo."

"What tattoo?"

"He has a big tattoo of a dollar sign on his left bicep. He always wears tank tops or T-shirts with the left sleeve cut off to show it off," Salvadoran flag said. Chicago and Budweiser nodded in assent.

"Just on his left arm?"

"Yes," Salvadoran flag said.

Cort wrote it down. "How can I find him?"

Chicago said, "He shows up at Don Juan's every Monday, around 7:00. To collect from a waitress."

"You sure?"

"She's my girlfriend."

Nice. Cort figured he had all he needed. He looked at the three and said, "So, what are your names?"

Budweiser and El Sal looked at Chicago. Chicago thought about it and said, "Michael Jordan."

Budweiser said, "Michael Jackson."

El Sal said, "George Bush."

Cort smiled. He thanked them and started walking back to the apartment building. He'd taken one step when it hit him. He pivoted. "Have you talked to the police?"

The three men shook their heads. Michael Jordan said, "No, the paramedics shooed us away. I tried to tell them, but they didn't speak Spanish."

Cort allowed himself a quick smile. He'd score a bucket load of chits from Homicide if he handed them eyeball witnesses.

His eyes swept across the three men. "Would you be willing to talk to a detective?"

Silence. Finally, Michael Jordan said, "We don't want any problems."

"Problems" meant immigration. Cort said, "The police are only interested in who killed Roberto."

Michael Jordan said, "How do we know?"

"You can trust me."

Michael Jordan cocked his head to the side. "Maybe, maybe not."

Cort looked at the other two men. No give in either of their faces. The cross around Michael Jackson's neck gave him an idea. "When you all went to Mass this morning, it was at Sacred Heart, right?"

The three men nodded.

Cort thought about asking them to wait, decided it might spook them. "Thanks." He turned and began jogging east on

Park Road, toward 16th Street.

Brad Bellinger hustled onto the street and held up a palm. With his dark wavy hair, blue eyes, and square jaw, Bellinger bore an unsettling resemblance to a full-sized Ken doll.

Cort pulled up. Bellinger said, "Get anything good from those guys?"

Each of the local TV news outfits had a cheesy promotional slogan. The slogan for Bellinger's station was, "We report to you!"

Cort pointed his index finger at Bellinger. "You report to me!"

Bellinger's eyebrows went up in surprise. Cort turned and resumed jogging.

"I promise, if you help the police, no harm will come to you," Father Dave said in Spanish. A sheen of perspiration covered his forehead. Father Dave and Cort had sprinted over together.

The three men said nothing.

Cort chimed in, "The police want the killer. And they wouldn't dare do anything against you if you're . . ." he paused, trying to find the right word, "represented by Father Dave."

Father Dave put a hand on Cort's shoulder. "You can trust Cortez. He wrote that article about the church."

At Father Dave's request, a church secretary had typed a translation of the piece, Xeroxed hundreds of copies, and distributed them to parishioners.

Michael Jordan's eyes flashed with recognition. "You wrote that?"

"Yes."

Michael Jordan nodded. "Okay."

Cort said, "Good. I'll get the detective." He ambled across the street, pleased with himself. He'd earn beaucoup chits with Homicide for hooking them up with the key witnesses.

His editors would suffer massive strokes, then fire him for violating journalistic ethics as they dropped to the floor, if they ever learned about half the deals he cut on the street. They had no idea. Cort knew if he played strictly by the book, he'd end up parroting useless press releases.

He was halfway across the street when a stout, fiftyish man in a tight tan suit, white shirt, brown tie, and brown loafers stepped out of the building.

Detective Rocky Piazza—two hundred and twenty pounds of grief.

Cort stopped in his tracks and groaned.

Piazza was built like a fire hydrant. Unfortunately, he was about as intelligent as one. He had curly, sandy-colored hair, chubby chipmunk cheeks, and brown eyes that were set a little too close together. Piazza's ruddy complexion turned beet red when he was riled up. Cort knew because Piazza turned beet red every time their paths crossed.

In two years on the beat, Cort had encountered all of the Homicides. Most were cordial. Some were indifferent. A few had become sources. Piazza, however, was overtly hostile. They'd first met at a murder scene in Columbia Heights. When Cort introduced himself, Piazza had snarled, "I know who you are. You're like a fucking cancer."

Halfway down the walkway, Piazza paused to say something to the crime scene techs, then continued toward the front gate.

Cort thought about it. Not even Piazza was dumb enough to turn his back on three eyeball witnesses . . .

He hit the sidewalk as Piazza pulled the yellow crime

scene tape over his head and stepped through the gate. "Detective Piazza, I have something—"

Piazza looked at Cort as if he was something he'd scraped off the bottom of his shoe. "Call PIO," he grunted—the department's Public Information Office. Cop-speak for "fuck off"; the boys in PIO worked bankers' hours.

"I have some—"

Piazza chested up to Cort as his face went beet red. He pointed a stubby index finger in Cort's face, fury in his eyes.

"I said, call PIO. I'm not talking to you, understand?" Piazza pivoted and marched to his sedan.

Plaintively, Cort said, "But I'm trying to help you." Piazza ignored him. As the detective slid into the car and slammed the door shut, Cort cried out, "I've got witnesses!"

Piazza pulled away from the curb.

"Goddamn moron," Cort muttered as the sedan rolled away. He looked over and saw Father Dave turn up his palms in a "What's going on?" gesture. Michael Jordan and his friends looked puzzled.

Slowly, Cort walked toward them, marveling at the purity of Piazza's stupidity, wondering what he'd tell Father Dave and the witnesses, wishing that Phil Harrick was there.

Harrick. He was working midnights this week.

Cort pulled his cell phone out of his satchel and punched in the numbers to Harrick's pager, which he'd memorized. He put the phone to his ear and the pager chirped. Cort punched in the number to his cell phone, punctuated it by hitting 9-1-1, then sent the page as he reached Father Dave.

The priest said, "Is there a problem? The officer didn't look too happy."

"No problem," Cort replied, nonchalantly. "That detective has to get back to headquarters, but I just paged another

investigator. One of the best on the force, and he's bilingual."
To the workers, in Spanish: "Don't worry, the detective's on
his way. He's Latino, he'll speak to you in Spanish."

Father Dave said, "Well, okay." The workers nodded.
Cort threw them a tight little smile.

Three minutes later, Cort's cell phone rang. He stepped
just out of earshot of the others. "Phil, thanks for calling back
so quickly. Where are you?"

"I'm on Georgia Avenue, I've been working my network all
night. I'm headin' over to see my girl Darlene now. What's up?"

Phil was a detective with NSID, the citywide Narcotics
and Special Investigations Division. His network consisted of
winos, dope fiends, hookers, gamblers, and street-level crack
slingers, along with legitimate business owners and straight-
arrow residents. His wife and five-year-old daughter were at
home in Arlington.

Darlene was a slender redheaded Assistant U.S. Attorney
who prosecuted gang conspiracies. She lived in Capitol Hill.
Darlene was Phil's side dish.

"I'm in Mount Pleasant, and I've got a *situation*."

Cort explained quickly, about the murder, Father Dave
and the three witnesses, and Piazza.

"Rockhead Piazza," Phil said. "Imbecile."

"Felony-stupid," Cort agreed.

"They still there?"

"Yeah, Father Dave too. But I don't think they'll be hanging around long. I don't think they'll cooperate if they're not
interviewed tonight." Cort paused, letting the idea sink in.
Then, "Look, I know you're not Homicide, but could you
take their statements. They saw the killer. This could be a
quick lock-up."

Phil sighed.

Cort said, "Come on, this is a real murder. The victim and one of his buddies have gang tattoos, but they're working guys now. This doesn't vibe gang beef."

Phil thought about it.

Cort said, "I'll get good play on this one."

Phil was Cort's best source. Phil liked press. In a resigned tone of voice, he conceded, "All right. I'll call over to Homicide and smooth things out with Rockhead or whoever's running the shift. I'll tell them I got a tip. Can you keep those witnesses there for five minutes?"

Cort looked over to Father Dave and the three witnesses and gave them a thumbs-up. The four men nodded back.

"Yeah."

"Darlene's been waiting up. She's gonna be pissed."

Phil killed the flashing cherry light on the dash of his unmarked sedan and pulled up across from the corner where Cort, Father Dave, and the three witnesses were waiting.

Cort ambled over and met him as he stepped out of the sedan.

Phil was a little taller, a little leaner, and, at forty, seven years older than Cort. His black hair was tinged with gray and thinning on top. He had thick eyebrows, brown eyes, and a neat mustache. His mother was Costa Rican, his father was Dutch, and Phil was fair-skinned.

Cort was five-foot-nine, with olive skin, brown eyes, and wavy black hair. If Phil were darker, or if Cort were lighter, they might have passed for brothers.

Phil wore white canvas Converse high-tops, faded blue jeans, a yellow polo shirt, and a thin blue nylon jacket. The get-up made him look like a suburban dad.

Cort knew otherwise; the front of the jacket covered

Phil's shoulder rig, which contained his department-issued Glock 9. The back of the jacket concealed the leather-covered metal sap and handcuffs that were always clipped to the back of his waistband. A .32 Smith & Wesson revolver was strapped to his right ankle.

"You know Father Dave?" Cort said as they crossed the street.

"*Of* him."

"I'll introduce you. I told the witnesses that you aren't interested in their immigration status."

Cort made the introductions. Phil shook hands with everyone.

Father Dave said, in Spanish, "These gentlemen would like to help the investigation. But they don't want to bring any legal trouble onto themselves."

In impeccable Spanish, Phil responded, "I want to find the killer. There won't be any problems."

Father Dave nodded. Chicago nodded. Phil pulled a notebook and pen from his jacket.

Cort said, "Excuse me, I need to check in with the office." He walked across the street, pulled the cell phone out of his satchel, and pretended to make a call. He didn't want to be within earshot of Phil's interviews. It could boomerang.

Cort had met Phil a year before, at a drug raid in the Barry Farms public housing project in Southeast. Two weeks later, Phil invited him to a drug raid in the Trinidad section of Northeast. Phil and his squad were decked out in Ninja outfits and bulletproof vests. He told Cort to stay close. Phil's squad stormed a two-story row house. Three slingers surrendered. A fourth ran upstairs. Phil, another cop, and Cort chased him. They found him inside a bedroom, straddling a window ledge. The punk tried to worm his way off the ledge.

Phil holstered his Glock, flew across the room, and grabbed his ankle; the other cop dropped his shotgun, sprinted over, and grabbed the other ankle. Cort stepped close and took notes. The punk pulled a piece from his waistband and, hanging upside down, squeezed off two shots. Wood and plaster exploded. Phil pulled his Glock and shot the punk's toe off. The slinger dropped his piece and screamed. Phil and the other cop pulled him inside. The punk's foot spewed blood like a small geyser. Phil tied his ski mask around the toe stump. The punk spit at Phil. Phil picked up the shotgun and slammed the butt into the punk's groin. Phil said, "Listen, *Ty-rone*, you don't ever shoot at the *po-lice*." Phil then looked up and saw Cort scribbling. He saw his fellow cop eyeballing Cort, looking *real* nervous. Phil braced Cort and led him into the hallway. "For the record, I fired my weapon to protect you, my partner, and myself. And that groin shot was off-the-record." Cort snapped to the Big Picture. He could nail Phil. Write one great story. And no cop would ever talk to him again. He slipped his notebook inside his black leather jacket. "What groin shot?"

A week later, Toeless Tyrone's public defender hit Cort with a subpoena. The P.D. wanted Cort to validate Tyrone as a civil-rights victim. The *Trib's* in-house attorney stiff-armed the subpoena with a blizzard of motions. Cort sweated it for a month. A hearing was held. The judge sided with the *Trib*. Toeless Tyrone pleaded out to a gun violation and assault on a police officer.

Cort learned a valuable lesson: Keep some distance from the story. Don't put yourself in position to be jammed up.

Cort watched Phil wrap up his interviews. Phil would have let him listen. But suppose Gato's defense attorney found out? He'd ask what Cort had heard. He'd ask if he knew how a narcotics man ended up on a homicide. He'd expose Cort's role. Better not to take that chance.

Phil slipped his notebook and pen inside his jacket and shook hands with the witnesses and Father Dave. The priest accompanied the Salvadorans as they walked toward their building.

Cort ambled over to Phil. "What do you think?"

"Gotta get this lowlife motherfucker."

Cort's eyebrows went up. He'd never seen Phil take a case personally. "You seem ticked off."

"I am. I don't think this is a gang beef. These guys seem straight. Gato knows they can't retaliate because they're undocumented. He's a parasite, victimizing his own people. I've got more respect for a hit man. A hitter knows someone might come back."

Cort licked his upper lip. "Do you have to hand this off to Rockhead?"

"Nah, Rockhead won't care, so long as he gets credit for the clearance."

"What now?"

Phil turned and pointed at Don Juan's Restaurant. "Our boy makes a regular pickup every Monday from a waitress at Don Juan's. Always shows between 7 and 7:30. I'll talk to the waitress and stake out the place. Nail him there."

"Okay if I hang out inside Don Juan's tomorrow?"

"It's a public place."

"One more thing. If you get him—" Phil shot Cort a look. "I mean, *when* you get him, could you play up the *coyote* angle in the charging document?"

Chuck Ross might balk at publishing the shakedown scenario from three unnamed sources. But a police charging document was golden.

Phil caught the drift. "I'll write it in haiku if you want."
He broke into a wide grin. "What?"

"I just realized—this is my first *coyote* hunt."

Cort stood on Mount Pleasant Street across from Don Juan's
fifteen minutes before 7:00, thinking, *Uh-oh*.

A dozen young men were trashing and torching a fried
chicken joint a block south of the restaurant. Another angry
horde was milling about nearby, itching for action.

Most of the young men wore bandanas across their
mouths. Some were swigging from beer bottles. A TV cameraman on the sidewalk zeroed in on the burning chicken
joint.

Tension from the previous night's riot had been percolat-
ing all day, and now it was boiling over. Cort had assumed the
cops would lock down the neighborhood with a massive show
of force. Three other *Tribune* reporters and a photographer
were roaming around the area. Cort figured the scene was
covered and he'd be free to shadow Phil.

Cort figured wrong. On the way over, he had listened to
a radio interview with the new mayor. She said that showing
too much force might be provocative.

A block south, a Metro bus paused at a stop sign on its
way across Mount Pleasant Street. A dozen men rushed the
bus, pelting it with bricks and bottles. Someone yelled, "Fuck
the police!"

Cort reached into his satchel for his cell phone as his
pager went off; Alonzo Reed's number came up. Alonzo was
the City editor. Cort punched the digits.

"Where are you?"

"Mount Pleasant Street, about a block from the fried
chicken place."

"It's on TV. What's happening now?"

A block south of the besieged bus, eighty cops in gas masks and full riot gear materialized. The mob gravitated toward the cops. Some of the rioters wielded long metal rods like spears: yanked-out street signs.

"A mob's forming. There's cops in riot gear out here now. Looks like they're about to square off."

"Stay with the mob."

"What?"

"No matter what, stay with the mob until it's over."

Cort couldn't argue. "Will do."

He clicked off, and started to punch in Phil's pager number. Maybe they could devise an alternate plan. He'd hit three digits when a riot cop with a bullhorn announced, "*You are unlawfully assembled. Disperse now.*"

From behind, Cort heard a handful of voices chanting, gently, "*Paz, queremos paz.*" Peace, we want peace. Cort turned. Father Dave was leading a half dozen church people on a march into the bedlam. They were holding hands, with the priest at one end.

Cort slipped the phone into his bag and hustled over. Ten cops loaded their tear-gas shotguns. In his mind's eye, he flashed on a mug shot of Ruben Salazar. Salazar had been a prominent *Los Angeles Times* columnist in the 1960s. He was shot dead by a sheriff's tear-gas projectile after covering an antiwar march. Tear-gas projectiles were basically ten-inch bullets.

"Father, they're about to fire tear gas. Maybe you all should veer off."

Without breaking stride, Father Dave braced Cort on the shoulder. "I appreciate your concern, Cortez. Sometimes, you just gotta have faith."

Cort turned in time to see the riot cops level their shotguns at the mob. To his left, he spotted a short brick wall on the side of a corner apartment. He thought about Ruben Salazar. He sprinted and dove behind the wall as the cops fired.

Chaos: The rioters and Father Dave and his group turned and hightailed it away from the thick, dark smoke.

Cort was on his knees, the tear gas burning his eyes, his lungs. He couldn't breathe. He stumbled to his feet. Choking, gagging, he weaved his way one block west, to 16th Street. He paused and bent at the waist. He wiped his eyes and jogged north for one block on 16th, then hooked a left back onto Mount Pleasant Street. Had to stick with the mob.

Half the mob had scattered, the rest were now in the street. Someone lit a Molotov cocktail. Someone else tossed a brick through the front windshield of a Toyota sedan. The Molotov flew into the sedan; the interior went up in flames. A TV cameraman backpedaled on the sidewalk.

Cort was reaching into his satchel for his notebook when he noticed a muscular Latino wielding a metal spear over his right shoulder in the middle of the street, thirty feet away. The man had a blue bandana over his mouth. He wore jeans and a black tank top. His hair was slicked back and he had a tattoo on his left bicep: a big dollar sign.

Gato.

Cort scanned the street, looking for Phil, for a random uniformed cop. No Phil, no uniforms, just turmoil.

The sunlight dimmed. Twilight was descending.

Word would get around the neighborhood that a cop was looking for Gato. He might even know already. Gato would be in the wind the next day, on his way to El Salvador.

"Goddamnit."

This half-assed, adrenaline-drenched, crazy idea popped into Cort's head: Maybe he could get a quote from Gato. A pro forma denial. Maybe delay him. What's the worst that could happen?

Cort yelled, "Gato!"

Gato turned, looked at him. "Gato!" Cort held up his hand.

Gato cocked his head to the side, studying Cort now. Three seconds later, he looked away, turned his attention back to the street.

Something inside Cort snapped: "Hey, Gato. *Asesino.*" Assassin.

Gato's head snapped toward Cort like an agitated cobra. His face went dark. He started sprinting toward Cort, clutching the metal rod like a lance, rage in his eyes.

Cort's heart skipped a beat, maybe two.

Gato was closing fast. He got within twenty feet, fifteen, ten . . .

Cort quickly slipped his satchel off his shoulder—maybe if he timed it just right he could sidestep the rod and slam Gato in the head, knock him off balance. Maybe.

Gato closed in. Cort locked in on the sharp tip of the rod—it was aimed at his chest, there would be no chance to even take a swing at Gato . . .

He half-closed his eyes, started to throw up a truncated Hail Mary.

He saw a flash of movement on the right. He heard a thump, then another. He braced for the tip of the spear. It never came. He opened his eyes.

Gato was sprawled facedown on the street, the rod clanging on the sidewalk at Cort's feet.

Phil Harrick stood over Gato, clutching his leather-over-metal sap in his right hand. Phil put his knee into the small of Gato's back. Smoothly, quickly, he slipped the sap into the back of his waistband, brought out the cuffs, and snapped them on.

Cort said, "Where'd you come from?"

Phil stood up. "I was tracking Gato in the crowd, waiting for my chance. Then you called him out. Good thing I had the angle. Ballsy move."

Cort was about to say, "*Stupid* move." Instead, he said, "Sometimes, you just gotta have faith."

JEANETTE

BY JIM BEANE

Deanwood, N.E.

I should've listened to Pop. He warned me off Jeanette right away, said she was nothing but trouble, but I was too far gone from the first time I saw her to ever listen.

"Jackie, she's a snake pit," Pop said, like she was the bottom of evil.

Last fall, Pop and I painted the office where Jeanette worked. That's when we met. Her boss, a guy named Olivet, operated a chop shop in the far Northeast corner of the city, in Deanwood. Olivet kept two steps ahead of the law and two steps behind Jeanette. Before I knew her a week, she told me she hated him, hated his hands always trying to touch her, hated his eyes undressing her.

"Quit," I told her, like I knew what to do.

"And do what?" she fired back.

I couldn't say.

She called herself a secretary, but I never saw her type one word. Olivet spent his days yakking on the phone, and watching Jeanette's ass. He leaned his chair back, propped his feet on his cluttered desk, plastered the phone to his ear, and followed every move her hips made with reptile eyes. If Jeanette bent over at the file cabinets, he moved, but only for a better view. Her body made your mouth water.

The first day on the job, Pop dropped a daub of paint on the corner of Olivet's desk, and the slob let him have all hell.

Jeanette slid between me and Olivet, before I acted stupid, and held her finger to her lips, for my eyes only. She strolled across the room to the files, opened the bottom drawer, bent at the waist, and swelled inside her skirt. And Olivet gasped. Jeanette swayed her hips to the music piped in through speakers mounted in the ceiling. And Olivet forgot all about Pop. I thanked her when she brushed past me. She blew me a kiss.

"Call me," she whispered.

Pop stared at me the whole ride home.

"She wants more than you got," he said in the alley behind our house on 12th Street. He'd already had too many beers. After my mother ran off, he soured on all women.

"You don't know her," I said.

"A slut's a slut, it don't matter what you feel below your belly."

Nothing he said could change her lips blowing that kiss. Nothing.

Jeanette started bringing me fresh coffee every morning when we got to the job.

"Jesus Christ, he can't work when you do that," Olivet said.

"I take care of those that take care of me," she replied, glancing at me to make sure I heard.

After a few dates and a Christmas ring, she started in about Olivet.

"He don't deserve all that money," she said, "his boys in the garage do all the work. He just counts it, the fat prick." She laid her open hand on my inside thigh.

By Valentine's Day, she was talking about Olivet's money like it should be ours.

"Think about us with that money, Jackie," she said. "We

could get away, baby, far away." It didn't take her hand long to convince me.

"We can't live without that money, Jackie."

"I don't know how to get it."

"Find somebody who can."

I turned away from her.

"Or I will," she said, and drew her hand away.

A couple of days later, I told her I knew a guy could take that money, you know, trying to impress her, like I was connected to more than a lousy paint brush. I dropped Michael Fannon's name, a guy from my brother's old gang.

"Call him," she said.

I didn't contact him right away, Michael wouldn't remember me. I tried to ignore her. But she stayed after me. Call him. Call him. Call him.

When I did, he didn't know me, but then I mentioned Richie, and he pretended to remember me. I told him about Olivet, the chop shop, the money, and Jeanette. He got interested, fast.

"Ripping off criminals works best," he said. "Less chance getting caught, and they deal in cash. I'll get back to you." He hung up without a goodbye.

He called me back a month or so later, on Friday night, my twenty-first birthday, April 5, the day after some cracker killed King in Memphis and the blacks set fire to the city.

"Now's the time," he told me, "the cops got their hands full."

Jeanette and I had big plans for my birthday, but they went to hell like everything else when King got shot.

"Come by anyway," she told me on the phone, "we'll do something." She didn't need to ask me twice.

"Keep out of downtown," Pop said when I left the house.

He glued himself to the TV and muttered about the welfare sons-of-bitches burning his old stomping grounds.

I drove Pop's van to Jeanette's apartment around 10:00. Her straight black hair shimmered in the hall light when she opened her apartment door. She wore a skirt the size of a hand towel. All her leg showed. Pink fuzz stood out from her sweater like she was electrified, and when she knew I was staring, she pulled the sweater down so tight I had to look away. A half-assed picnic dinner sat on her counter top, and she said we should go to McMillen Reservoir, park on Hobart, in front of Pop's old place, and celebrate my birthday.

"Forget about everything but us," she said, and she got close to me and reached her hand around my ass.

Pop was right, you can't think below your belt.

I figured the reservoir was safe. The blacks wouldn't burn anything near Howard University. We found an empty spot in front of the house where Pop grew up, and parked. Jeanette pointed at the mirrored moon reflected on the reservoir.

"Romantic," she said. Compared to Edgewood Terrace, where she lived, and Michigan Park, where I lived, she was right. We hadn't known much else.

Jeanette piled Pop's paint tarps flat on top of each other, covering the floor of the van, and tucked a clean sheet around the outside corners, like a real bed. She laid two pillows and an old quilt on top, then shed her clothes and stripped off mine. Pop's van had no windows in the back. We crawled under the quilt. She pulled at me, impatient, wild, and when she was ready, she pushed me flat on my back and guided me inside her. She made me swear to do anything for her love. Swear. And swear. And swear.

When we dressed, we sat in the front seat and rolled the windows down. An orange glow lit the sky above Howard.

Smells, like fire jobs before new paint, drifted through the van. Smoke leeched from between Howard's big brick buildings and rolled across 5th Street, smothering McMillen's still surface like cemetery fog. I cracked two beers, lit a smoke and another off it, and clicked on the radio. I searched for that new Smokey Robinson song, but the shit going down all over the city screamed out on every station. I was wrong about Howard. 7th Street burned as hot as 14th.

Jeanette's eyes glazed over.

"I got to get out of here" she said. "I'll die here." She waved her hand across the windshield. "We'll all die here."

We stayed on Hobart until 4 a.m. The fires never went out, and I never mentioned Michael's call.

The next morning, Pop and I loaded the van for work, and he told me that Michael had called after I left. He wanted to know why Michael "that piece of shit jailbird" was calling after me. Pop made it real clear, when Richie enlisted, that he didn't want to see any of Richie's gang again.

"What, that scumbag wants to sing you Happy Birthday?" Pop said.

My only brush with crime, shoplifting from the five-and-dime on Monroe Street, had been dealt with swift and sure. One of the clerks, who had a crush on Richie, ratted me out. I was in third grade at Saint Gertrude's.

Richie beat my ass and said he'd do worse if he caught me again. From then on, my criminal activity stayed limited to stealing Pop's change. High school ended and I signed on with Pop's paint crew. A couple of years passed and Pop dumped his crew. From then on, it was just me and him and the sick smell of paint.

I didn't tell Pop that I'd called Michael first. Pop would never understand. I called Michael because I promised I'd do anything for her love. I hoped he'd never call back.

But King got killed, the cops got busy, and Michael got hungry.

"Perfect," Jeanette said when I finally did tell her, "Olivet's stashing more money than ever. He's fencing for the looters. They been bringing stuff since they torched downtown. The safe under his desk is fat with cash."

"Where are the cops?" I said.

"You think the squares from out in the burbs would come by at night shopping for their wives and girlfriends if cops were a problem? And Olivet keeps counting that money, alone, late, after midnight, when everybody's stopped coming around. Big money, Jackie, for everything we want, and all the cops across the river."

I called Michael back and told him what Jeanette said, and about the alley that Pop and I used to get into Olivet's back lot. Olivet's lot filled the triangle between the train tracks and Kenilworth Avenue, where they almost collided, and stretched alongside the back fences of Deanwood's gasoline alley garages.

"Smart girl," he said. "I know her?"

I didn't answer.

Deanwood's a quiet place, street after street filled with squat brick and cinderblock duplexes, and none too nice apartments. Pop called Michigan Park a move up from Hobart Place. Nobody moved up to Deanwood, that was clear. The only single houses were country shacks thrown up by the colored farm boys who came looking for city jobs, money jobs. Everything looked beat.

Olivet's alley lay half hidden behind brush grown wild around the tracks. It dead-ended into Olivet's back lot. He didn't bother with a gate or fence. He wasn't worried about keeping anybody out. I told Michael that the whole time Pop and I worked painting Olivet's office, we never saw a soul use that alley, coming or going.

"Tonight's the night," Michael said on Saturday when I got him on the phone, "the city's still hot. Get the key from your girl and meet me at Chick Hall's." Honky-tonk whites gathered at Chick Hall's Surf Club, a shitty storefront bar just over the line in P.G. County. Jeanette loved Chick Hall's.

I told her the plan and she handed me the key to Olivet's back door. She kissed me on the mouth and said she knew the safe was full. Then her eyes narrowed and she asked, "When do I meet Michael?"

"Hasn't come up," I said. I didn't like how quick she was to ask that.

"How about tonight, how about I ride with you to the meet? I'll drive Pop's van home and pick you up after it's over."

"Michael might not go for it," I said, hedging.

She closed her fingers around my arm and pulled me tight to her. On tiptoes, she kissed me again and let my hands roam.

"C'mon, Jackie, we'll have some fun later," she said, and pushed me off, playing. Her fingertips grazed across my zipper. She was driving Pop's van to Chick Hall's that night around 11:00. She always got her way.

On our way there, we passed a group of kids hanging out at the intersection of Bladensburg and South Dakota, in front of Highball Liquors, too late for kids so young to be out. They were yelling at each car passing by. I felt better. With cops around, no kids do that.

When we turned through the light, the kid nearest my window screamed, "Honky!" He flipped me the finger and pumped his fist in the air. Jeanette pushed the gas a little harder.

Chick Hall's was near Peace Cross, in a strip of crummy stores on Bladensburg Road. Ten miles past Chick's was all country.

We pulled into the lot, behind the bar, and I glanced over at Jeanette. The glare from an alley streetlamp sprayed across her face. She slid the tip of her tongue between closed lips and moved her head side to side, searching the stretch of empty lots.

She picked a spot next to the dumpster, in the darkest corner, and cut the engine. A dark sedan, hidden in the night shadows, blinked its lights once, and the doors sprung open. Michael and two strangers spilled out.

Jeanette watched Michael lead his crew across the lot toward us. They looked like killers, dressed in black from head to toe. Jeanette licked her lips.

"He's handsome," she said. She wouldn't take her eyes off Michael, and leaned forward in her seat.

"Michael said alone," I reminded her. She looked at me like she'd forgotten who I was.

"Does it matter?" she said. I wished my brother Richie was one of them. Jeanette jumped from Pop's van, slammed the door, and propped herself against the front fender. I moved quick, to be by her side. Michael walked right up to us without saying a word. The two with him split apart and flanked us. Michael glanced at me, then nodded his head to the guy near my shoulder.

"That's Ray," he said, and the guy's face pinched together like a smile hurt him. Michael called the other guy his boy, and said his name was Dee. A thick rope of scar cut through Dee's right eye.

"You the smart girl?" Michael said to Jeanette. He moved closer like he might sniff at her, like some dog.

"Maybe," she said, "smart enough." Michael's eyes traveled from her ankles to her eyes.

"Surprised I hadn't noticed you before," he said.

"That's okay, I'll be around."

"Cut the shit, Romeo," Ray said to Michael, "we got work to do."

A noise, like a laugh, came from Dee. Jeanette looked at Ray like I'd seen her look at bugs.

"You got the key?" Michael said to me, but still stared at Jeanette. She reached into her pocket to retrieve it. Her jacket opened and she drew in a deep breath and pushed her breasts out. Michael didn't miss a thing. She held the key between her thumb and index finger and extended her hand toward Michael. He held his hand still, palm up. When the key came close, he touched the side of her hand with his fingers, and she dropped the key.

"Be careful," she said. I wanted her talking to me, but she wasn't.

"Don't worry," Michael said.

I sneaked my arm around Jeanette's waist and pulled her closer to me. Michael didn't blink. She couldn't keep from staring.

"Let's go," he said.

I tried to kiss Jeanette, but she tilted her face away, like she did with fresh makeup, and blew a kiss. I followed the three of them across the lot to the dark sedan.

Michael tossed me the keys. He jumped in the front seat and motioned me behind the wheel. Ray perched in back. Dee stared at me from the rearview mirror. The scar jagged through his eye and left his eyeball milk-white, like a boiled egg. He shifted in the seat and the twin barrels of a sawed-off shotgun poked out between the buttons of his overcoat. He took his time covering them up.

"See what you want, boy," he said.

Michael motioned me to start the car. "Do the speed limit and don't run any lights."

"I thought you weren't worried about cops," I said.

"I'm not. Just drive and shut the fuck up. I'll do the thinking."

Pop called it right about Michael, he was no friend, but it was too late. Richie wasn't around this time to bail me out. I took Bladensburg to Kenilworth heading toward the city, and passed commercial buildings and scrap joints left stranded on empty streets. I thought about Jeanette's sweet lips against mine and mashed down on the gas.

"Easy," Ray said. Hot breath laced with stale booze pushed against the back of my ear. I let off the gas and he settled into the backseat. I scoped every intersection for law, but no cops were in sight.

At the D.C. line, I turned off Kenilworth onto Eastern Avenue and headed into Deanwood. Before we came to the tracks, I turned right onto Olive Street and slowed down to a crawl. Olive dead-ended into Polk, and Olivet's alley opened across the intersection. All the houses and apartments sat dark, like everyone had turned in, like real people, like Pop.

I glanced again in the rearview mirror and saw Dee's milk eye blink once, slow motion, then his good eye zeroed into mine. The shotgun lay across his thighs.

"Eyes on the road," Ray said, nudging me in the shoulder.

We stopped at Polk, facing the alley. To the left, a walkway disappeared under the tracks into a concrete tunnel, black from soot off the overhead trains. The last garage in gasoline alley was half a block to my right. The streetlights were out.

"Let's go," Michael said.

I cut the lights and coasted across Polk onto the gravel alley. The night swallowed us up. I kept my foot off the gas, careful not to tap the brakes, afraid of the red glare. Loose stones grumbled beneath the sedan's weight. The weeds from the tracks side of the alley swept against my side of the sedan, grabbing, like living things trying to hold me back.

I steered a little closer to the fences that separated us from the garages. Nothing stirred.

"There's his light," I said, and pointed ahead to the familiar white-washed building that appeared from the darkness like a ghost.

"Stop here," Ray said.

I touched the brakes and winced, waiting for the red glare.

"Ray disconnected the lights," Michael said, and chuckled to himself. Ray said something about me under his breath.

"Make a U-turn," Michael directed. I looked up at the little patch of yellow light shining through the door that led to Jeanette's and my future.

"Face out the alley and keep the engine running," Michael said, "we won't be long."

I adjusted the rearview so I could watch the landing at the top of the metal stairs and the door with the light. Olivet's Cadillac snugged close against the side of the building, hiding beneath the stairs.

Michael swiveled in his seat and faced the others. Dee slipped a shell in each barrel and snapped the shotgun closed. The hair at my neck stood up. They lingered outside the car for a second, talking too soft for me to hear, then I watched them creep across the lot to the bottom of the stairs.

I could've started the car and taken off. If I waited until they climbed the stairs and went inside, I could've hauled ass. They couldn't stop me.

But Jeanette wanted Olivet's money, bad, and if I took off, she and I turned to shit. The air inside the sedan drew close, hot. I opened the window for relief. *Don't run*, I repeated to myself, over and over.

Michael led the way up the metal stairs. He held the key in his left hand, extended. A handgun dangled from his other, I could see the chrome. Ray raised his own gun. Dee followed, two steps behind, the sawed-off cradled against his chest.

"Port arms," Richie called it, when he showed off his army drills. He used a broomstick instead of a rifle, but Pop and I got the idea. Maybe Dee was in the army, maybe that's how he got that scar. Maybe he knew Richie.

Michael stopped at the last step, below the landing, and pushed the key into the lock. He lay flat against the building, hidden from the square of light in the door. When the door opened, they shoved inside.

My hand reached for the shifter, I pumped the clutch once, but couldn't put it in gear. Not without Jeanette.

I leaned across the seat to roll Michael's window down, and a loud sound, like a cannon, exploded the night. I buried myself into the seat, low, and peeked over the back to see out the rear window. Michael burst through the door at the top of the landing and charged down the flight of metal stairs. A bulging sack swung from his gunless hand. Ray came right behind him, fast, and Dee so close he nearly fell over Ray. All three hit the drive running and moved across the lot toward me.

The smell of burnt gunpowder came off them when they piled into the sedan.

"Go, go, go!" Michael yelled, and I punched the gas. We lurched down the alley, tires squealing, and left rubber on Polk where the gravel drive ended. I took a screeching left, and pulled on the headlights.

"Take Kenilworth," Michael said, and I smashed the gas pedal to the floor. Dee broke the sawed-off open and dumped the cartridges into his hand. He caught me watching him in the rearview.

"Mind your business, boy," he said. Michael and Ray stared out their side windows, unsmiling, nodding their heads slow, like they were in a trance.

Thoughts of Jeanette raced through my brain during the ride to Chick's. Olivet's money. Her money. Fuck the money. All I cared about was Jeanette. She loved me, not the money.

Jeanette was waiting for us in Pop's van. The lots were empty. She'd parked in the same spot beside the dumpster. I pulled in next to her.

She slunk out of the van into the glare of our headlights. Her skirt hiked up and showed the whites of her thighs. I climbed out of the sedan fast, but she looked right past me, even as I moved beside her.

"How'd it go?" she asked Michael.

"Why you asking him?" I said.

"Good." Michael held up the fat sack.

He didn't look at anyone but Jeanette when he spoke. He handed her the sack and she unrolled the top and looked inside. She touched the sleeve of Michael's coat.

"They shot him," I said, grabbing at her attention, and Ray told me to shut the fuck up. I lost Dee behind me in the shadow of the dumpster.

Jeanette glanced at me, but spoke to Michael. "You shot Olivet?" She sounded pissed, like Michael had deliberately disobeyed.

"Let's go, Jeanette," I said and grabbed her wrist. Forget Michael's sack of money, we needed to be gone. I tugged her arm. Cops don't wait to track down killers, no matter how long the city fires burned.

She didn't move.

"Let's go," I said. I tried to make my voice strong, but even to myself I sounded weak.

"Get your hands off me," she said, and jerked away. She looked like the sight of me might make her sick.

Michael reached out to her and she went to him. He pulled her close.

"You shot him?" she said, her voice bedroom soft.

"The fat slob wouldn't open the safe." Michael lifted his arm and Jeanette cozied into his chest beneath it. She put her open hand on his belly. "Smart girl," he said. His eyes burned right through me.

My heart closed down, I couldn't breathe, I lunged toward Jeanette with both hands. Jeanette. My Jeanette.

"Who does he think he is?" she said, shrieking, dodging me. Something drove into the side of my skull and I sank to the lot like rocks in water.

All three men came on me like vultures. I couldn't do anything.

"Fucker came after my girl," Michael said.

The first kick caught me below the ribs, and I felt myself lift off the asphalt parking lot. I saw the shotgun stock coming and it caught me on the bridge of my nose and felt like it tore half my face away. Then the blood, my blood, spraying everywhere, and the smell of copper filled my head. I tried to stand but couldn't make myself move. A boot heel crushed the fingers of my left hand, and I screamed, but no sound came. My teeth were gone and my tongue filled my mouth. A jumping foot snapped my forearm like a dried stick. Dee lifted my head by my hair and looked into my face. I saw the blur of Jeanette tight against Michael's chest.

"You still living, motherfucker," Dee said, and let my hair go. My face thudded hard against the asphalt, splashing in my own blood. He stomped my jaw, twice, and my body shuddered. Then, all sense was gone.

Olivet lived. So did I.

He fingered Michael's gang and they fingered me, to cut down their own sentences. It cost me four on a three-to-five.

Visitor days came and went. I got some calls. Pop came once a month, my public defender twice in four, but not Jeanette.

Never Jeanette.

PART IV

The Hill & The Edge

THE BOTTOM LINE

BY JAMES GRADY

Capitol Hill, N.E./S.E.

The Capitol building glowed in the night like a white icing cake.

Can't believe I'm here, thought Joel Rudd as he drove toward that fortress on a hill. The car wheels rumbled his eyes to the passenger he'd picked up at a prestigious downtown hotel. She had the edgy burn of a 1940s movie star. Used the name Lena.

As they neared Capitol Hill, she said: "So you're the Senator's number one boy."

"I'm his Administrative Assistant, his Chief of Staff. A long way from *boy*."

"Is this ride *assisting* or *administering?*"

"Call it the end of a long day."

Joel had made his play earlier, when sunset pinked the marble Capitol. Legislative Director Dick Harvie and Personal Secretary Mimi sat with Joel on the leather couch in the Senator's inner office, sipped cold beers while they waited for their boss.

Senator Carl Ness strode into his office, filled a glass with vodka and ice.

"Here's to us fools on a hill," toasted the Senator. "We got through another day without wrecking the country."

They went over the schedule Mimi'd beamed to the BlackBerry the Senator carried along with two cell phones—

the taxpayer provided one for official calls, the private one wrapped in blue tape for conversations nobody wanted logged in public records.

The Senator told Dick and Mimi: "Joel will drive me home."

Meaning: *Leave us now.*

The Senator and Joel sat alone in an office once assigned to assassinated RFK.

Senator Ness said, "Fuck it, I'm not making *give-me-money* calls tonight."

"We'll raise enough for reelection," replied Joel.

"Nobody ever has enough cash." The Senator frowned. "You look . . . shaky."

"Did you call out to the state today and talk to Joyce?"

"She had that school award thing over in Personville. I'll call her after you drop me off tonight. Maybe she'll even pick up the phone."

No comment, thought Joel, who knew all about wives, having never had one. Then he said, "We're facing two issues. First is the Committee vote on the F-77 fighter program. It's down to which firm wins, United Tech or Z-Systems, no real differences between either company's bird."

The Senator shook his head. "We got zero enemies with an Air Force so powerful that we need a new war bird."

Spring it now, thought Joel. He said: "Second, you've got to be Senate sponsor for an aid package, only $8 million and change, for refugee camps in Sudan—"

The Senator sighed.

"—only $8 million, but it'll save 10,000 starving people."

"Foreigners. Hell, *African* foreigners. Not our constituents."

"Our folks are still lucky."

"High as back-home unemployment is, never call them *lucky*. Our opposition is drooling to smear me as a 'big spender'. A 'tax-and-spend' guy ain't who we can reelect." Ice clinked in the Senator's glass. "That trip got to you, didn't it?"

Joel remembered wails from raped women now "safe" inside a barbed-wire desert refugee camp. Life fading from the face of a skeletal eight-year-old boy. Buzzing flies.

The Senator said: "You didn't need to bring me that white canvas sack. Like a flour sack, only it's a body bag for dead kids. Didn't need to give me that sack."

"I wanted you to remember."

"I already wake up every morning with too much to forget." The Senator sipped his drink. "You gotta drive tonight."

"I know. I'll hit the bathroom before we—"

"It's not just me who you got to drive."

Joel sank back into the leather chair. "I thought we were through with all that. What if there's a problem?"

"Won't be. Out-of-town Joyce won't know. Would probably feel relieved."

"Bullshit."

"Yeah, but it's bullshit that works." The Senator looked away. "Tonight isn't . . . personal."

"Oh, *great*."

"Who do you want to pick her up? Me, when every cell phone in town is a camera? Some mailroom geek who's got nothing invested in us except a job that pays him less than he could make bartending? A taxi with logbooks?"

"I didn't sign on for this."

"It's gonna happen. All you get to do is choose how."

So after driving the Senator home, Joel played chauffeur.

His passenger said: "Aren't you going to ask?"

"I got no questions for your answers."

"Bullshit. You're *all* questions. Probably been getting away with that for years."

"Why are you a whore?"

"I'm good at it. What's your excuse?"

"I don't need one. I've got a great job."

"So I see." She looked out the car window. "You're driving me."

He sped past the Senator's huge town house. Drove into a courtyard of two-story dwellings created as stables and slave quarters. Now most of those boxes were homes for the thin slice of Congress' 20,000-plus employees who lived on Capitol Hill.

Joel stopped at the Senator's back door. Slapped a key onto the dashboard.

She scooped up the key. "Don't catch cold out here."

Long and lean and not looking back, she disappeared into that town house rehabbed years after the city-gutting King-assassination riots.

Joel sped to his own house five blocks away. He lived alone. Stood on the maroon rug in his living room with its Smithsonian art prints and National Park Service black-and-white poster of a mustang in a blizzard. He charged upstairs, wrestled off his tie.

The cell phone filled his shirt pocket like a stone.

Joel looked out his bedroom window to the night.

Capitol Hill is a geography of mind, will, and luck. Gang turf carved by the blades of Congress. What matters on the Hill might not count in Chicago or Paris, not in the mile-away White House or at the Supreme Court, where Joel said the motto etched on that law cathedral should read: *"Equal justice under the five-to-four decision."* Yet, what happens on Capitol Hill might change the world. As Joel had told his protégé Dick: *"Up here, the bottom line never changes."*

Joel's cell phone rang after 112 minutes. He said: "I'll be right there."

She stood alone in the night alley.

"You could have gotten mugged out there," said Joel as she huddled beside him. "Or worse."

"So what."

He sped away from that back door. Stopped the car at the end of the alley. Idled.

"Next time, get your boss *café au* Viagra."

Crimson flames roared in Joel's head.

She said: "Are we going to sit here and stare at the road?"

"Tell me where to go."

"So much to say, so little time."

"I need to know—"

"But you never get to."

"I know what I'm doing!"

"Congratulations," she said. "How do you like it so far?"

"Don't fuck with me."

"I wouldn't take your business."

"And you're all business."

"What's your label? Politics?"

"Look, all I want is . . ." He stared out the windshield.

"Oh. I see. It's about what you want." Her hand pulled on the emergency brake. She drew toward him like a slow falling star.

"What are you doing?" he said as her face floated closer, closer.

"Guess."

Her mouth covered his. He tasted lightning. She drew back. Met his gaze as he managed to say: "I thought girls like you never kissed on the mouth."

She raged at him, both hands slapping.

Joel shook her. Lena's hair flew wild in the streetlight's glow. She fought free and he let her. She didn't run or look away, and he saw her. Felt her shiver.

Streets of fire drove them to his living room.

She ripped his shirt. Wore black lingerie. Her bare legs clamped around Joel's waist as he laid her down on the living room's maroon rug.

Two hours or a lifetime later, they lay naked in the white sheets of his bed.

Her hand stroked his cheek. "What were your women like yesterday?"

"All I see are characters in movies."

"How do they look?" she said.

"Smart. Funny. Successful. Pretty. Like the kind of woman a man needs."

"Couldn't fix them, could you?" She said: "Don't save me. And don't make me your personal Jesus."

Joel smiled. "Jesus was a man."

"Don't be so limited."

"Who knew you were so full of *don'ts*."

"I'm about out," she said. "How about you?"

"All I know is this is going to drive me crazy."

Lena sealed that with her kiss.

Come morning, Dick grinned when Joel finally walked past his desk: "Get lost coming to work?"

"Whatever," said Joel. "What's happening?"

"Money wars," said Dick. "We've got three weeks to decide our F-77 vote."

"What's up with the Aid to Sudan bill?"

"They should have waited on that over there," said Dick,

nodding toward the House side of the Hill. "Made sure they had a champion over here."

Joel said nothing about his visits to the key House staffer for the bill's author, nothing about urging speed on the bill. Now, to Dick, he said, "Polish our armor."

"The boss went for that? It's the right thing to do, but he's so freaked about reelection I can't believe he'll stick his neck out on something for nothing."

"He's not there yet," said Joel. "But be ready."

Mimi buzzed Joel: *The boss wants you.*

The Senator sat behind his desk. Looked up as Joel entered the private office.

"About last night." The Senator shrugged. "We all have our needs."

"Really." Joel walked out.

The Senator's eyes burned Joel's neck through the door he shut behind him. At Mimi's desk, Joel told her, "Call Joyce wherever she is. Get her back in town."

"Home to her husband? Not likely."

"Mrs. Senator loves her job as much as he loves his. Reelection on the horizon, gossip about his solo ways . . . Joyce knows we all gotta do what we all gotta do."

The workday wall clock stretched Joel tighter with every sweep of its red second hand. He left the office for home as soon as he could. She showed up seven minutes early. Stood on his stoop holding a pizza box and a clunky cloth purse. Hair floating free, she wore no makeup or perfume, a hooded sweatshirt under a denim jacket, torn blue jeans on slim legs and black-and-white sneakers.

"This is nothing but me," said Lena.

He pulled her inside.

Ninety minutes later, they ate cold pizza while sitting

naked on his bed.

"Your arms," she said. "How did an indoor guy get such a tan?"

He told her about Sudan, the refugee camp, the three-day "fact finding" trip that he blew up to a two-week tour in Hell that the State Department finally insisted he abandon.

"The worst part was seeing the faces of real people fall away from the helicopter as it lifted me up. I saw their eyes. I saw them believe my promises."

"You're exactly who belongs in this town. Get out while you can."

"What about you?"

"Where can I go? I started out letting guys be generous to a hot girl who didn't want a slave-labor job or a soul-sucking career. Then one day you realize that you added it up all wrong and you're stuck being your score."

Joel cupped her wet face. "Who you are right now is all you need."

She shook her head no. "Remember Sudan? You've either got power or vultures get you. Plus, the shit I've done has to be worth it. Has to get me beyond it with *enough* so nobody can touch me. Except you. The best I am is being who you want."

Thursday night she only called to say she couldn't see him.

Friday night her *plans* were to be *not there*, but he called her so many times that she relented. Said she'd see him around midnight.

Lena rang his doorbell at ten minutes into tomorrow. Stood on his doorstep looking like a magazine ad, all hair and lips and sheathed legs in a black dress that plunged between her teardrop breasts. Her eyes were broken windows.

She stalked upstairs to his bathroom and closed the door.

He sat on the bed. Listened to the shower run for twenty minutes. *The hot water tank must be empty.*

He found her huddled on the floor of the tub, naked, icy liquid bullets spraying down on her as she looked at him, sobbed, "Not enough soap in the whole damn world."

He stepped into the shower and pulled her up, held her in that cold, cold rain.

By the next afternoon, smiles softened her jaggedness. They walked past Saturday shoppers who'd come from the Eastern Market food stands where J. Edgar Hoover sacked groceries as a boy. Joel tried to show her the secret grotto tucked into the Senate side of the Capitol grounds, but Homeland Security had kicked the terrorist alert level up to YELLOW. Even his Senate staff ID wasn't enough to get her past SWAT-geared Capitol Hill cops swarming around America's democracy factory.

"It's okay." She squeezed his hand. "Take me home."

And he knew she meant to his house.

Sunday, she urged him to do one thing she'd never sold and they did.

Monday, he went to work.

"Getting *down*," Dick said, as he opened the *Washington Post* on Joel's desk. "Here on A20, a full-page ad from United Tech salutes their planes with '*American-built technology.*' Then on Page A24, a quarter-page ad where Z-Systems proudly announces their F-77A '*simulator*' performed flight tests with '*superlative success.*'

"And," continued Dick, "here's an '*According to government sources*' news story about a General Accountability Office '*investigation*' into cost-overruns by Z-Systems on their flying tanker. Of course, no mention of which Congressman or Senator ordered GAO to kick Z-Systems' butt or why the story got leaked."

"Seen it before," said Joel.

"Yeah," said Dick. "Our boss ambushed me this morning at the coffee pot. Told me that he doesn't care which company he votes for."

Joel said: "Did he go off again on reelection?"

"Naw, but speaking of running, that Sudan relief bill ain't got no legs."

"They'll show up any day now. Trust me."

"Always," said Dick.

That night, as Joel's kitchen echoed with laughter, Lena's cell phone buzzed. She said, "Excuse me." Walked as far away as she could. Came back in ten minutes. Said, "I've got to go." Left him alone with his nightmares.

Tuesday evening she was sitting on his front stoop with a smile that lit her face.

Wednesday her restlessness woke him with the dawn. She wore only his tattered high school football jersey. Told him: "I can't do this anymore."

Joel felt his ceiling fly away.

"I can't leave you," said Lena. "I can't go back and do what I do. And I won't let my whole life until now add up to worse than nothing."

"If it's about money—"

"No! If it's your money, then you're just like all the rest. I can't let you be that!"

"What about me? You say you protect yourself against psycho killers and getting . . . and I have to believe you. But you fuck other men and it's like you let them rape you! Can't you—"

"Start all over?" He heard the tremor in her voice. "Baby, I ain't got the time. All I've done is like a long black cloud swelling up behind me. I'm running out of sky."

He held her and she sobbed. The sun came up and she lay awake on his heart.

Victory at work that day meant he and Dick brokered a deal to give air polluters a six percent rollback of fines instead of the seventeen percent proposed by his Senator's opponents. Joel linked a freelance cameraman he'd cajoled into filming the refugee camp to a network news producer who owed Joel. As he and Dick walked their boss to a Roll Call, the Senator told Joel: "Nobody wants your Sudan relief bill. I can't put my brand on a dead horse." Joel pleaded: "You can make it work." Senator Ness looked at Joel, shrugged.

Later, Dick told Joel: "Least he left you with hope."

"Hope isn't enough on the Hill."

"I know. Up here, the bottom line never changes: It's what you can get done." Dick added: "Still, working on the Hill is the right thing for guys like us to do. The last best place where we can get paid to fight the good fight."

"Yeah," said Joel, who'd preached that gospel to Dick once upon a time.

After work Joel found Lena on his couch, her hands wrapped around a bottle of Jack Daniel's.

"I got a phone call today," she said. "From your Senator. Didn't take it."

Joel took a swig of bourbon.

"I stared at my cell phone screen and realized something: I have his number."

"Leave him out of this. Leave him alone."

"No, he's in this with us. He's got my number, but I've got

his. And the number of the guy who hooked up me and the Senator."

"What guy?" said Joel.

"This guy, this lobbyist. He's gay, so . . . No *business* between us. Don't know how, but he hooked up with your Senator."

"I can't be with him all the time," said Joel. "What's the guy's name?"

"Frank Greene."

A bulldog who wears Wall Street suits. Joel said: "I didn't know Frank was gay."

"It's not who he is," said Lena, "it's what he offered me."

She leaned closer. "Frank told me that if I could get the Senator to tell me who he was going to vote for on a military planes contract—"

"The F-77 authorization bill."

"Yeah. Frank offered me $5,000 if I got your boss to say who he was voting for."

Joel took a swig from the bottle.

"My idea," she said, "is that if five grand is a fee for just knowing about a deal, what would it be worth to a guy like Frank to be able to broker that deal?"

Joel's stomach churned sour acid.

"You told me all about it!" said Lena. "It's not like this vote makes any difference. It's not about America or national defense or fighting evil."

"We can't be about this."

"We're not! We're about us. This is about getting us free."

"It's for you."

"Yeah, it's for me. And you said you want me. I'll always be who I was, but this way I have something to show for it. This buys me a getaway. Here."

"Not enough," he whispered. "We're not worth enough to do this."

"What other chance do we have? I'm changing my life for us. What about you?"

He walked to his window full of night. Stared out at the city he'd chosen to make his home. He searched the darkness outside. Faced what he'd never embraced.

"Only one way we can do this," said Joel. "We need to make doing what's wrong be for more right than just us."

After he told her *how,* she said: "I'll set it up."

"Won't work," he said. "Frank won't believe just you. Buy just you."

"I don't want you touching—"

He stroked her hair. "Too late."

Joel nodded to her cell phone. "Make the call."

"What about the Senator?"

"Nobody needs him," said Joel.

But two nights later, Joel sat in his car with the bulldog in a Wall Street suit who said: "Hey, fucko, I need the Senator."

Across the street waited Capitol Hill's neighborhood ballfield-sized Lincoln Park that 198 years after the signing of the Declaration of Independence became D.C.'s first public site for any statue honoring a woman or an African-American.

"It's not about what you need," said Joel. "It's about what I can do."

"You don't get to vote in Committee. Or on the Floor."

"Not in the flesh, but I'm the spirit moving the man."

"This town's full of people who died thinking they were somebody else."

"You get close to him," said Joel, "the odds go up that we'll all get caught."

Frank Greene drummed his fingers on Joel's dashboard. "$100,000."

"My price includes more than cash. There's a relief bill for Sudan that's come over from the House on a wing and a prayer. You're going to angel that prayer. Muscle that bill into a workable law."

"This is a money town and you want me to save the world? What's the catch?"

"No catch. But I get to deliver my guy to lead the charge in the Senate."

"One hand cleans the other, huh?"

Yellow headlights silhouetted them sitting in the car as a cop drove past two more men sharing secrets in D.C.'s dark night.

"Believe what you gotta believe," said the bulldog. "But deliver what you sell."

"Don't you trust me?" Joel shook his head at the man's silence. "Me too. That's why I have to see motion on your side before I deliver from mine."

"What do you mean *motion*? I call you in a few days, tell you which company, you lock your man down, I deliver the cash through the babe."

"Never call her again. If you see her on the street, walk on by. And make me see what I need to see."

On the following Wednesday, Mimi dropped a "Dear Colleague" letter on Joel's desk, a mass mailing to all law-makers on Capitol Hill from the Congressman who'd authored the Sudan relief measure and was now proud to announce that a caucus of business and labor groups had organized to support the bill.

Letter in hand, Joel walked to the suite Mimi shared with Press Secretary Ricki.

Mimi was on the phone. "Good to talk to you, Glenn." She mouthed the name *Parker* to Joel. "The Senator will be sorry to have missed your call, but Joel's standing right here."

Joel took the phone. "Glenn, how are you?"

"How I am is stuck. Not sure we should be talking—legally."

"The law says there's no problem with a citizen calling his Senator's office—one time, anyway. They let guys like us touch base for free."

"Free?" Glenn laughed. "Then FYI, a bunch of the Senator's friends out here plus some folks back in D.C. just formed an independent educational committee so voters realize who to touch the computer screen for next time."

Dead air filled the phone call between the Senator's D.C. office and the bank president's phone back home in the capital of the Senator's state.

Until Joel said: "That sounds like great news, but you're right, it's possibly of a partisan nature, so we can't talk about it on this publicly funded phone, or from this taxpayer-owned office."

Joel gave him a phone number for the town house that the party's Senatorial Campaign Committee rented across the street from the Senate, told Glenn to call him there in an hour.

Mimi said: "Is this one of those things I don't know about?"

Joel knocked on the brown door to the Senator's private suite, didn't wait for a "Come in" before he did, and closed the door behind him.

Senator Carl Ness sat with suit jacket off, tie loosened, three cell phones and BlackBerry on the massive desk, as he worked his way through a stack of papers.

"You talk to Glenn Parker recently?" said Joel.

The Senator shrugged. "Joyce ran into him at that Bay City pancake breakfast for the Girl Scouts."

"And I suppose they chatted about how things are and how they could be better."

"God bless the First Amendment. People can talk."

"Did you give Joyce her script?"

"She's been at this a long time. She knows what to say." The Senator smiled. "What are you upset about? None of us left any fingerprints."

"Don't ever pull a stunt like that again without first running it by me."

"Hey, I am the Senator." He raised his hand. "Point taken, but this is a done deal."

Joel dropped the "Dear Colleague" Sudan letter on his boss' desk. "If you lead the charge for that bill over here, you're going to make a lot of important people happy."

"Who will I make mad?"

"Nobody who can hurt you."

The Senator leaned back in his chair. "We live in a brutal world. It's incumbent upon us as Americans and human beings to do all we can to help innocent men and—no: *innocent children*—who violence, evil, and greed have *blah blah blah*." The Senator raised a warning finger. "Don't get me in trouble on this."

"Me?" said Joel. "Get you in trouble? That's not the way it's always been."

Later, walking back from the Campaign Committee's house, Joel detoured to a Union Station pay phone. He called the bulldog, said: "Yes."

"You can still back out," whispered Lena that night in his bed.

"No we can't," said Joel.

The U.S. mail brought a package to his home the next day—a disposable cell phone that buzzed in his pocket three days later. Joel put the cell phone to his ear.

A bulldog said: "Is this who it should be?"

"Probably," said Joel.

"Z-Systems. I repeat, Z-Systems."

After work that night Joel arranged to go out for a beer with Dick and their Committee staffer Trudy. They went to one of only four bars that survived the deluge of ferns-and-cloth-napkins gentrification that laundered Capitol Hill in the 1990s, a booths-and-stools joint with Hank Williams *wannabe's* in the jukebox. A stuffed owl spread its wings above the bar mirror. Congressional aides loved the bar: It reminded them of a blue-collar *real world* they imagined they could still claim as their roots.

"Is it just me," said Trudy, "or are we the oldest Hill staffers in here?"

"Congress runs on the blood of twenty-five-year-olds," said Joel. "Guys two jumps up like us are usually thinking about getting out, back to the real world and on to big bucks."

Trudy asked: "How many people on your staff are from D.C.?"

"One," said Joel.

"We aren't like ordinary factory towns," said Dick.

"We aren't like any town anywhere," said Joel.

They drank cold beer. Joel let Trudy think it was her idea to meet with the Senator. Those four playmakers huddled the next morning.

Senator Ness said: "Give me your recommends."

"The companies' planes are essentially equal," said Trudy. "But the future looks best with United Tech. United's bird is more bucks per copy, but Z-Systems' bid is a low estimate that they'll recoup in cost-overruns. Plus, Z-Systems has that GAO probe."

Dick said: "Are you telling us that United Tech is more honest than Z-Systems?"

Even Trudy laughed.

"I say that the GAO investigation of Z-Systems means they're the best choice," said Dick. "They won't be so inclined to try a rip while the watchdogs are in their shop. Plus, Z-Systems is the cheaper *right now* and we pay for our pick with *right now* dollars."

The Senator said. "Joel?"

"Read the headline," said Joel. "'*Senator Ness Votes Against Low Bidder on Jillion-Dollar Contract.*' It's hard to explain to the voters why it looks like you chose to overspend their tax dollars. I say it comes down to good politics married to good government. If you add up everything, your best choice is Z-Systems."

"Makes sense," said the Senator.

"Okay," said Dick. "Z-Systems it is. How about I draft a letter of commitment to the Committee Chairman?"

Trudy said: "Great idea."

"Yeah, Dick," said the Senator, "except I'm voting for United Tech."

Dick blurted: "You said Z-Systems made sense."

"But," said the Senator as Joel fought terror, "it makes more sense and better government to build for the future. The political stuff's gotta take a backseat."

Dick said: "So do I draft the letter?"

Buy time. Joel said: "Let's think that play through, hold off until tomorrow."

Joel walked the Senator to a vote, then hurried through

the tunnels honeycombing the Hill beneath the Capitol to use the Campaign Committee phone and call back-home banker Glenn Parker.

"Glenn, our friends in your new group," said Joel. "Are they a bunch of guys from United Tech?"

Glenn said: "No. Are we expecting any?"

"Beats me," said Joel. "It's a free country."

That night, he sat on his living room couch with Lena. Streetlamps filtering through his dirty windows cut across them with light and shadows.

"After the Senator bucked me for United, knowing that committee had just formed out in the state, I thought maybe I'd catch him having done his own side deal. He's played cagey like that before."

Joel shook his head. "But now he's choosing what's best for the country, the hell with reelection. That's why I went to work for him. He may be a personal jerk, but he stands up for what he believes. The damn son of a bitch."

"What if you can't get the Senator to change his mind?" asked Lena.

"Then we're fucked."

"You could make it up to Frank Greene on some other vote some other time."

"There is no other time," said Joel. "If I fuck him on this, he'll need to fuck me. Plus more. To keep his pride, his clout. Keep himself safe."

"What are you talking about?" she said.

"This is a tough town."

Joel woke up under a cloudy sky. He let Mimi play out the morning office rituals. Then told the Senator: "Change your mind. Go for Z-Systems."

"Let's get Dick in on this," said the Senator, pushing the intercom button.

After Dick joined them, the Senator said: "Joel wants me to change my mind and go with Z-Systems."

Dick asked Joel: "Why?"

"United Tech is the future, but today is tomorrow."

Dick shrugged. "Whatever that means, we agree."

Senator Ness sighed. "Okay, I'll vote for Z-Systems. Let's get on to stuff we can give a shit about."

"I think I can get TV showing you rescuing starving kids," said Joel. He wanted to shout for joy. He wanted to cry for shame. He did his job, called the TV producer with "news" that prompted the producer to ask for a "deadline" chance that Joel granted.

Joel, Dick, Press Secretary Ricki, and the Senator huddled in his office.

"Just because they film our guy doesn't mean they'll use it," said Ricki.

"Great visuals have a better chance of making the news menu," said Joel. "Plus, if it bleeds, it leads, but—*I've got it!* The white sack. The burial bag for kids from the refugee camp!"

"Perfect!" said Ricki.

"Picture it, Senator," said Joel. "You do the usual interview sit-down they want to film this afternoon, wait for the right moment . . . then pull the white sack out of your suit jacket pocket. That gives them action and the illusion of a *gotchya*—news film is all about gotchyas. You'll be anointed a caring, crusading hero on network TV."

Ricki said: "So where's this sack?"

The three aides looked at the Senator.

Who said: "*Ahh . . .*"

Joel snapped: "Don't tell me you lost it."

The Senator said: "Thing creeped me—*wait!* It's on the pile to get auctioned off at a fundraiser or shipped to the state university's archives. The sack's at my house."

Joel said: "The interview's in three hours. You've got Agriculture mark-up in twenty-five minutes. You can cut out early. Dick, do that commitment letter now. Get him out of the Committee meeting with plenty of time for you two to get to his place, get the sack, come back. I like the idea of you two walking: You'll roughen up for the camera."

Seventeen minutes later, Dick showed Joel the commitment letter.

"Z-Systems it is," said Joel. "Make him sign it, run copies, and bring it all to me."

As soon as he was alone, Joel dialed the disposable cell phone.

"Yeah?" said the bulldog who answered Joel's call.

"Yeah," said Joel. "Now what about the rest of your end?"

"Ninety minutes. Your house." He hung up before Joel could say no.

Joel punched in a second phone number. When Lena answered her cell, he asked: "Where are you?"

"Your place. Where else."

"Get out of there. The bulldog is on his way."

Knock, on Joel's office door, and Dick came in: "Our boss signed on the line."

"I'll walk you two over." Joel put the signed letter and copies in his suit pocket.

Dick's frown said he thought that was peculiar, but *hey:* they were on the move.

Joel made sure they entered the right hearing room, then hurried outside.

An ocean of gray clouds rolled over the Capitol dome. Wind flapped Joel's suit jacket as he walked past Hill cops, past tourists who were realizing that visiting this site was like hiking to a *kabuki* play but not understanding Japanese. An orange public school bus crammed with inner-city D.C. kids passed him on the way to their classroom that had a hole in its ceiling the size of a coffin.

He found Lena in his living room.

"I won't let you do this alone," she said. "Why is he coming here?"

"To show me he knows where I live."

"Can we get away?"

"Sure," he said. "Anywhere you want to go."

"Here," she said, nuzzling his chest. "I want to go right here."

"After this, it can be just us."

He felt her nod. "I can be somebody else. I can dye my hair."

The doorbell rang.

Rain drops spit at Joel when he let the bulldog in his house.

The lobbyist stared at them. "You two make a helluva pair."

"Don't you talk about us." Lena hugged her arms across her chest.

Frank Greene shrugged. "What do you got for me?"

Joel handed him a photocopy. As the bulldog studied that piece of paper, Joel heard the clatter of wind and rain storming against his living room windows.

"Our turn," said Lena.

"About that." The bulldog tossed a thick envelope to Lena. "Tough luck."

"What do you mean?" said Joel.

"Changing circumstances require compromises. Means that your appropriation is cut fifty percent to fifty thou."

"You can't screw us," said Lena.

"Fifty K is way more than you've been paid for screwing before." The lobbyist turned to the Senate aide. Shrugged in a fashion that an amateur might mistake for an apology. "This town. What can you do?"

"I didn't sign on for this," said Joel.

"You signed up for everything the moment you let her in your car."

"Stop it!" screamed Lena.

The bulldog thrust his finger at her. "You don't give orders."

Joel pushed the lobbyist's arm away from Lena.

"What are you going to do?" growled the bulldog. "You got what I gave you."

Joel replied: "And all you've got for sure is a piece of paper."

"Oh, you think so?" The bulldog snapped at Lena. "You think so, too?"

"Shut up!" She shook the envelope in Greene's face. "You think I did it for this?"

Lena threw the envelope away. It landed on the couch by her bulky cloth purse.

"Why you did whatever is your problem."

Joel said: "Leave her alone."

"Oh, come on." said the bulldog. "Don't you get it?"

Joel said: "I get that we've only gotten half of what was promised."

"You sure you want the rest?"

"Shut up!" Lena lunged toward the couch, her purse, the money envelope. "You can't fuck us like this!"

"Babe, getting fucked is your whole life."

"Not now!" Lena cradled the envelope and her clunky purse. "Not for us."

"*Whoa*, stop the way the world's been working, 'cause suddenly you decided you got yourself an *us*? Let's see."

"No. Don't!"

Like a mad dog, the lobbyist whirled to Joel. "You want it all?"

"Shut up." said Lena. "Stop!"

The bulldog surged toward her Joel, growled: "You want what you really got?"

Out of her purse jerked Lena's hand holding a snub-nosed revolver *Bam!*

Window panes flashed and vibrated with the gunshot.

From outside, it seemed only like the storm.

Joel knew he must have heard the bang, seen the gunshot flash, but he felt like he had fallen back into himself after being far away. Now, suddenly, he was right here, in his living room, Lena holding a pistol, Frank Greene clutching his left side.

"You bitch!" yelled Frank. "Gonna kill you."

Frank staggered toward her.

Bam! Bam!

Frank crumpled to the maroon rug. Window panes rattled.

Lena whispered: "It shot him."

Joel crouched to touch the lobbyist's motionless neck. Then Joel's hand shook and wouldn't stop. His whole body trembled.

Lena pulled him up to her embrace. "I'll call the police," she said. "Tell them the truth."

"What good would that do?"

"Even you can't fix this."

"But it can be managed."

"Joel, no. What he did, said, what he was going to—"

"What matters is what happens right now," Joel told her.

He filled her eyes as she told him: "I never thought it would go this way. I love you."

"Yeah. But now that's not enough."

He pocketed the gun. Had her help him roll the dead man up in the maroon rug.

Joel put on a hooded raincoat. Ran outside in the storm. Drove his car into the alley, parked by his trash cans. Lena let him in the back door. Helped him shoulder the rolled-up maroon rug, stagger through the rain, cram it into his car's trunk.

Inside his house, water dripped off them to tap on the bare wood floor.

"Take the money." He stuffed the envelope in her cloth purse. "Go home. You weren't here. Barely know me. I'll call when it's safe."

He drove her to nearby Union Station. Stopped where the few people running past them had eyes only for their own escape from the storm.

"Go," he told her crying eyes. "I'll call as soon as I can."

She hugged him so tight he almost died. Ran from his car toward the subway escalator. Turned to look back at him through gray sheets of driving rain. He memorized her standing there washed by all the tears in town.

The escalator fed her to the underground.

Go, he told himself. No speeding tickets. No accidents. Off the Hill: Virginia? Maryland? A country road. A quarry filled by a dead lake. A ditch with rocks that could be rolled. Wipe the gun. Throw the wallet, cell phones—*cell phones: what is it about*—never mind. Ditch evidence everywhere but on the Hill.

Ring! His cell phone, not the disposable he'd need to dump.

Can't *not* answer.

Dick's voice in his ear: "Joel, where the hell are you?"

Sell the truth when you can: "In my car. On the Hill. Got places to go."

"Yeah," said Dick, "like here to the boss' house, pronto."

"Why?"

"Because of the rain, man. It's like a hurricane."

"But—"

"No *buts*, or our butts are in a sling. We got here just as it started spitting. Finding the white sack took awhile. Now we gotta get back to the Capitol in time for the interview in the TV press gallery. Looking rough for a good TV Q is cool, but looking like a drowned rat blows, so you need to swing by here and give us a ride."

"What about the Senator's car?"

"In the shop, and in this storm, no way can we get a taxi. If you don't come get us, we'll lose the chance to get the Sudan bill on TV and spin the PR we need to win."

Rain drummed the roof of Joel's car. Flooded his windshield.

"Yeah," he said into the cell phone, "Ness's got to take this ride."

Joel double-parked in front of the Senator's town house.

Two men hurried through the rain to his car. The Senator wore a trenchcoat, jumped in the front seat. Dick tumbled into the back.

"Where's your umbrella?" said Joel.

"Somebody else always has one," said the Senator.

"Go!" said Dick. "We're going to be late."

Joel stepped on the gas.

Ca-lump.

Dick said: "What was that?"

The rearview mirror showed Dick turning to look toward the car's trunk.

"D.C. streets," blurted Joel. "Roughest roads around."

Joel steered his car into a right-turn-on-red. Water wooshed under his tires. Potholes slammed the wheels. The wipers went *whump whump.*

"Turn on the defrost," ordered the Senator. "You can barely see."

The engine fan whirred an invisible wind up the fogged windshield.

"Look out!" yelled Dick.

A yellow smear slid past their surging car.

"You almost hit that cop!" said Dick.

A neon red starburst filled Joel's windshield.

"What the hell?" said Dick as Joel slammed on the brakes.

Three Capitol Hill cops in yellow rain slickers blocked the road. One cop stabbed a popped flare into the wet mirror blacktop. Two others stalked toward the halted vehicle.

Joel lowered his window. Spray from the storm wet his face.

"Sir, shut off your vehicle!" yelled the older cop, while the younger one kept his right hand thrust inside his yellow slicker. "Now!"

A laser dot of red light refracted through the windshield to kiss Joel's chest.

Joel shifted to park and killed his engine. The red dot danced on Joel's chest as two cops moved to his side of the car.

"Sir!" yelled the lead cop. "The officer back there ordered you to halt."

"I didn't see him. I'm driving Senator Ness."

The older cop snapped a flashlight beam on the Senator's face.

Gonna be all right, thought Joel. *Gonna make it now.*

"He's him," said the cop's younger partner.

"Sorry Senator," said the ranking officer, "I didn't see you, but . . . Doesn't matter. Homeland Security just bumped us up to ORANGE Alert."

"Fuck Homeland Security!" yelled the Senator. "This is Capitol Hill, I'm a Senator, we're in charge, let us pass."

"Sir . . . our scenarios include a Senator being snatched in a terrorist attack."

"That's ridiculous."

"So is four jetliners being hijacked into flying bombs. I'm sorry, but you entered our secured zone so now you all have to step out of the vehicle before you proceed."

Joel yelled: "In this damn storm?"

"Come on," said Dick. "We can still make it."

The black Senate staffer stepped out of the car, kept his hands in plain sight.

"Fuck me." The Senator stepped into the rain.

Through the water-blurred windshield, Joel saw three more yellow-slickered cops march toward the car. One carried an umbrella. One carried a pole with a mirror for examining the underside of vehicles.

The senior cop told the driver: "Everyone must exit the vehicle."

Joel Rudd stood on the road, arms out like Jesus, face turned up to the falling rain.

Senator Carl Ness stood under an umbrella held by a yellow-slickered cop and, like his law-writing aide Dick Harvie, stared at the Capitol Hill wizard they worked with who suddenly seemed to have gone insane.

"Sir, we need to pop the trunk. Check it. Then you can go."

"No," said Joel. "I'm going nowhere. I'm already there."

The older cop said: "We're just following the rules."

Joel turned his flooded face toward that guardian of law and order. "Rules. I know about them. In my trunk you'll find a body."

"*What?*" chorused the cop, the U.S. Senator, and the legislative director.

"A lobbyist named Frank Greene. Shot dead."

Rain beat down on them. Flares sputtered. Police radios crackled routine reports.

Until a cop opened Joel's trunk, announced: "He's right."

The younger cop slid his hand back inside his yellow slicker.

An officer lifted his radio, but his sergeant ordered: "Keep this off the air."

Senator Ness yelled at Joel: "What have you done?"

Joel stared at the man he knew so well, had served so long. A thousand calculations churned behind the Senator's frantic expression. Through the raging storm, Joel saw the spirit inside that man as clearly as he saw the spirit in himself.

Carl Ness reached inside his suit and pulled out a white sack.

"Do you see what you've done?" said the politician. "Do you see what you've put at risk? Ten thousand lives and you stand there flushing them down the drain."

A cop exchanged his radio for a cell phone.

The Senator shook the white sack. "Now it'll take all I've got to make this happen."

Suddenly Joel saw it all through the pouring rain. *Cell phone. Fingerprints.* The cell phone in the cop's hand as he reported in. The third cell phone on the Senator's desk when there should have been only two. A sequence where a bulldog and a politician set up a "shaky" crusader with a desperate dream girl who they'd schooled. Joel positioned to structure the corrupt deal over the Senator's "opposition" in front of witnesses Trudy and Dick. If anyone ever cried corruption, the guilty fingerprints would belong to fall guy Joel. The Senator's "independent" campaign committee set up to reap a windfall from the contract winners. The payoff to Joel and Lena was chump change to distract him, keep him quiet, drive more nails into his frame.

The white sack waited in the Senator's fist for what Joel would say.

The whole, unprovable, public truth wouldn't save Joel. Would cut the balls off a Senator so that he kept his job but had no power. Would thus sentence 10,000 people to starvation. Destroy a woman desperate to be free.

Capitol Hill's bottom line: *It's what you can get done.*

Thunder boomed. Joel never saw the flash. His words tasted like smoke. "The creep got shot because he welched on paying me for fixing the warplane vote."

"Wait," said the youngest cop. "Shouldn't we read him his rights?"

No one can prove me wrong, thought Joel. Or will want to.

Clarity shimmered through the hissing red glow of the flares, the spinning blue-and-blood lights on arriving police cars, the storm-slick skull-white glow off the Capitol dome. Joel envisioned Lena grimly marching through a D.C. airport. He wondered where she'd go. The color of her hair.

"My fall!" cried Joel.

"What'd he say?" yelled the older cop.

Whose partner yelled back: "He said it was his fault!"

But Senator Ness's face said he'd heard Joel's offer. A look of pure understanding passed between them.

Like the noble boss of a doomed sinner, the Senator told Joel: "I'll do all I can."

Joel's nod sealed their redemptive bargain.

"Cuff him," ordered the older cop.

Bare steel clamped around Joel's wrists.

Dick Harvie lunged toward the prisoner who'd taught him how democracy works.

"Murder," said Dick, the word burning in his eyes. "I get that. But how could you, you of all people, how dare you sell out all the best dreams up here."

Joel said: "Everybody gets a hill."

STIFFED

BY DAVID SLATER

Thomas Circle, N.W.

The restaurant had emptied after the Friday lunch shift, so Gibson shoved open the battered back door to get a quick taste of sunshine. He leaned against the chain-link fence, pulled his lunch tips out of his pocket, and slowly counted the crumpled bills. Seventeen lousy dollars.

He plopped down on an overturned five-gallon pickle bucket and lit a Camel to mask the dumpster's ripeness. He added some numbers in his head, trying to figure out how much he had earned that week. He needed at least another thousand by the end of the month or he was going to lose his apartment. But if he was going to continue living off his eight-dollar-an-hour salary while putting his tips toward the thousand-dollar goal, there was no way that seventeen bucks was going to cut it.

He still had to man the grill until the next guy came on in a few hours, but he figured that there wouldn't be many more tips coming his way that day. The afternoons had been slow lately as the stifling summer heat settled over D.C.

The heavy door groaned opened and Karen, the day waitress, walked squinting into the sunshine. "There you are," she said. "Want to make a few extra bucks?"

"What are you talking about?"

"I'm supposed to hang around till the next girl comes in

at 5:00. But I was hoping to get over the Bay Bridge before it backs up. You want to hold down the fort?"

"You think I can work the grill and wait on tables too?"

"Come on, Gibson, look at how dead it's been. You can handle it for a couple of hours."

Gibson shrugged his shoulders. What the hell. He had been counting on pocketing more than fifty bucks from the day's lunch shift, and this might get him there.

"Give me a couple minutes to finish this cigarette," he said, "and I'll be out."

The Shelbourne Grill was a dying breed for the neighborhood just below Thomas Circle. Nothing fancy or modern: People came in for made-from-scratch onion rings and fat burgers, grilled behind the bar by the same guys who served the beer. The crane-strewn neighborhood was upgrading fast, but the Shelbourne hadn't seen much change in its four decades. It was narrow and dark, with seating for around sixty at a worn bar, six uncomfortable wooden booths, and a row of two-tops. The prices were low and the place only accepted cash, even though ten times a day they had to send customers scurrying to the ATM machine at the corner bank across the street.

Working as a combined grillman/bartender took some getting used to for Gibson. In the fourteen years since high school, he had bounced around a lot of restaurant kitchens, but this was the first place where he had worked behind the bar and around customers. When he first took the job, he wasn't sure he was going to be able to put up with the patrons' bullshit, but he had been doing it for more than a year now without any major hassles.

Gibson only worked the lunch shift, and most of the customers he dealt with were generally all right: low-key folks from the neighborhood or from the offices on 15th Street, most of whom would rather read a book or paper than talk anyway. But according to Williamson, who had worked dinners at the Shelbourne for a nearly a decade, an increasing number of twenty-somethings had been stopping in at night for a cheap tune-up, in part because of *City Paper* ads placed by Barry, the young owner who had inherited the place from his father around eight months earlier.

Gibson had dealt with some of these kids during his afternoon shifts. He found most of them impatient and a couple of them obnoxious, but so far he had managed to keep things in check. The tips, which cooks never saw at most restaurants, gave him a reason to watch his temper. And that motivation had intensified since he learned five months ago that his apartment building was turning into co-ops. Now, his only chance of holding onto his place, the place he had lived in ever since his mom passed away a decade ago, was if he came up with the down payment by the end of the month.

He stood at the end of the bar and poured himself a cup of coffee. The tables were all empty and so was the bar, except for McManus, the college kid that Gibson had just carried all through the lunch shift. He was a preppy little snot who moved in slow motion behind the bar and didn't even care enough to cut a sandwich on a bias. The word was that he had been hired because he was a family friend of the owner. That seemed logical, because Barry wasn't much older than McManus and, in Gibson's eyes, was just as worthless. Barry was probably locked in his upstairs office at that very moment, jerking off as usual to a copy of *Golf Digest*.

Gibson looked down the bar at McManus, who was reading the sports section with his crisp red Nationals cap turned backwards on his head. Asswipe didn't even know enough to go home after punching out on a beautiful Friday afternoon. He looked up at Gibson and waved his empty Budweiser bottle.

"Gibster, can I get another one of these?"

Gibson, who was half-heartedly filling the salt and peppers, sighed and rolled his eyes. "Fine with me if you want to drink up your tips." He grabbed a beer from the cooler and put it in front of McManus, who nodded and said, "That lunch shift sucked today, didn't it?"

"You're telling me. Seventeen dollars in tips ain't working for me."

"I heard that," said McManus. "Not when I'm only making ten bucks an hour."

Gibson walked back toward him. "Did you say ten bucks an hour?"

"Yeah, man, can you believe that? I tried to get more out of Barry but he wasn't budging. Said that's the max for a starting cook." He turned back to his newspaper, not noticing the color rising in Gibson's face.

Just then, as if on cue, Barry appeared on the stairway.

"Gibson, where's Karen?" he asked, as he sauntered toward the bar.

"She took off twenty minutes ago."

"She left already? Who the hell told her she could do that?"

"I guess I thought you did," said Gibson.

Barry turned his back, began walking to the stairway, and called out over his shoulder, "Come up to my office. Now."

Gibson hung back for a few minutes, refilling the toothpick containers so he could gather his thoughts. Then he walked upstairs, knocked on the door, and pushed it open. Barry pulled his feet off the desk and tried to pretend he had been doing paperwork. But Gibson saw the *Sporting News* peeking out from under the spreadsheets.

"So, did you and Karen even think of asking me before she took off?"

"I told you: I thought she had cleared it with you."

"Bullshit." Barry stood up, turned his back, and pretended to swing a club at a golf ball. "It's too late for me to do anything about it at this point, Gibson. But I've got paperwork to do, so I'm not gonna help you if you get in the weeds."

Gibson stared at him in disbelief, thinking, *This idiot is probably five years younger than I am. He's got a big-ass college ring, a fifty-dollar haircut, and a dive restaurant that his daddy bought him, but he doesn't know the difference between a saucepan and a colander. And he doesn't know how lucky he is that I don't smack that smirk off his face.*

"It's gonna stay slow, Barry. I can handle it," he said. "Anyway, I thought you'd appreciate it. I've been here since 10 a.m."

"Oh yeah? You've been here since 10? Guess what? I'll be here until we lock the doors at 10 p.m. tonight, and then for another hour closing up. So please don't tell me what I'm going to appreciate. What I'll appreciate is if the waitresses wait on the tables and the cooks do the cooking." He turned and eyeballed Gibson. "You're a mess, too. Put on a clean apron. And from now on, shave before you come to work." He momentarily turned back to his paperwork, then looked up at Gibson as he stood there, seething. "Something else?"

"Yeah. Actually, there is. How come that little shit down there is making two bucks more an hour than I am?"

Barry inhaled deeply, his eyes narrowing. "Why is it your business what anyone else is making?"

"Because I'm supposed to be the head lunch cook. I've

been here for a year now and I've never missed a shift. That kid is just here for his summer break."

"That kid works half as many hours as you and is saving for college."

"By drinking Budweisers at 2 in the afternoon at my bar?"

"Gibson, it's *my* bar, and unless you're ready to punch out for good, you better get your ass behind it right now."

Gibson shook his head in disbelief. "You know that's not right, Barry."

Barry sat back down at his desk and again leaned over his imaginary paperwork. "The only thing I know is that you better leave my office now, Gibson."

Gibson didn't close the door behind him as he left the room. Downstairs, McManus was gone, and three singles were under his empty longneck—just enough to cover the staff price of his two beers.

Everything went fine for the first half hour or so. Three parties filtered through and Gibson made an extra eleven bucks. He sipped his coffee, felt a tingle across his forehead from the caffeine, and thought about his plight. He took out of his back pocket the folded up piece of paper he'd carried for five months, with the scrawled figures that traced his pursuit of the elusive down payment.

Just then a party of four banged through the front door. Two lantern-jawed young men with a blonde and brunette, all in their early twenties and still in their work clothes. The guys had loosened their ties. The girls wore unflattering suits, but Gibson quickly noticed they had opened their blouses a button or two.

Gibson had seen the two guys in there before. They dressed like little Congressmen but he could still smell the frat house on them. He figured they had gotten off early from their jobs on Capitol Hill, since they were all suited up when the rest of the young D.C. work force sported the casual Friday look most summer weekdays. Gibson silently cursed the recent *Roll Call* article about D.C.'s cheap watering holes. Most of the Hill rats were harmless enough, but these two guys were definitely the types who thought they owned the world just because they worked for self-serving blowhards who qualified as celebrities in D.C.

Because Gibson was going to be solo for another hour and a half, he waved them to a table at the back of the room, near the bar. That way, he wouldn't have to run to the length of the floor and back to fetch their drinks and food. But they plopped themselves down at the booth that was farthest from him, in the front of the restaurant, pulling a chair from another table so one of the guys could spread out at the end of the table.

Gibson walked over to their table to drop off menus and get their drink order.

"How're you all doing today?" he asked.

"Bring us four Sam Adams," said the one of the kids, without even looking at Gibson. He had what sounded to Gibson like a Massachusetts accent. He was chunky, but looked comfortable and confident in his suit and tie. Like the other kid, he was sporting that short hairstyle Gibson was starting to detest, where the hair was combed forward and sloped up in front.

"And two orders of onion rings," said his friend, a taller, thinner kid who somehow managed to look down his nose at Gibson even while sitting at a table. "We'll order the rest when you get back." No *pleases* or *thank yous*.

I've seen this act before, thought Gibson. They're going

to show off for their girls by acting like big-timers. In a god-damn burger joint.

While he wrote down their order, he noticed the brunette checking out the thick homemade tattoo on the thumb webbing of his left hand. Gibson wished he could change lots of things in his life, but this tattoo wasn't one of them. He did it himself the day before his mom's funeral, with just a broken ink pen and a needle with thread tightened around the tip. He was proud of its clarity and proud that he had used his mom's initials—D.G.—instead of the much less inspired MOM.

Back at the bar, he threw two bowlfuls of onion rings into the fryer basket and slipped it into the hot oil. When he placed their beers in front of them, the junior Kennedy didn't look up from his story. ". . . So this stupid constituent actually thought the Congressman was the one who had replied to his letter." He smirked. "As if."

A few minutes later, Gibson returned with their steaming onion rings. This time, the kid interrupted his story long enough to say, "Why don't you just bring us another round now? And quarters for the jukebox." He handed him two singles, and a long afternoon got longer.

They ordered their food, and while Gibson threw the burgers on the grill and garnished their plates, two more tables walked through the door—both deuces. But the kids from the Hill continued to act like Gibson was their personal servant, keeping him running for rounds of beer, mustard, napkins. Their empties piled up in the middle of the table, but they wouldn't let him clear the bottles because they wanted everyone to see how many beers they had pounded. And when he went to take away their plates, they didn't help him out at all, instead making him go through contortions to get around the bottles to the dishes.

Gibson dumped the dishes in the bus pan behind the bar and leaned against the beer cooler. He clenched his jaw and breathed hard through his nose. I'm a cook, not a waiter, he thought. In almost every kitchen he had worked in before coming to the Shelbourne, the cook was the king. As long as the plates went out full and came back empty, nobody gave a shit if he had an occasional temper tantrum. And he never had to put up with haughty, demanding customers—only the occasional bitchy waitress, which was easy enough to squelch by slowing down their orders until they learned who was boss.

Now, because he was saving for a down payment, he had to grin and bear insults from the same sort of dickheads who were driving up prices all through the neighborhood? Gibson's stomach churned as he went to wait on another table. The taller kid from the Hill called out "Yo!" to him as he walked by, then held up his beer and pointed to it. Gibson signaled "one minute" to the new table, turned around, and went back behind the bar. He pulled out a cold one and brought it to the guy. Before Gibson could hustle off to wait on the other table, the brunette said, "I'll have another one, too."

"Okay," Gibson said, breathing deeply. "Anyone else ready?"

They all ignored him, as Junior, who was making his move on the blonde, launched into another story.

Gibson hustled behind the bar and brought the brunette her beer. As he started to move off to the table that was waiting, Junior looked up from the blonde long enough to say, "I'll have another beer, too."

Gibson was just about to lose his temper, when he looked over at the table and saw the tall kid elbow the brunette.

They were both giggling like grade-schoolers. At first Gibson thought it was only because they were getting a load on. But then he realized that the guys were busting his balls and keeping him running on purpose. They thought he was here for their amusement.

He looked hard at the tall kid and then at the jerks who surrounded him. He knew that in a just world this was where he told Junior and his buddy what he thought of them and their idiotic gelled hair, right before he made them bob for apples in the deep fat fryer. But instead, he clenched his jaw and thought about how big their check was and how much he needed the tip. Somehow, he managed to walk away to wait on the other table.

The rest of the shift was no better. By the time Williamson arrived to relieve him, Merle Haggard was blasting and Junior and the blonde were dancing awkwardly in the narrow aisle by the jukebox. No one ever danced at the Shelbourne. Gibson had to slide around them, loaded with dishes, every time he went to a table. His shirt was soaked with sweat and stained with ketchup.

Williamson took one look at him and said, "Rough one, huh?"

"You don't know the half of it," he replied through clenched teeth.

He finished up all his parties while Williamson restocked the garnishes behind the bar. The big party asked Gibson for their check and he brought it to them with a forced smile. It totalled $104—not much for four people who had been eating and drinking for a few hours, but a lot for the Shelbourne, where a burger cost only six bucks. When he got back behind the bar, he watched the guys look long and hard at the check, trying to focus on it.

The table bucked up. It took them awhile. He walked over and they handed him the check and a thick mess of bills. "I'll be right back with your change," he said.

They were already getting up from the table. "It's all yours, sport," said the tall one, who actually slapped him on the back. Gibson thanked them.

He got back behind the bar to the register and counted it, facing the bills out of habit. He counted it once, then again, thinking that some bills must have been stuck together. There was $112 in his hand. Eight bucks on 104. Not even ten percent, after what they put him through.

He walked fast to the front door, pulling his apron over his head as he went. By the time he got to the street, they were nowhere in sight. He continued to look for a few minutes, then went back inside the restaurant and into the kitchen to calm down.

Willie B., the prep guy, had just started his shift, and was slicing and peeling a bag full of fat white Georgia onions. A Backyard Band go-go tune blasted from a flour-covered boom box on the shelf above his stainless steel prep table. Gibson stormed past him and was about to punch out and head home. But instead he turned and barreled up the stairs to the office.

Barry opened the door and looked up at him. "Everything all right?"

"Yo man, you gotta do something for me!"

"What are you talking about?"

"Barry, you gotta give me more money or start giving me some good night shifts. I need money and you owe me."

Barry's eyes narrowed. "How do you figure that?"

"You've been underpaying me since I've been here. I'm telling you, I need money, man! They're gonna kick me out of my apartment."

"Now you listen to me, Gibson. I don't owe you shit. I offered you eight bucks an hour on good faith and you accepted it. And as for better shifts . . ." He hesitated, then took a breath and said, "Listen, Gibson, I don't want to be any crueler about this than I have to. But you're lucky I even let you behind the bar on day shifts. You're really not the type of guy I want out in the front of the house with the kind of customers I'm starting to get at this place."

"What're you saying?" said Gibson. "You've—"

"Gibson, just call it a day. Go home and think about whether you want this job—the way I've set it up. If you come back Monday, I'll know you do. If not . . . honestly, I don't give a flying fuck."

Gibson crossed Thomas Circle and trudged through the neighborhood. A woman with a broken flower in her tangled hair sat on the wall of Luther Place Memorial Church, belting out a song that Gibson didn't recognize. He walked past brick town houses and an apartment building with a sign that read "*Starting in the low-400s!*" as if that were something to be excited about. Office workers and tourists didn't bother with this part of 14th Street, but for Gibson it was home, and it bothered him that even here a new upscale furniture store was bumping up against his favorite chicken joint.

He got home around 6:30, went straight into the bedroom, and threw a wad of bills on top of his worn dresser. Not counting his hourly, he ended up making sixty-two dollars, which was more than he thought he'd end up with when he headed out in the morning. But all he could think about was the platter of shit sandwiches he was force-fed all day by those fucking Hill punks and that asshole Barry.

* * *

He climbed into a hot shower. His skin tingled, then got used to the burning spray. As the water ran over his head, a rank smell of burgers and fryer grease filled the shower stall, like he was one of those freeze-dried meals you eat while camping. He ran the water full blast on his head for a couple more minutes until the smell disappeared. But the steam couldn't ease his anger and shame, or the pressure he felt behind his eyes.

He had to get out of the apartment, so he slogged down 14th toward Franklin Square. On the way, he dropped into a small liquor store for a forty-ounce beer. With his back to K Street, he sat down on a bench in the square, staring at the towering statue of John Barry in his cape and commodore's hat. After five months of near sobriety, the beer tasted incredible.

While Gibson drank from the bottle, which was still wrapped in brown paper, he looked up at the office buildings surrounding the square, and then at the new luxury apartment building on 14th. He thought about the home where he had grown up in Arlington, right across Key Bridge. His old man, an honest, hard-working guy, had lost that place—and killed his wife's spirit in the process—by running up around $15,000 in debt. Twenty years later, even a small bungalow there went for more than half a million. Where's the fairness in that, Gibson wondered.

He watched a skeletal man with a scraggly beard rifle through a trashcan, and thought for the fiftieth time that day about the money he had to come up with by the end of the month. Gibson finally admitted to himself that there was no way he would be able to raise enough scratch in time.

He was restless, so he walked a block along K, stopped in at A-1 Wines and Liquors for another forty, and grabbed a bench at McPherson Square. Across the park he saw a man huddled inside a dirty hooded sweatshirt next to a mismatched set of Samsonite luggage and a stuffed black trash bag. Over his shoulder, straight down Vermont, the top half of the Washington Monument was visible above a clump of trees.

The streetlights cast an eerie hue over the park. Gibson leaned back, stretched out his tired legs, and sipped slowly from the bottle. Late-night businessmen and tourists from the nearby hotels avoided him as they crossed through the circle, on their way to the subway stop on the corner.

A little past 10:30, he polished off his third forty. He had been doing numbers in his head again, thinking about how many hours he had worked over the past year at the Shelbourne. At forty hours a week for roughly fifty weeks, he calculated that he'd put in around 2,000 hours over the past year. He multiplied that by the two bucks an hour that he figured Barry had cheated him out of, and arrived at the tidy sum of $4,000. Money that he could have easily saved. Money that would have enabled him to reach his down payment.

He twisted the open end of the damp brown bag tight around the thin neck of the empty bottle. He reckoned that $4,000 might be in the range of what the Shelbourne was going to do that day, since they rang nearly a grand on a decent lunch and at least two or three times that on a Friday night.

He crossed K Street and walked slowly back toward the restaurant, still grasping the heavy, empty bottle by the neck through the bag. Across the street from the Shelbourne, he found a spot, half submerged in shadow and half lit by a streetlamp, which gave him a good view of the front door. A few minutes after 11:00, the restaurant's interior lights went out. Barry emerged and pulled the heavy wooden door shut tight behind him.

Gibson knew that Barry's backpack contained the zippered bag that the owner slipped into the bank's night deposit slot each evening. Barry double-checked the lock on the front door, then crossed the quiet street to walk the half-block to the bank. Gibson stepped back fully into the darkness.

Barry's footsteps grew louder as he approached, the heels of his boots clapping on the sidewalk. Soon he was inches from Gibson, his eyes focused straight ahead. As Barry passed, Gibson moved out behind him and swung the bottle violently, connecting with the back of Barry's head. To Gibson, things seemed to be moving in soothing slow motion. Blood jumped into the light of the streetlamp, and Barry's body thudded to the ground.

Gibson's heart beat rubbery in his chest, but he was otherwise calm as he reached for the backpack lying beside Barry's still form. The colors on the street were vibrant and clear. The night breeze was pleasant on his face.

For the first time that day, Gibson felt at peace. His headache, and the weight upon his shoulders, had lifted.

THE MESSENGER OF SOULSVILLE
BY NORMAN KELLEY
Cardozo, N.W.

Connie D'Ambrosio rose from her slumber and slowly rubbed her tingly right ass cheek. Normally she would have smiled remembering the sensation from the powerful slaps her posterior had welcomed the night before; she would have looked at herself in the full-length mirror and marveled at the reddish splotches on her rump. Connie had told her new lover, Douglas, that this was the only thing that carried over in her blood from Sicily, it having been invaded by the Moors, George S. Patton, and others over the centuries.

She was proud of her Mediterranean heritage, especially with people like Fellini, Sophia Loren, and Marcello Mastroianni on the world scene. Her olive complexion, a hint of melanin, meant she could pass for anything from the old, Old World: Arab, Jew, Spaniard, Greek, a southern-coast French woman, or even a Gypsy. With a head full of deep curls and raven-black hair, she knew that she was one generation away from not being considered white. When she had explained to Douglas the previous night the numerous ways in which Italian-Americans had been discriminated against (before becoming officially designated as "white" like Jews and Slavs), he merely smiled and gave her some serious tongue, working her in a way that only a saxophone player could.

But this morning there was a new sensation. It wasn't the morning afterglow from their lovemaking, or even the receding skin-burn of a wondrous butt-slapping. No. This was an extremely localized sensation pinpointed just below the curve of her luscious right ass cheek.

She instinctively reached for the bed's linen, only to discover that no sheets or blankets were covering her. Then she felt something else over her: burlap. She was wearing a burlap gown? The texture of the cloth almost made her ill. The thought of such a vulgar fabric touching her skin, covering her body, was beyond the pale. The finest linen, fabrics of the highest order, had graced her since birth. Constance D'Ambrosio was to the manor born: one built on the numerous misfortunes of former associates of her father, Carmine D'Ambrosio, a businessman of indeterminate affairs.

Sensing something was wrong, she rolled over to reach for the night lamp on the evening table. The cold concrete smacked her hard as she hit the floor.

"I don't like this fucking dream," she moaned in her Jersey-girl accent that only revealed itself under the most extreme circumstances. Slowly, she sat up and began collecting her wits, adjusting her eyesight to the darkness. She noticed a shaft of dim light slashing through the room, but what truly caught her attention was a shiny reflection off some polished surface. *Two* polished surfaces. Within seconds her mind began filling in the blanks and she realized that those surfaces were her shoes.

Connie tried to rise, but her foot slipped, landing her on her rump, shooting pain to the tingly spot. "Damn it."

"Are you all right?" inquired a man's voice from over by the shoes.

Connie scrambled backward upon the bed and drew her legs in. "Who are you? What's going on?"

"Don't be alarmed," said the man. "No one is going to hurt you."

"Where am I?" She lowered her volume. "Where's Douglas? *Do you know who I am?*"

"Yes," said the figure sitting quietly in the darkness. "That's why you were brought here."

"Then you know who my father is and what he'll do to anyone who lays a hand on me! He'll—"

"Does that include Douglas?"

Connie said nothing.

"I'm sure he doesn't know about Douglas, nor would he approve of your taste for . . . what do your people call us, *mouliani?*"

The stains of Connie's lust were conveyed in a series of photos that the man slid to her across the concrete floor. Though it was dark in the room, she could make out enough of the images to recognize herself in a series of explicit con-tortions with her black lover. She fleetingly recalled those moments of pleasure, but the wondrous feelings turned to shame and self-recrimination as she imagined her father see-ing the photos. Don D'Ambrosio was a man of respect.

"Miss D'Ambrosio," continued the man from the shad-ows, "we have a situation that requires your assistance."

"My assistance?!" she shot back. "You kidnapped me! That's what this is about, isn't it? How much do you want? Do you think that you'll live long enough to get it from my father? He'll—"

"Not if he sees the photos," interrupted the voice. It was cool and cunning. Connie had become familiar with the tim-bre of black men's voices, and he sounded like one, only edu-cated.

The photos meant blackmail. He was right: Her father

would have a genuinely violent reaction if he saw them. Whatever situation she was in, she would have to get herself out of it.

"What is it that you want?"

"This is a delicate situation, Miss D'Ambrosio. We want you to call your father."

"What?" She shook her head in bewilderment. "No." The fear had set in. She knew the consequences of breaching her family's honor.

"Your father has taken something that belongs to another man, and he wants it returned."

"I don't understand."

"You're a hostage, Miss D'Ambrosio. Your father and his associates have taken something that doesn't belong to them, and the rightful owners want it back. At the right time, all you have to do is make a phone call to your father and ask him to return it. Nothing else will be required of you; you'll get the photos and negatives."

"Return *what?*" replied the woman. "I wake up in a sack and you hold me responsible for something I didn't take?!"

The man stood and stepped back into the deeper shadows of the room. She heard him knock three times on a door, then a dead bolt sliding.

"Sophia Devereaux."

"What? Who the hell is tha— Hey!"

The light that entered the room was quickly extinguished, but it silhouetted the man's lean body in a dark suit as he left.

"Wait!" She rushed to the door, almost tripping over the burlap gown. "Look, I'll do it!" She pounded with her small fists. "Just get me some clothes! Get me some real clothes! GET ME SOME REAL CLOTHES!"

* * *

Dr. Minister Mallory Rex's footsteps echoed through the cavernous basement as he made his way past the warren of rooms to the stairs leading him away from the devil's bitch that the Messenger had instructed him to cage. When he got to the ground floor of Washington, D.C.'s Temple of Ife No. 1, he told the chief sister, Maaloulou, to get the captive something better than burlap.

"After all, she is our guest, and we Afrikans always attend to our guests' needs. As is our custom."

"As is our custom," replied the dark woman dressed in white from head to toe, then she bowed her head.

The doctor minister continued through the temple, nodding to the other brothers and sisters he passed as he thought about the situation that had been handed him. And he thought the situation was beneath him.

Dr. Minister Mallory Rex made them feel proud. He was a former officer in the United States Marine Corps, a war hero cashiered for sleeping with a fellow officer's wife—a yacoub's bitch. He had fallen within the white man's military, but had risen and moved forward with a new mission after reading Dr. Isaiah Afrika's words in *Rise Ye Mighty Race: A Message to the New Blackman.* Dr. Isaiah Afrika had laid the foundation for the Original Kingdom of Afrika based on a conflation of Yoruba and Islam: *Izlam*. Now it was the relentless recruiting, mesmerizing telegenic appearances, and stylistic zeal of Dr. Rex that captivated the faithful and put fear into the hearts of yacoubs, the nation of white devils. And who knew their trickery and deceitfulness better than one who had served faithfully during his years as a "lost Negro"— *nigorant but loyal,* as the Messenger of Izlam once said of the sleeping blacks he called the "walking dead."

Thus far the operation had gone according to plan. The she-devil, while taking her lusts, was unaware that her new lover, Douglas, a follower of the Original Kingdom of Afrika, was under orders to bring her in. Inebriated, she didn't feel a thing, thinking she was being pinched and stroked, when he inserted a small needle into her rumptious tush, putting her soundly to sleep. Hiding her inside his double-bass case, Douglas wheeled her from his apartment on 16th Street onto U Street, in the direction of the temple near the corner of 14th. No one would have thought anything was untoward, certainly not a colored musician rolling his instrument down a street of clubs, southern fried joints, and gut-bucket gospel storefronts. These establishments stretched west from the Howard Theater area to the social axis of U and 14th streets, the heart of Soulsville. It was the center of "third places," the loci between work and home for the city's colored population, the best place for the Temple of Ife to recruit the walking dead.

Dr. Rex knocked on the double doors leading to the Messenger's meditation chamber and waited for the word. Upon hearing it, he removed his shoes, entered a large room with a gurgling fountain in the center, and bowed to the figure in white who sat divining the wisdom of Olodumare with cowrie shells.

"May our Lord and Father be with you," said Rex.

"And He unto you, my son," answered the Messenger, without looking up. He counted several shells and moved them around. "It's been written that you have received some wisdom."

"Yes," said Rex, who walked over to the old man's desk and pressed a button. Water ushered forth from the fountain more loudly.

[FBI Agent 1: Damn it, that smart-assed nigger turned up the volume again.

FBI Agent 2: Hoover is going to have our butts if we bring in more flushing toilets!]

Rex placed himself in front of the man who had made blackness a badge of honor. For untold minutes the master and teacher uttered not a word, letting the sound of water wash over them and empty their heads.

Rex slowly opened his eyes and presented a koan to the Messenger: "Why?"

The old man said nothing at first, his dried lips unparted. The student knew something was coming by the way the old man's Adam's apple began to move above his collar.

"Because the Blackman has to become a man of respect."

Man of respect, thought Rex as he crossed U Street, stopping by Brother's Shoe Shine Shop to pick up a copy of the *Evening Star.*

"Good seeing you, brother minister," said Herman, the legless newsie, looking up to Rex from his platform affixed to four wheels. Herman had always considered himself half a man until he met Dr. Minister Mallory Rex, the only black man in America who truly confronted the devils. He and the denizens of Soulsville, while most of them God-fearing Christians, had welcomed back the black prince from exile after his intemperate remarks brought the Kingdom scorn and opprobrium during the nation's mourning of the white devils' fallen leader. He had been cast aside for nearly a year, watching lesser men attempt to claim his position, "trying to rap like Rex" but falling flat on their faces. The Kingdom's numbers were down. Recruitment had flattened, and the coffers were less than full. It was Rex who added a kind of severe glamour and dash to the humorless black men in white robes who preached Izlam on the street corners of America's urban bantustans while Uncle Tom ministers called for reconciliation and integration. It was the "mighty Rex" who the brothers proclaimed "cool and slick," and who the sister women, O.K.A. and not, wished would park his shoes beneath their beds.

Rex understood his new mission: He was on a test. Would he do the dirty work of the Kingdom?

"Peace," he said to the half-man.

As he walked toward his appointment, the prince of Soulsville observed that U Street was having its streetcar tracks removed—a sign that the sleepy little city was maturing. The Metropolitan Board was laying down the beginnings of a subway system like New York's.

This stretch of northwest D.C., from 11th Street west to 18th, had seen better days. It was, as one book Rex had read suggested, its own "secret city." Earlier, a better tone of Negroes had resided there, but the influx of rough-and-tumble Southern blacks had changed the place and driven them away. It now had the odor of real people; it was a place of beauty parlors, fried hair, and big-hipped bouffant-do sisters. Men still wore hats but the new looks, the "James Brown" process and the "Afro," were making barbers anxious. There was a different mood in the air; the elders called it "funky" and the youths ran with it. Soul Brother No. 1 had announced a "brand-new bag," and civil-rights cats working for SNCC hung out at Ben's Chili Bowl, with kids constantly coming in and out of the three cinemas along the way: the Lincoln, the Republic, and the Booker T.

D.C. was different. D.C. was *country*, and that meant a slower sense of reality—colored people time, heightened by the lush foliage of the area and its legendary humidity. The whole city had the feel of a village since the buildings were no more than three stories high in residential areas and ten or less in the commercial districts. It was a chocolate city, a city in which over seventy percent of the population was colored, invisible to the master class that lived there and ignored by the indifferent tourists visiting the national edifices.

But D.C. was also a city of an aspiring middle class that was branching out from Le Droit Park, Shaw, and U Street, to the tree-shaded "Gold Coast" of upper 16th Street. There resided the "big-ticket Negroes" that Rex rallied against in the oasis of Meridian Hill Park, cited in the past as one of the most beautiful landscaped parks in the country. On a warm spring day, when the heat brought out the richness in colored people's skin, making them glow, the Original Kingdom of Afrika would hold its annual Kingdom's Day in this park, creating a huge Afrikan village in the heart of bourgie D.C. Hundreds of vendors would lay out their wares in stalls, and it was at the Groove Records pavilion on Kingdom's Day that Dr. Minister Mallory Rex had first met Sophia Devereaux.

And he well remembered her when he slid into the booth at Ben's Chili Bowl across from her brother, Lorenzo Devereaux. Rex told the record producer that phase one had been completed and that the Messenger approved of the recording that Groove Records was making of his speeches.

Ten years younger than the man facing him, Lorenzo Devereaux shifted the conversation to the real agenda for the meeting: the mob's encroachment on all that his family had achieved. Groove Records had been on a steady roll of soul and sweaty R&B hit records since the 1950s, and these days even the "legit" labels were salivating over their work, wondering how they were doing it: making music *and* money. Now these wop bastards thought they could just walk in and take over their company because "niggers ain't shit and had no protection."

Three days earlier, Lorenzo had met with his step-mother and half-brother, Leon, to discuss the family crisis. Sophia, his half-sister, had been kidnapped by the Gambino family of New Jersey, headed by Carmine D'Ambrosio.

"We need to get some back-up," Lorenzo urged. "We're going to get some black people who aren't afraid of the mob."

O.K.A.

"Are you crazy!!" Leon had recently assumed the position of president of Groove Records and did not like the idea at all. He wanted to call in the police.

"Yeah, sure," said Lorenzo, stubbing out his Chesterfield in an ashtray. "Go to the cops, the FBI, the same people who been spying on Daddy and Mama for years! I say we handle this *our* way. I have a contact with the Kingdom."

"You're crazy, man!" Leon protested.

But Leon had no real plan other than calling the police. Either capitulate or ask the cops to handle it. It wasn't fair, he thought. He was just supposed to handle record deals, make money, cruise around in his Cadillac, and go to bed with red-bone lovelies . . . and show up his bastard half-brother, Lorenzo. In Leon's eyes, Lo resented the fact that their father had chosen him to run the firm, despite the fact that Leon's own mother thought the half-brother should be at the helm. Perhaps Lo was more competent as an executive, but doesn't blood—full blood—count for something?

Betty Lou Compton, the legendary jazz pianist and composer, the woman who had rescued Groove from the dark days of the Red Scare, was silent. This was a gamble. Her daughter's life, certainly more important than the record company, was in the balance. Yet she understood, as did Lorenzo, that the kidnapping was a form of humiliation, that a family such as the Devereaux could not fully protect itself on its own. The police and the FBI would likely be indifferent, given the accusations the bureau had made against them in the past. They wouldn't even protect those poor civilrights demonstrators who were beaten during freedom rides in the South. It was rumored that Hoover thought Martha Reeves's "Dancing in the Streets" was an underground call for riots and demonstrations.

"Mama!" said Leon, who could see that her slow response to shutting down the crazy idea meant she was considering it. "We're talking about Sophia. Lo can talk all that foolishness about the Kingdom, but she ain't his sister."

"Lorenzo has been just as much of a brother to her as you," defended his mother. "I don't recall you changing her diapers, mister. When have you ever taken a real interest in anyone in this family? You got your position as the president of Groove, but the first sign of trouble . . . ? You're willing to cut a deal with them!"

"We're talking about the Mafia!" said Leon.

"And they bleed like anyone else," countered Lorenzo. "I know how we can checkmate them."

"How?! How you gonna do that? Huh? We only have a few days for Sophia—"

The door opened and in wheeled Rayford Devereaux, the wounded Lear who had retired as the founding president of Groove Records years ago to work on his book. When Betty Lou had recently decided to leave the company's helm to return to composing, that's when the mob had spotted something fat and unprotected for the taking.

"What are you two arguing over now?" asked Rayford as he approached them. The very sight of their father in a wheel chair underscored how his two years in prison had broken and discouraged him. He had finally given up, after battling for years to prove that black music was the social glue keeping Negroes together.

No one had yet mentioned to him that the center of his heart had been stolen.

"Daddy," said Lorenzo, "something has happened." Lorenzo peered around the room and his eyes settled on Leon, who, as the chief executive of Groove Records, ought to be the bearer of bad news. Leon looked away.

"Sophia has been kidnapped," said Lorenzo.

Their father's white eyebrows met in the middle of his forehead as he turned to his wife, who only nodded yes.

"Who?"

"The mob. Carmine D'Ambrosio," replied Betty Lou. "They have given us seventy-two hours to make a decision. They want to be our, uhm, partners."

"You mean our *masters*," corrected her husband. He turned to the CEO of his patrimony. "What's your plan, son?"

"Plan? Uh . . ." Leon stammered.

"You got something up your sleeve or not?!"

"Daddy, it's the mob," explained Leon. "They just want the company—parts of it."

"I'll give them every bit of money we have to get my baby girl back, but they ain't getting their hands on this firm! No deal."

"They'll kill her . . ." started Leon, shocked at his father's ruthlessness. He thought it had been drained out of him.

Rayford Devereaux looked at his son and realized at that very moment that he had made a terrible mistake. Leon saw Groove Records only as a business, not an empire or dynasty, certainly not a way of life, a trust. He himself may have been a tired old nigger in the eyes of many, but he had become such the old way: arrested by the government and beaten in jail because he refused to denounce some of his artists as Communist. He spent two years in jail for Contempt of Congress, and many a patriotic Negro had stomped his ass in bids for early release.

"Son, this is a ship, the USS Groove, and we're officers. We go down with the ship. Money? Let them Italian crackers have it, but they will not get this company. Not even over Sophia's body! This is our heritage."

Leon gaped at his mother.

Betty, however, saw a miracle: Her husband was back. The old Rayford Devereaux, who won her heart forty years before when she was a college student under his tutelage, had empowered her to defy her blues-hating, preacher-crazy father. That man had re-emerged . . . but at the price of her daughter?

"Lorenzo has an idea, Ray," said Betty. "It's risky."

"Hell," said Rayford, "if Kennedy could risk the goddamn world over Cuba and make the Russians pull their missiles out of Dodge, I'll take a chance."

"Yeah, for your record company," muttered Leon.

Lorenzo told his father the idea: Call in the Original Kingdom of Afrika. Seeing that the new chief executive of Groove Records had no other idea or plan, Rayford Devereaux dispatched Lorenzo to the temple immediately. Time was tight.

* * *

"*WHAT?*" said Jimmy Falco. "Are you sure? . . . Damn . . . Okay . . . Yeah, I see . . . I understand . . . Right. Gotcha."

Jimmy "the Hydrant" hung up the pay phone at a Maryland rest stop just outside of the District line. He watched the cars along the highway and couldn't shake off what he'd heard. He had to whack the bitch. It was fortunate that he had brought along Ricci, the sick bastard. It was one thing to follow orders, but Ricci was the kind of sick fuck who actually enjoyed hurting people.

Jimmy got into his black Buick and returned to the place where he and Ricci were keeping the colored gal. When he had first heard the assignment, he was excited. Wow, he thought, the daughter of the owners of his favorite R&B label. Jimmy loved R&B; his hero, from his own tribe, was Louis Prima, the Italian-American who sounded colored because he had grown up in New Orleans. As a street-corner boy, one of the last Italians who lived in East Harlem before the spics took it over, Jimmy Falco had sung on stoops with his group, Spics & Spades. Darker than most Italians, he passed for PR, and fucked as many of them as he did Italian gals. Colored women? Shit, he couldn't get enough: sweet, dark butter.

After the two hoods grabbed the girl blocks away from Howard University earlier that week, they had driven out to Maryland and put a lid on her. She was scared crazy. She should be. Ricci was as big as the Hydrant was short, though the latter was in charge. Five-foot-four, one hundred seventy pounds of muscle and man, Jimmy was on the rise as a soldier and future crew leader; he followed orders, but did so with style and stealth. Whenever he put some sucker to sleep, he carried out his assignment as painlessly as possible.

But whacking a dame? Orders were orders. The business transaction didn't go right, and something new had come up.

When he turned the bend onto the gravel road, he could see stars winking at him through the trees above. The air was clean, unlike stinky New York. He parked, then pulled his squat muscular body out of the car, lit a Camel, and trudged toward the little bungalow. He would give Ricci the order to waste her. When he reached the door, he knocked on it three times but heard nothing. He looked around, placed his hand on his heater, and knocked again. Still no response. He put his ear to the door and listened.

That motherfucker.

Jimmy darted around to the side of the bungalow and peeked into the window of the bedroom where the hostage was being kept. Ricci, a towering hulk, was having his way with the girl, who was sitting on the bed with her arms and legs bound.

Jimmy cursed himself for leaving Ricci with her. Ricci had talked about doing something to her, but they both knew that anything untoward with a hostage was strictly forbidden unless sanctioned by the don.

Now, Jimmy had an extremely serious disciplinary problem on his hands; it was a good thing that Ricci wasn't a "made" man. The Hydrant went to the back door and quietly jimmied the lock. Crossing the room without a sound, he pulled out his silencer and affixed it to his piece.

When Ricci heard his name, he knew instantly he was dead. But reflex action made him go for his holster. The Hydrant plugged him four times: one in the head, two to his heart, and the fourth blew off his putz.

The colored gal screamed her head off until Jimmy told her to shut up and pulled her into the living room. She was in shock, having been struck a few times by Ricci before he molested her.

Exhausted and disoriented, Jimmy decided to report the sudden turn of events. Jimmy untied her legs and told her to grab her shoes. They were heading out.

Back at the rest stop, he parked the car and looked at her.

"I'm sorry about what happened," he said. "That was very unprofessional. That's why he was punished. I have to make a call. If you even try to get out of the car, I'll have to take care of you the way I took care of him. Do you understand?"

The girl was still in shock but had enough awareness to grasp what the short but handsomely ugly man was saying. Jimmy left the car, made his calls, and was back in. He looked at the colored gal again and thought about what he had to do, something that sickened him.

As they approached D.C., two other cars joined them and they drove together to Union Station. Late at night, under the sleepy eyes of indifferent travelers, an exchange was made: a life for a life.

Connie D'Ambrosio, dressed in a chic Chanel suit, was escorted by Dr. Minister Mallory Rex and his chief lieutenant; keeping security were several well-dressed black men known as the Sword of Izlam. Sophia Devereaux, dressed in the dungaree slacks and red cashmere sweater she had been wearing for days, was escorted by Jimmy the Hydrant; they were backed up by several Gambino hoods.

The two men in charge said nothing. They each nodded, prompting their hostages to cross over to their respective rescuers.

Finally, Jimmy spoke: "Mr. D'Ambrosio wishes for me to convey his apologies to the Devereaux family about this *misunderstanding*, and assures you that it will never happen again."

"It better not," came the curt reply from the minister. He turned around, taking Sophia with him, his security team covering their backs.

Both parties vanished as the early morning sun seeped through the large windows of the train station.

Jimmy and two other members of the Gambino family headed north with Connie, who held the photos and negatives in her purse, greatly relieved that the whole situation was over. She talked about the "spades" and how they had kept her locked up. The boring food they served her . . . how stupid those *moulianis* were. She carried on for a while in this manner.

The car soon pulled back onto the gravel road and came to a stop at the bungalow. Jimmy, sitting up front, told the driver and the other guy, Marcos, to go inside and collect Ricci's body, which would be stuffed into the trunk.

The Hydrant didn't understand what hit him: It was very unprofessional, but he started to cry. He was spent.

"What's the matter, Jimmy?" asked Connie, who treated the lug as one of many "uncles."

"Nothing," he choked. When Connie reached forward to console him, he grabbed her arm and pulled her over the seat before she could feel his stiletto cutting her throat.

"Why?" asked Rex.

The Messenger had sent the photos of Connie D'Ambrosio cavorting with Douglas to her father. The Messenger knew that her father would be compelled to murder her to avenge his honor as a man of respect. The deal was that the young woman would call her father and tell him she was being held in exchange for another person—nothing more.

Rex felt that sending the photos was a betrayal, and that the young woman, though a she-devil, had been needlessly sacrificed. "We gave our word," he said. "That means something."

"My son," reflected the Messenger, feeling triumphant, "*you* gave *your* word. Besides, one's word only means something if the other person is worthy of receiving it."

As a gift, the Messenger handed Rex a copy of one of his favorite books: Machiavelli's *The Prince*.

Dr. Minister Mallory Rex withdrew from his teacher's chamber. He had been firmly reinstated, with good standing, into the O.K.A., and the Messenger's son, Kwami, would become an executive at Groove Records. But as he walked through the halls of the Temple of Ife No. 1, taking in the admiring gazes of those he passed, the minister wondered what the cost was to his soul, and how long would he keep it.

Time would tell.

THE DUPE

BY JIM FUSILLI

K Street, N.W.

T hough it was not quite 1 o'clock, the Bombay Club was already filled to capacity for Sunday brunch. Its décor reminiscent of a British officers' lounge in occupied India, the restaurant's dining room shimmered with the buzz of convivial conversation from the customary mix of Senators, Congressmen, White House aides, K Street lobbyists, TV pundits, and print journalists. The insiders acknowledged each other discretely.

Surrounded by the whiff of coriander and piano jazz played with stately reserve, Jordan Port sat at the bar, his back to the clipped cordiality. He hunched into his camel's hair topcoat, its collar turned high, incredulous still that Mendes had invited him to where he was no longer welcomed.

Port had known Mendes for decades; he interned under her at the *Des Moines Register*, and she edited his first book, *Restoring the Soul of America*, a surprising bestseller that had made him all the more useful in the eyes of his handlers. Though the two had lunch together earlier in the week, he accepted her email invitation to the Bombay Club because he needed her. Taking a circuitous route that revealed his desperation, he arrived at the restaurant two blocks from the White House grounds well aware she was likely his last friend.

Sweating under his violet shirt and black cashmere blazer, Port anxiously surveyed the room through the veined mirror behind the bar. He saw a half dozen people with whom he'd had dinner at their homes, and there were at least that many with whom he had shared a dais at a conference or a podium at a rally.

They are shunning me, he thought. Every one of them.

And all he had done was write a new book, one that could be summarized by what Ronald Reagan said some thirty years ago:

"When we begin thinking of government as *we* instead of *they*, we've been here too long."

"Mr. Port?"

He turned to find a young Indian man, a rail-thin busboy.

"Mr. Port," he said compliantly, "a message, please, from Ms. Mendes. She prefers for you to wait outside."

Port looked into the man's dark eyes for a sign of sincerity. He wondered if the restaurant's manager had been asked to send him elsewhere.

"Please, sir," said the Indian man with a sweep of his arm. "The lady is waiting."

Port nodded, left the bar stool, and headed out onto Connecticut Avenue.

He was greeted there by pale sunlight and a sinewy black man who crossed the avenue to approach him. The black man wore a vest with the yellow logo of a company that owned a chain of parking garages. The winter wind rippled the sleeves of his white shirt.

He towered over Port, who was as lithe and delicate as a young teen.

"She's in Room 523 at the St. Regis," he said, repeating the room number.

Port shivered and dropped his hands into his coat pockets. "I don't understand. The St. Regis—"

"Ana Mendes," he said directly. "You'd better go now."

Port nodded and began to walk briskly toward I Street.

When Port turned the corner, the valet dashed back across Connecticut Avenue to the garage where the Indian busboy was behind the wheel of a black Cadillac Escalade. The valet removed the uniform top he'd been given and tossed it behind the front seat.

The busboy drove quickly toward I Street, but not so fast as to overtake Port.

The St. Regis was one block away.

Five days earlier, Port was summoned to Off the Record, a clubby bar in the basement of the Hay Adams Hotel. Douglas Weil Jr. was waiting, and with a wave he called him to a cherrywood table set deep in a dark corner. Framed political cartoons and caricatures rested on the wall above Weil's neat salt-and-pepper hair.

Weil had ordered a 2001 Viognier from a Virginia winery, and he poured Port a glass as his guest crossed the crowded room and eased into the banquette.

"Thank you for coming on such short notice, Jordie," he said.

"Always a pleasure, Doug," he replied cheerfully, concealing his nervousness.

They were both in their mid-forties, but Port's famed boyishness and Weil's grinding sense of purpose made them seem years apart.

Before Port could reply, Weil said, "My father is disappointed, Jordie."

Port waited for Weil to fill his glass before he offered a silent toast.

Weil returned the gesture, though his eyes were slits. "I

read the manuscript," he said, as the glasses met. "You are way, way out of line."

"What did your father say?" He sipped the delightful wine, a favorite for its taste rich in peaches and apricots, and heady floral bouquet. "He knows we have to take back—"

The thickset Weil leaned toward his guest. "Don't, Jordie," he said, through gritted teeth. "I read it. I don't want to have to hear it."

Port had known a warning was coming, and he surmised it might be Weil who delivered it. Off the Record, a favorite of the city's political insiders, was a suitable venue: All of Washington would know he'd been chastised, and thus responsibility for his actions couldn't be attributed to the American Center for Culture in Communications, of which Doug was president and his father founder and chairman emeritus.

But Port believed Weil could be swayed. "The principles your father shared with President Reagan mean nothing to these people, Doug. You know this."

Jutted chin hovering above the table candle, Weil said, "Don't be a simpleton, Jordie. We have what we've worked toward for more than thirty years. No one is walking away from it because of you."

"When Ronald Reagan said a balanced budget was essential to restoring America, Doug, the deficit was $66 billion," Port continued. "Today, it's more than ten times that—after Clinton brought it to zero."

"Jordie . . ."

The K Street lobbyists and White House staffers who peered with curiosity at the two men couldn't tell from appearances what they were saying. They saw the twinkle in Port's pale-blue eyes and his dimpled smile, an expression familiar to millions of Americans from talk shows, book jackets, magazines, and newspapers. All seemed well.

"Middle America is being compelled to act against its own interests," Port said, as he returned the chilled glass to the table. "They need tax relief, affordable health insurance, a promise fulfilled on Social Security . . . Doug, the ACCC can help them. We can help—"

"Oh Lord." Weil sat back, resting his folded hands against his vest.

"We've moved light years from what Ronald Reagan believed, and what I believe."

"Are you kidding?" Weil sat upright and plopped his hands on the table. "Jordie, do you think we give a good goddamn what you believe?"

Port started to reply, but stopped when Weil lifted the bottle to refill his guest's glass.

"Listen, we plucked you out of the cornfield because we knew you would do what you were told," Weil said, as the golden wine flowed. "You've still got that farm-fed puppy look, but by now, people have been trained to know what's coming out of your mouth before you open it. Hell, you go off message and they'll shut you down."

For effect, Weil laughed, reached across the table, and punched Port on the shoulder with the side of his fist. Not for a moment would he let Port know he was concerned. The manuscript Port had written used Reagan's words and ideals to challenge the direction the Right had taken since the opportunity of 9/11. Once Mendes massaged the prose and smoothed out his newfound fanaticism, the book would be another Jordan Port bestseller. That could be deadly dangerous, a blueprint for a moderate coalition.

"So here's how it works, Jordie. We're going to issue a

press release telling people you're on sabbatical. You're going up to the cabin our money bought you in the Casper Mountains to write another book. You won't answer the phone and there'll be no email. You'll return when we tell you and we'll give you your next manuscript."

"Wait a minute, Doug, I—"

Anticipating the protest, Weil held up his hand. "Don't worry. Mendes will be involved. She'll make it sound enough like you."

"I wrote those books, Doug. You can't—"

"The words are yours, sure; yours and Mendes's. But not the ideas."

Weil took a short sip of the wine he considered pretentious and feminine, holding the glass by its stem.

"If it was up to me, we'd be done with you," he said, as Port looked on in silence. "But my father likes you. You helped us get Hollywood on board and you helped us turn around the FCC. But the end is in sight if you don't wise up."

Port did not so much as blink.

"Think you'd be happy working your way back up to the copy desk in Davenport, Jordie?" Weil asked. "No, I would think not."

The next day, Port joined Ana Mendes for lunch downstairs at Red Sage, a smart restaurant with a Southwestern theme. He ordered the salmon paillard, and his former mentor the pecan-crusted chicken dusted with red chili. In her briefcase was his latest manuscript, *Betraying Ourselves*.

"Ana, if he could've gotten away with it, he would've shot me right there," Port said, sipping the Sancerre he'd ordered.

"Wrung your neck is more like it," Mendes replied. "Jordie, what were you thinking?"

She recommended him out of college for his first full-time job at the *Quad Cities Times*. Something about Jordie brought out a tenderness in her, and so they kept in touch and she felt a sense of pride when he became the paper's film critic. She followed his career when he moved to Fox's KLJB-TV, and in 1991 she wrote a reference letter to the ACCC. He was telegenic, personable, reasonably bright, and she knew Ronald Reagan was his hero. A true believer, he'd be a perfect public face for Douglas Weil's political action committee.

Some years later, she asked one of Weil's lawyers why they'd decided on Jordan Port.

He fit the profile, she was told. His father, a son of a Roosevelt Democrat, was described as aloof and unsympathetic, and he died when Port was nine years old. In turn, Port spent his school days and early career in an unwitting search for praise and validation, particularly from older, plainspoken men. They knew he'd adore Douglas Weil, whose warm, folksy manner belied his cunning and drive.

The clincher was his behavior as a film critic. Port gulped down every perk offered by every studio, from a sixty-nine-cent pen to a flight to Nice for Cannes. He'd convinced himself he had to do so for the job, not once questioning whether he really needed a foot-high figurine of Schwarzenegger as T2 for his desk, Molly Ringwald's voice on his answering machine . . .

This kid was waiting to be bought, the lawyer said.

Mendes now sat across from Port and saw fear and determination mingling in his eyes.

"Jordie, there are faster ways if you want to kill yourself—"

She stopped short, remembering Port's mother had committed suicide.

"It's all true, Ana. I challenge you to tell me it's not."

Mendes sighed. "Jordie, this town is fucked. You're not

going to get anything done here. This book . . . I can't make it happen."

"I can take it to New York," he said.

"Jordie, ask yourself if you want to blow up the bridge. Ask yourself if you have *any* friends on the Left."

"Ana, I want to do what's right," he said earnestly. "Reagan's legacy—"

"Jordie, will you . . . Jordie, stop," she said sternly. They were a block from the Treasury Department, a short walk from K Street, and she was no longer certain she could match a face with a title. Looking around, she whispered, "Jordie, there's no right or wrong. There's no dissent and no discussion. There is what is."

"They mock Reagan," Port said, ignoring his salmon. "They call his philosophies 'paleo-conservatism.' They say his lessons don't apply."

"Jordie, I know," she said tiredly. "I read your manuscript. So did Randy."

Randy Dawson, her boss and stepson of a nationally syndicated columnist. The house, Patriot Publishing, was a subsidiary of a marketing firm funded by the pharmaceutical industry and an ad-hoc coalition of brokerage firms.

Port said, "I'm sick of going to these luncheons where they praise Reagan in public and then mock him when the paying guests leave."

"Jordie, will you listen to yourself? I know you almost twenty-five years and you're lecturing me," she said.

She reached across the table and held his hand. "Please. You have to stop. You have no chance of success. They will bury you. Do yourself a favor and burn the manuscript."

"I can't," he said, drawing up. "Someone will publish it. It's good and it's right."

"Jordie, I'm trying to help you. You have to under—"

Port's cell phone rang.

It was Douglas Weil Jr., and he asked Port if he was alone.

Without knowing it, Port had stood and was now next to the table. Last night, whenever he closed his eyes to sleep, Weil was there, teeth bared.

Mendes saw him quiver.

"Find a corner," Weil told him.

Port walked to one of the private dining rooms, and he shut the door behind him.

"You've booked yourself on MSNBC tomorrow night," Weil said.

"Yes. Yes, I did."

"Cancel," Weil said forcefully.

"Doug, I can't. I'm—"

"Cancel," he repeated and cut the line.

When Port returned to the table, he saw it had been cleared.

Mendes was gone.

Jordan Port was in the lead-off slot on MSNBC's *Hardball*. The producers knew him well—the appearance was Port's seventy-third in the past fifteen years. There hadn't been a more charming Clinton basher.

The guest host, with whom Port had scuba dived in the Caymans, called him Jordie. On air, he referred to him as "still one of Washington's young wise men."

He threw Port the softball he asked for.

"You've written a book Washington doesn't want to see in print. Am I right?"

Eleven minutes later, Port ended his comments with a quote from Ronald Reagan:

"When we begin thinking of government as *we* instead of *they*, we've been here too long."

As he stepped into darkness outside the MSNBC offices on Nebraska Avenue, Port's cell phone rang.

A senior producer from *Larry King Live*, who excoriated him for going elsewhere. She then cheerfully invited him to appear tomorrow night, asking if he'd messenger the manuscript to her.

Friday was a dead night for news, Port knew. But he figured he could parlay a *King* appearance into fodder for Sunday's TV roundtables and shout fests. He'd send the show a chapter, but he'd hold the work close until he went to New York on Monday to find a high-powered agent. The media buzz would give him wings.

No sooner had he cut the line than the phone rang again.

The caller, whose voice he couldn't recognize, gave him the address of a website and a password. In the e-address, the name *jordanport* came after the second backslash.

Heart pounding, Port raced his ACCC-owned Lexus back to Dupont Circle. He parked at a fire hydrant, the car's flashers flickering on his nineteenth-century red-brick row house.

Running into his dark apartment, he ignored the blinking light of his answering machine and scurried to his desk, still wearing his camel's hair topcoat and the blue blazer, blue shirt, and blue-and-pink club tie he'd chosen for his *Hardball* appearance.

His hands shaking, it took him several tries before he typed the correct address. He'd kept trying to put an ampersand between the letters.

Finally, the screen went blank, and then it flashed a site for S&M aficionados.

Port used the password he'd been given, drove down two pages, and found photos of a burly man in leather, cat-o'-nine-tails dangling from his broad fist. On a table, face burrowed into a short stack of towels, was a naked man whose butt had been whipped raw.

The next photo showed the man's face, and it was Port's.

Port's face, as clear as if in a Sears portrait, though he had never—not once—participated in such activity.

Much of Washington assumed Port was gay, but he wasn't. He had little interest in sex, and hadn't been with anyone in almost five years.

But there he was, in every photo.

Including several on the final page where the burly man in black-leather chaps was sodomizing him.

In the harsh light of the monitor, Port sat with his mouth hung open. His mind raced as he stared at the images.

He jumped when his cell phone in his pocket rang.

The same man who'd called earlier said, "Make it right on *Larry King* and the site comes down. Fuck up and the password comes off."

Anxious, distraught, Port arrived at the CNN offices on First Avenue for the interview. A hard-driving storm pounded the city since dawn and though it had passed, he wore a Burberry trenchcoat over his suit, shirt, and tie. He wanted to give the impression that he spent the day running from meeting to meeting, but in truth he hadn't left his apartment, answering the door only for the CNN messenger.

When the interview ended, he planned to stay at the Dupont 5 Cinema for as long as they'd allow, dodging calls by watching movies, hiding in the dark, preparing to flee by train to New York.

The segment producer, a young Asian woman in a khaki crewneck sweater and ill-fitting cargo slacks, met him at Security.

"What are you doing here?" She held a silver clipboard. "You're cancelled."

Port frowned. "No, I—"

"The ACCC called," she said. "You're not feeling well, you're under some kind of stress . . ."

Port tried to smile. "I'm right here, Hisa."

She touched his coat sleeve. "You look awful, Jordie."

She was right: dread, a second sleepless night; listening to footsteps in the apartment above, cars on Riggs Place . . .

"But I can do it, Hisa." He bucked up, thrusting out his chest. "Raring to go. Dependable as always."

She looked at him. Agitated, fidgeting in place . . .

Her boss told her the pages he sent were an incoherent rant.

He saw confusion and sympathy on her face.

"Yeah, I'd better go," he said, sagging. "I don't know. This flu . . ."

"Rest easy, Jordie," she told him, as she turned to scurry back to the elevator.

Five hours and two films later, Jordie arrived home.

The password no longer worked on the S&M site, and he permitted himself to think they'd taken the photos down. The thought lasted seconds.

He had several emails, but one immediately caught his eye. The subject line read, *Urgent!* From Ana Mendes via her home AOL e-address.

"Jordie," she wrote, *"I must see you. News! Meet me at the Bombay Club, Sunday, 1 p.m. Happy, happy."* It was signed, AM.

The signature and the "*Happy, happy*" made it real for Port.

Years and years ago, he ran into Mendes at an *Editor &
Publisher* conference in Chicago. Drinks, sentiment, more
drinks; two people alone, despite the glad-handing at the
banquet and bar. He wanted her—the embrace mattered, the
affection—and she thought, *Why not?* Up to her room, and
afterwards, as he lay with his head on her sweat-soaked
shoulder, she asked, "Happy?"

"Happy, happy," he replied.

Port stared at the email, and he permitted himself to
think she had spoken to her boss, who somehow got to
Douglas Weil Sr. at ACCC. A book promoting Ronald
Reagan and his ideals was what America needed now. We
ought to pull away from these guys, Mr. Weil. They've only
got a couple of years left anyway, and the country's not going
to keep tacking right . . .

The thought lasted seconds.

It took Port less than three minutes to hustle through the
early-afternoon chill to the St. Regis, and another two to
reach the fifth floor. Room 523 was in the center of the long,
rose-carpeted corridor that was lined with white floral-pattern
wallpaper.

Not once did he ask himself why Mendes wanted to meet
in a hotel when she had a town house in Georgetown.

Port knocked on the unlocked door.

Then he stepped inside.

He saw the red bedspread had been tossed aside, and the
bed was in shambles. On the off-white wall beyond the bed
was an array of blood spatter. Blood was smeared from the
center of the stains to the floor where Mendes lay. A dime-
sized hole was above her right eye.

Port retreated in shock, stumbling against the desk chair, his arms flailing. He stopped when he hit the closet door.

Bringing his hands to his mouth, Port shuddered and he felt weak, and he understood.

Standing in a silence broken only by the hum of the heating system, he tried to remember what he had touched and who had seen him in the lobby or on 16th Street. Then he went over and looked at Mendes, a friend who had tried to warn him.

She wore a black chemise and was naked below the waist.

In death, she seemed terrified. Ana Mendes, the most self-possessed woman he'd ever known.

As he turned from her, he saw on the desk an almost-empty bottle of wine, a 2001 Viognier from a Virginia winery. There were two glasses, a mouthful of golden wine remaining in each, and he was sure one of the glasses wore his fingerprints, gathered days earlier at Off the Record.

Port hurried to the bathroom, grabbed a hand towel, and—

The front door opened, and Port was joined by the Indian busboy and the black man from valet parking.

The black man spoke with cool assurance, as the man from India barred the door.

"You have no possibility of escape," said the black man. "But you are left with a choice."

Port's mouth had dried and he struggled to speak. "I didn't—"

"Your call, Mr. Port."

Port noticed they were both wearing latex gloves.

"First choice: You killed her in a fit of rage brought on by the depression that's been responsible for your erratic behavior."

"I didn't—I wasn't angry with Ana. I—"

"You argued at Red Sage. Several people noticed that she left when you took a phone call."

"That's not—"

"Dozens of threatening emails to her from your ACCC computer. Calls from your ACCC cell phone."

The Indian man stepped next to his associate. "You quarreled because you learned Ms. Mendes had written a book about you."

"About *me?*" he asked, his voice cracking.

The man counted on his thin fingers. "Your attempt to blackmail Douglas Weil and the ACCC with your latest manuscript. Your mental decline. Your troubled childhood. Your reputation at the newspaper. The sadomasochism . . ."

The black man now had a gun in his hand. With the silencer, the barrel seemed more than a foot long.

"I've read this book by Ms. Mendes," said the Indian man. "Fascinating. Who would've known? This will surely profit Patriot Publishing."

Said the black man, "If I shoot you from here, it's the second choice: You were killed with Ms. Mendes when your tryst was interrupted. A jealous ex, a robbery? Someone with an obsession . . ."

"An obsession," the Indian man repeated.

"Or I step up, put the gun to your temple, and make it look like murder-suicide. If so, Ms. Mendes's manuscript is released, the S&M website . . . Your psychological records. Anecdotes. Your name will become synonymous with a spokesman gone mad.

Said the Indian man, "A *Jordan Port* is a pig looking for a new trough."

Port's mind reeled. He could see it unfolding—the

headlines, the patter on talk radio, *schadenfreude*, the mounting disgrace; reporters invading Davenport to interview his step-mother, neighbors and high-school teachers to track down rumors fed them by Doug Weil's PR machine.

"But I don't deserve . . . I don't want to die," he said meekly, his voice dripping resignation.

"Mr. Port," said the Indian man, "you are already dead. It's a matter now of how you are remembered."

The black man raised his arm.

"Take off your clothes, Mr. Port. Let's do it right."

As his tears began to flow, Jordan Port slowly removed his camel's hair coat.

The Indian man hung it in the closet next to Mendes's suit.

ABOUT THE CONTRIBUTORS:

ROBERT ANDREWS, a former Green Beret and CIA officer, has lived in Washington, D.C. for over thirty years. His last three novels, *A Murder of Honor, A Murder of Promise,* and *A Murder of Justice,* feature Frank Kearney and Jose Phelps, homicide detectives in the Metropolitan Police Department.

B.J. Andrews

JIM BEANE was born at Garfield Hospital in Washington, D.C. and spent his early childhood in Michigan Park near the city line. He grew up in the 'burbs. His stories have appeared in the *Baltimore Review,* the *Potomac Review,* and the *Long Story.* He lives in Prince George's County, Maryland with his wife and daughters.

Judy Licht

RUBEN CASTANEDA covered the D.C. crime beat for the *Washington Post* from 1989 through the mid-1990s. He has also written for the *Washington Post Magazine,* the *California Journal,* and *Hispanic Magazine.* A native of Los Angeles, Castaneda, forty-four, lives in Washington.

Stuart Hovell

RICHARD CURREY grew up in Washington, D.C. and environs and lives there today. His stories have appeared in *O. Henry, Pushcart,* and *Best American Short Story* collections, aired on National Public Radio's *Selected Shorts* series, and performed at Symphony Space in New York. His novel *Lost Highway* was reissued in 2005 in print and as an audiobook.

Vivian Ronay

JIM FUSILLI is the author of the award-winning Terry Orr series, which includes *Hard, Hard City,* which was named winner of the Gumshoe Award for Best Novel of 2004, as well as *Closing Time, A Well-Known Secret,* and *Tribeca Blues.* He also writes for the *Wall Street Journal* and is a contributor to National Public Radio's *All Things Considered.*

Andrei Jackamets

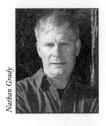

JAMES GRADY is the author of *Six Days of the Condor* and a dozen other novels. He has worked as a national investigative reporter and a U.S. Senate aide, and has published several award-winning short stories. Grady received France's Grand Prix du Roman Noir in 2001 and Italy's Raymond Chandler medal in 2004. He lives inside D.C.'s Beltway.

JENNIFER HOWARD, a native of Washington, D.C., grew up in the Palisades section of town, around the corner from the old MacArthur Theatre. Her fiction, essays, reviews, and features have appeared in the *Washington Post* (where she was a contributing editor from 1995–2005), *VQR*, the *Boston Review, Slate*, the *Blue Moon Review, Salon, New York Magazine*, and other publications. She now lives on Capitol Hill with her husband, the writer Mark Trainer, and their two children.

LESTER IRBY was born and raised in Northeast D.C. He was first arrested at age thirteen and later spent more than thirty years in federal prison for crimes ranging from bank robberies to two prison escapes. Irby wrote "God Don't Like Ugly" while incarcerated in the Lewisberg Federal Penitentiary. He was released on parole in May 2005 and currently resides in Southeast D.C.

KENJI JASPER was born and raised in the nation's capital and currently lives in Brooklyn. He is a regular contributor to National Public Radio's *Morning Edition* and has written articles for *Savoy, Essence, VIBE*, the *Village Voice*, the *Charlotte Observer*, and Africana.com. He is the author of three novels, *Dark, Dakota Grand*, and *Seeking Salamanca Mitchell*.

NORMAN KELLEY is the author of three "noir soul" novels featuring Nina Halligan: *Black Heat, The Big Mango*, and *A Phat Death*. He is also the author of *The Head Negro in Charge Syndrome: The Dead End of Black Politics*, as well as the editor of *R&B (Rhythm and Business): The Political Economy of Black Music*. He was born and raised in D.C. and currently lives in Brooklyn, New York.

LAURA LIPPMAN is best-known for her award-winning Tess Monaghan series, set forty miles to the north of Washington, D.C. She spent part of her childhood just outside the District line when her father was the Washington correspondent for the *Atlanta Constitution*. Lippman still frequents the city, home to some of her favorite people and restaurants.

Jim Burger

JIM PATTON grew up a D.C. suburb, then moved to the Left Coast. Back in the area after many years, he finds the summers even more stifling, the traffic more maddening. Worst of all, Shirley Povich is gone.

Yalcin Erhan

GEORGE PELECANOS is a screenwriter, independent-film producer, award-winning journalist, and the author of the bestselling series of Derek Strange novels set in and around Washington, D.C., where he lives with his wife and children.

Jim Saab

QUINTIN PETERSON is a twenty-four-year veteran police officer with the Metropolitan Police Department of Washington, D.C., where he is currently assigned to its Office of Public Information as a media liaison officer. He is the author of several plays and screenplays and two crime novels, *SIN (Special Investigations Network)* and *The Wages of SIN*.

Kevin Palmer

DAVID SLATER is originally from the Jersey Meadowlands, and has called D.C. home for more than two decades. During that time, he has worked in several dive restaurants and, for the last fifteen years, in environmental conservation. He currently lives with his wife and two kids in the Clarendon section of Arlington, Virginia.

Cecelia Slater

Jagatjyoti Khalsa

ROBERT WISDOM grew up in the Petworth area of Northwest Washington, back when D.C. was still a town. He attended D.C. public schools and graduated from St. Albans. He was called _Bobby_ growing up, which gave way to _Bob_ in the world after D.C., got the nickname _Bayobey_ from his Brazilian capoeira master, and currently plays a character named _Bunny_ on HBO's _The Wire_. He's all about the B's.

Also available from the Akashic Books Noir Series

BROOKLYN NOIR
edited by Tim McLoughlin
350 pages, a trade paperback original, $15.95
*Winner of Shamus Award, Anthony Award, Robert L. Fish
Memorial Award; Finalist for Edgar Award, Pushcart Prize

Twenty brand new crime stories from New York's punchiest borough. Contributors include: Pete Hamill, Arthur Nersesian, Maggie Estep, Nelson George, Neal Pollack, Sidney Offit, Ken Bruen, and others.

"*Brooklyn Noir* is such a stunningly perfect combination that you can't believe you haven't read an anthology like this before. But trust me—you haven't. Story after story is a revelation, filled with the requisite sense of place, but also the perfect twists that crime stories demand. The writing is flat-out superb, filled with lines that will sing in your head for a long time to come."
—Laura Lippman, winner of the Edgar, Agatha, and Shamus awards

BROOKLYN NOIR 2: THE CLASSICS
edited by Tim McLoughlin
309 pages, trade paperback, $15.95

Brooklyn Noir is back with a vengeance, this time with masters of yore mixing with the young blood: H.P. Lovecraft, Lawrence Block, Donald Westlake, Pete Hamill, Jonathan Lethem, Colson Whitehead, Irwin Shaw, Carolyn Wheat, Thomas Wolfe, Hubert Selby, Stanley Ellin, Gilbert Sorrentino, Maggie Estep, and Salvatore La Puma.

CHICAGO NOIR
edited by Neal Pollack
252 pages, a trade paperback original, $14.95

Chicago Noir is populated by hired killers and jazzmen, drunks and dreamers, corrupt cops and ticket scalpers and junkies. It's the Chicago that the Department of Tourism doesn't want you to see, a place where hard cases face their sad fates, and pay for their sins in blood. This isn't someone's dream of Chicago. It's not even a nightmare. It's just the real city, unfiltered. *Chicago Noir.*

Brand new stories by: Neal Pollack, Achy Obejas, Alexai Galaviz-Budziszewski, Adam Langer, Joe Meno, Peter Orner, Kevin Guilfoile, Bayo Ojikutu, Jeff Allen, Luciano Guerriero, Claire Zulkey, Andrew Ervin, M.K. Meyers, Todd Dills, C.J. Sullivan, Daniel Buckman, Amy Sayre-Roberts, and Jim Arndorfer.

BALTIMORE NOIR
edited by Laura Lippman
252 pages, a trade paperback original, $14.95

Brand new stories by: David Simon, Laura Lippman, Tim Cockey, Rob Hiaasen, Robert Ward, Sujata Massey, Jack Bludis, Rafael Alvarez, Marcia Talley, Joseph Wallace, Lisa Respers France, Charlie Stella, Sarah Weinman, Dan Fesperman, Jim Fusilli, and Ben Neihart.

LAURA LIPPMAN has lived in Baltimore most of her life and she would have spent even more time there if the editors of the Sun had agreed to hire her earlier. She attended public schools and has lived in several of the city's distinctive neighborhoods, including Dickeyville, Tuscany-Canterbury, Evergreen, and South Federal Hill.

SAN FRANCISCO NOIR
edited by Peter Maravelis
252 pages, a trade paperback original, $14.95

Brand new stories by: Domenic Stansberry, Barry Gifford, Eddie Muller, Robert Mailer Anderson, Michelle Tea, Peter Plate, Kate Braverman, David Corbett, Alejandro Murguía, Sin Soracco, Alvin Lu, Jon Longhi, Will Christopher Baer, Jim Nesbit, and David Henry Sterry.

DUBLIN NOIR
The Celtic Tiger vs. The Ugly American
edited by Ken Bruen
228 pages, a trade paperback original, $14.95

Brand new stories by: Ken Bruen, Eoin Colfer, Jason Starr, Laura Lippman, Olen Steinhauer, Peter Spiegelman, Kevin Wignall, Jim Fusilli, John Rickards, Patrick J. Lambe, Charlie Stella, Ray Banks, James O. Born, Sarah Weinman, Pat Mullan, Reed Farrel Coleman, Gary Phillips, Duane Swierczynski, and Craig McDonald.